ST. MARTIN'S

MINOTAUR

MYSTERIES

The Miracle Strip

—Nancy Bartholomew—

St. Martin's Paperbacks

THE MIRACLE STRIP

Copyright © 1998 by Nancy Bartholomew Long.
Excerpt from *Drag Strip* © 1999 by Nancy Bartholomew Long.

Library of Congress Catalog Card Number: 98-7330

ISBN: 0-312-97095-1

Printed in the United States of America

St. Martin's Press hardcover edition / September 1998
St. Martin's Paperbacks edition / October 1999

10 9 8 7 6 5 4 3 2 1

Acknowledgment

A first novel is a fragile creature, and *The Miracle Strip* is no exception. It would never have been written without the invaluable assistance, coaching, and advice of many people. Any mistakes that have been made are purely mine. I have taken liberties with the beautiful town of Panama City, moving people and places, adding buildings and streets where necessary and deleting some to suit my needs.

I could never do complete justice to the dedication and professionalism of the Panama City Police Department officers who assisted me in my research, in particular, Sargent Joe Hall, Detective Mark McClain, and Corporal Ed Eubanks. They answered hundreds of questions and let me ride with them as they went about their jobs protecting the lives and property of Panama City residents.

I am also indebted to a wonderful and loyal critique group: Wendy Greene, Nancy Gates, Ellen Hunter, Chris Farran, Carla Buckley, Pam Blackwood, and Charlotte Perkins. I am also deeply grateful to my agent, Irene Kraas, and my editor, Kelley Ragland, for having faith in Sierra Lavotini and me.

I wish to also acknowledge and thank the Greensboro, North Carolina, Police Department, and in particular Corporal J. F. Witt. Corporal Witt spent many hours answering technical and procedural questions, without hesitation and despite his busy schedule.

Thanks, too, to Nova Wyte and the staff of Club 9 1/2 Weeks in Atlanta, Georgia. Nova took me under her wing, and showed me the ropes. Dancers like Nova are few and far between.

Stuart Kaminsky befriended me when I needed guidance. He took time from his own busy writing schedule to mentor me and I will remember forever his kindness and wisdom.

Then there are the women in my life, the friends who stepped in and helped out when and where they could. They picked up the kids after school, or said, "I'll take them with me for a couple of hours, you go write." They let me whine, they shored up my courage, and they kicked me back out into the fray. Cathy, Johan, Susan, Ellen, Tru, Wendy, Wendy, and Anita . . . thank you.

And, as always, my heart, soul, and gratitude goes to my family. My boys ate a lot of noodles for the six months it took to write this book. My husband took up a lot of my slack and was a constant source of emotional support, as well as being my in-house editor. My extended family gathered around encouraging me and always reading, reading, reading. Thank you.

One

*W*hat happened to Arlo shouldn't have happened to a dog. Granted, Arlo was a shameless con and a flawless manipulator, but he was also brilliant and, in his way, lovable.

I've always liked a guy with charisma, and Arlo had plenty of it. I'm an exotic dancer for this little club in Panama City, Florida. It's a beach resort area, so you can believe I've heard all the lines and met all manner of men. It takes more than a line of talk to win me over, it takes nerve and daring, a certain glint to the eye that means herein lies a risk taker. I like that kind of spirit in all my friends, so it didn't particularly matter that Arlo was of the canine persuasion.

Arlo was a fixture at the Tiffany. He arrived on the scene with his owner, Denise, about a year ago. Denise tended bar and Arlo usually spent his time racked out at her feet. Everybody knew it, and everybody looked the other way, even the health inspector. Vincent, the boss, told the inspector that Denise was blind and that was why her dog worked with her. It didn't seem to matter that Arlo was a mutt of the most unrecognizable variety and not like your basic Seeing Eye dog. Arlo trotted over to the inspector, extended one of his paws to shake, and licked the guy's hand. Then Arlo proceeded to turn a backward flip and roll over three times like a circus dog.

"How the hell you teach him that?" the inspector boomed to Denise.

She looked him dead in the eye, widening her gorgeous green 20/20s, and cooed, "They sent him to me like that. I guess it's part of his training."

The health inspector was in love, with all of his six-foot-two brawny redneck being. Denise is a looker. She's got deep red hair and she's built tiny. Men see her and instantly they're all mush, wanting to take care of the frail little bird. We laugh about it; a lot. They don't know Denise can drink most heavyweights under the table and rides a '48 Harley Panhead. Arlo rides on the banana seat in back. Denise even had a little dog helmet custom-made for him, but I digress.

It was on a Saturday night, about two months ago, that Arlo disappeared. I remember because I'd been breaking in a new routine. See, the Tiffany ain't a strip joint. We are not low class. Vincent Gambuzzo, the owner, told us when he bought the place that we would not be about a bunch of naked girls giving a pole a workout while the music blared rock and roll at a million decibels. No, the Tiffany has standards; we appeal to a higher class of customer. That is why we choreograph our dances. We have costumes and themes and music you can relate to. So I remember my routines and I remember the night Arlo disappeared.

I was doing Little Bo Peep.

Two

The music started. "We are poor little lambs who have lost our way . . ." I wandered out wearing a blond ringlet wig, a full blue dress, and pantaloons. Vince got some stuffed sheep from a pawn shop somewhere and scattered them around the stage. They were in pretty bad shape. Moth-eaten. One was missing a leg and had to be propped against the blue-sky backdrop. I stepped out in front and peered into the audience.

"Oh, where are my lambs?" I called, stretching out my arms. "Come to Mama, little lambie pies."

That did it. These three traveling-salesman types came tumbling over one another in their rush to get to the stage. They were stopped by Bruno, the steroid-impaired bouncer, who informed them that they could go no closer. I'm peeling out of my dress by this point and standing in my little corset and pantaloons. Some of the men were baahing, and the rest were panting.

When I'm premiering an act, I look around the place to see how everyone's taking it. Denise gives me the thumbs-up if she likes it. Tonight she was crying. She didn't even look up. Her bar back was taking over, filling the drink orders, while she stood off to the side wiping her eyes. Arlo usually wandered out to the edge of the bar to watch the show, but he was nowhere to be seen. Is it my act? I wondered.

There was nothing for me to do but finish up and try

to get to Denise. I quickly lost the corset and pantaloons, stripping down to a lambskin G-string and rhinestone pasties. I stepped to the edge of the stage so's the fellas could get a real good glimpse of the pasties made up to look like lambs. Then I did my grand finale. It's old-fashioned but effective. I got the tassels on my pasties swinging so they rotated in opposite directions. An engineer told me one time it was a matter of force and gravity. He said with my 38DDs it was all momentum and propulsion. I say it's a gift; you either got it or you don't.

The three drunk salesmen were hooting and throwing bills up onto the stage. I turned around, bent over, and reached through my legs to grab the money off the floor. The crowd went wild. I straightened up, blew them a kiss, and sauntered offstage. Ralph, the stage manager, was waiting, holding my purple silk kimono.

"Another winner, Sierra," he said, helping me into my robe. "Them guys love the fairy tales."

"Yeah, right, Ralph," I answered as I headed toward the bar. "You're all little boys at heart."

Denise was still crying. Her back was turned to the customers and she was trying to act like she was arranging the bottles, but no one was fooled. Her regulars stared uncomfortably into their watered-down drinks, trying to act like they didn't know she was crying. If she kept this up, the place would be empty by eleven.

"Hey, so Little Bo Peep hold some childhood memories for you or what?"

Denise walked toward me, her pretty face blotchy and her eyes swollen with tears.

"He's gone, Sierra," she whispered. "Arlo's gone."

It took a moment for the words to sink in, then I moved forward and put my arms around her thin shoulders.

"Oh, Denise, I'm so sorry," I said, drawing her away from the bar. "What happened?"

I could envision poor little Arlo, roadkill outside the

Restful Haven Trailer Park. Worse yet, I thought, Arlo flying off the back of Denise's cycle, careening into a tree and landing in a sandy road ditch.

Denise shook her head. "It's not that, Sierra. Somebody took him."

Straight off, I got mad. After all, I've got a little Chihuahua, Fluffy, at home. If someone was to snatch her, well, it'd be like losing my own kid. The people here at the Tiffany, we're one another's family. The rest of the world tends not to accept us. I guess they see us as bottom feeders on the respect scale along with your prostitutes and lawyers. But we protect one another. If one of us has a problem, then we've all got a problem.

"Who'd want to take little Arlo?" I asked. "How'd they get him?"

"I don't know," she wailed. She fumbled around, rooting through her pockets, finally drawing out what I thought was a tissue.

"They left this," she said, handing me the crumpled, tear-wet piece of paper.

I couldn't read in the darkened bar. I led Denise back toward the employee area and stopped under one of the wall lights. There was no such thing as privacy at the Tiffany. Girls were pushing past us trying to get in and out of the dressing rooms. I spread the crumpled paper out with my hands and started reading.

IF YOU WANT TO SEE THE MUTT AGAIN, GET THE $100,000. DON'T CALL US, WE'LL CALL YOU.

It was just like the movies. The words had been cut from magazines, pasted onto the paper in uneven lines. But who would want to kidnap a dog and ask a barmaid to pay a hundred large?

I was about to ask that and a few hundred other questions, when I saw Vincent Gambuzzo bearing down on us like a Mack truck.

"Look," I said, "Vincent don't need to get in on this. Go on back to the bar, I'll run interference for you. When we get off tonight, we'll go over to your place and figure something out."

Denise was staring at Vincent like a deer caught in headlights. I gave her a little shove to get her moving, then turned to face the boss. I had the feeling Vincent would've mowed me down to get to Denise, just for the pleasure of reaming her out for leaving her post. Vincent was like that sometimes. If he thought he had the upper hand, he was all over you.

Vincent never had the upper hand with me. For one thing, in my black spike stilettos, I was a good four inches taller than him. For another, Vincent knew I had his number. When he bought the Tiffany, about a year ago, he tried to bluster his way around us girls, intimating that he was big-time connected. He'd sit around, all three hundred pounds of him, in his black suit, with the black silk shirt and tie, wearing these wraparound sunglasses, with it dark as Pharaoh's tomb in here, and let on he knew all these big wiseguys, like Lucky Pagnozzi and Stiff Red Runzi. I knew he didn't know anything.

You don't grow up in Philly without knowing every rank-and-file mobster by name and reputation. Lucky Pagnozzi was a nobody, didn't nobody I know ever hear of him. Now, Stiff Red Runzi, that was a name; only trouble was Stiff Red got his name after the fact. Stiff Red bit it outside a Fort Lauderdale restaurant sometime in the late seventies, secondary to a driveby whack from a rival family.

Vincent Gambuzzo, I found out, was the son of a small-time numbers guy. Buying the Tiffany was Vincent's attempt to make it big. So the first time Vincent attempts to mess with me, I lay it all out for him.

"Vincent," I say, "I admire what you're trying to do here, really I do. Turning the Tiffany into a high-class joint is a stroke of genius, but you're making a mistake."

Vincent kinda leans back in his chair, puffing up his

chest, getting ready for a fight.

"And how is that?" he asks, pitching his voice low like he's maybe Marlon Brando.

"Well," I say, "you start off good, but then you start bullying everybody around and treating me, your top act, like I'm a no-nothing no-talent. That will not get your staff to pull behind you. It will, however, piss us off."

Vincent's face turns red and his jaw starts pumping like the turnstile at Vets Stadium on the opening day of baseball season. Before he can blow, I continue.

"Furthermore, my last name's Lavotini, as in Moose Lavotini. You may have heard of him?"

All right, now, I admit that I am not related to Big Moose Lavotini, head of the Lavotini Syndicate out of Cape May, New Jersey, but Vincent didn't need to know that. I just paused and looked significant. Vincent took the bait and blanched. He didn't talk to me no more like I was lunch meat, and I didn't bring up that his so-called connections were bogus.

So when Vincent saw me in the hallway, he realized he wasn't going to get to Denise. Instead, he slowed up and stared at me from behind his sunglasses.

"Don't you got nothing better to do than block the hallway?" he grumbled.

Vincent had to save face some way. I shouldered past him and into the dressing room. It was five minutes until I had to be back on for the second show. I realized as I walked into the dressing room that I was still carrying Arlo's crumpled ransom note.

Three

$\mathcal{D}$enise didn't live far from the Tiffany. She'd lucked out moving to Panama City in the winter, off season to all but the snowbirds from Canada. She had an efficiency in the Blue Marlin, one of the little family motels that lined Highway 98, a main route to the beach. Denise managed to live there for off-season rent year-round by relieving the motel manager of front-desk duty one day a week.

We wandered past the pool, our faces lit with the weird incandescent glow that radiated from the underwater lights. Denise's little studio was at the far end of the court, right next to the ice machine and the motel laundry. It was April, spring break season, and the motel was pretty much at capacity. Parties seemed to be in full swing in many of the motel rooms, the music and mating calls of the young rednecks echoing off the enclosing walls of the complex.

Denise didn't seem to hear a thing. She stuck her key numbly in the lock, sighing as it wouldn't turn and she had to twist harder.

"Damn thing," she muttered impatiently.

"Want me to try?"

I turned the key in the lock and quickly realized the problem: Denise'd already unlocked it. I said nothing, turned the door handle, and pushed open the door. Even without turning the lights on, with only the dim glow from the neon tubes that framed each wing of the motel, I could see something was very wrong. It was either that or Denise was a bad housekeeper. The insides of the little efficiency were turned upside down. The mattress from the bed was flung against the wall, lamps were knocked over, and the contents of the dresser drawers decorated the tiny apartment.

"Oh my God," Denise gasped, sagging against my arm.

I reached around and fumbled for the light switch. With the overhead light on, I could see we had a much larger problem. The lump of sheets at the foot of the bed wasn't a lump of sheets. It was a body.

Denise tossed her cookies all over the sidewalk outside the room, narrowly missing my stilettos. I took a few steps inside the room, in part to avoid being splattered, in part to make sure the guy was really dead, not just hurt bad. There was no mistake. The man's hands were tied behind his back and blood had clotted around a small indentation at the base of his skull.

Behind me, I could hear Denise heave again as I looked around for the phone. I found it on the far side of the bed, ripped from the wall.

"Denise," I called, "is the office open?" I was on automatic pilot. I didn't want to stand still long enough to really get what had happened. I needed to move, to get help, to get away from the odor and the sight of a pale yellow body.

Denise coughed and straightened up. "Yeah," she said, "there should be someone in there."

"Well, we need a phone. Yours is out of order." I blew past her and headed up to the front office with Denise right behind me.

The police had to make their way through spring break traffic. I heard the siren long before I actually saw them weaving in and out of cars, passing pickup after pickup of half-clad, drunken college kids. Denise was sitting inside the office, sipping tea that her friend the manager had pressed upon us both. I was standing outside by the entrance, trying to suck enough air into my lungs to replace the smell of death. It didn't seem to be working.

Panama City sent three cars. The area was quickly sealed off, and before I knew it, Denise and I were leading the officers back to her room. This time I couldn't go inside. They let us go as far as the edge of the sidewalk. It must've made quite a picture. There I am, still in my stage makeup, my blond hair all piled up on top of my head, dressed in stiletto heels, towering over this young recruit with a buzz cut. Denise's there, looking tiny and frail, and stinking like vomit. The whole place is rapidly being cordoned off with crime scene tape, which, as it always does on TV, draws a crowd. And to top it off, there's a dead body on Denise's floor.

Denise was standing next to me, peering into her place and shaking, when the detective arrived. I knew it was him because of the way the uniforms started cutting out of his way, and how they right away let him past the tape and got busy. Up until he arrived they'd all just stood around, not doing much of anything.

The detective walked right up to the body.

"You guys get a shot of this yet?" he called to the crime scene team.

"Got it, Skipper," someone yelled out.

The detective stared at the guy's back for a moment, like he was thinking or something, then he leaned down and turned the guy over. Denise gasped again, her eyes widened.

"Oh God," she whispered.

"Oh God, what?" I asked. She looked terrified and even more pale. "You know him?"

Denise trembled violently. "No," she said. "I never saw the guy before."

The young recruit who'd written down our particulars

was standing next to Denise, watching. I don't know what he was thinking, but I was thinking, She knows that guy. The victim may have been a mess, his face bloody and discolored, but I could've sworn she knew him.

The detective called to the police officer who'd taken our statements and he trotted right up. I was trying to read their lips, but Denise had another agenda.

"Sierra," she hissed, yanking on my sleeve.

"Hush," I hissed back, "I'm trying to get what they're saying."

"Sierra!" Her voice was insistent.

"What?" I said, impatient to get back to eavesdropping. Denise looked around to make sure no one was listening.

"Don't say anything about Arlo," she said softly.

I turned all the way around, forgetting about the cops.

"Look, Denise, do you think this could have something to do with Arlo?"

Denise wouldn't look me in the eye. "I don't know."

"You don't know?" I said. "Listen, Denise, your dog disappears, then your place gets torn up and some guy's dead on your floor, and you don't know?" Out of the corner of my eye, I saw the police officer gesture toward us. "I think you oughta level with them, Denise."

Denise glared at me, the color rushing back into her face. "Look, Sierra, they got Arlo, all right? I don't give a rat's ass about anything else. They've got my dog and I'm not doing nothing to jeopardize getting him back."

The cop and the detective were starting toward us. I didn't have time to mention to Denise that there was the small matter of her being a barmaid and not having the ransom money.

Denise's eyes were filled with tears. "I mean it, Sierra," she whispered. "Keep your mouth shut about Arlo."

What else could I do?

* * *

Detective John Nailor wasn't my type. I knew it from the moment the officer with the clipboard introduced us. I don't mean he was unattractive—far from it. I'm only saying he was a little too clean-cut for my tastes, that's all. His hair was black and clipped short. He had deep brown eyes, the kind that don't miss details. He walked up and shook hands like he was at a business meeting, firm and efficient. He was wearing a navy blue suit that I could tell must have set him back plenty. His shirt was crisp and white, and to his credit, I didn't see one of those plastic pocket liners some men have to keep their pens from leaking. He smelled good, too.

Denise wouldn't look him in the eye. She stared down at the ground and was still shaking like a blender. Detective Nailor put his hand on Denise's shoulder like a big brother and started talking.

"Ms. Curtis, I know this has been hard on you, but I need to ask you some questions. I'd like you to come to the station and give a statement."

Denise shook her head. "Why?" she asked.

Nailor shrugged. "We find it easier to do it that way. I can type up your statement, get you to sign it, and we'll be through."

That's what he said, but his eyes were serious, and he watched Denise like maybe she was holding back. Maybe I was paranoid; after all, I'm not used to keeping secrets from cops. I didn't think he'd be such a bad guy to talk to, but it was Denise's secret to spill, not mine.

"Let's go, Denise," I said. "We'll give our statements and get it over with."

Nailor looked up at me and smiled. "That won't be necessary, Ms. Lavotini," he said firmly. "I only need to talk with Ms. Curtis. She's the resident. As I understand it, you were just visiting?"

He was smooth, this guy. The way he asked the question and then stared into my eyes made me feel guilty, and I hadn't even done anything. My dad used to look at me like that when he thought I was skipping school or giving the nuns a hard time. Most of the time my dad didn't even have anything on me; he'd only ask like that to see what I'd cop to, but that was then.

"That's right, Detective," I answered, "I was only visiting."

Denise stood up a little straighter and tossed her long red hair back over her shoulder.

"I'll be fine, Sierra," she said, her voice suddenly strong. "I'll call you later."

"Whatever," I answered.

I knew what they were doing. They were separating us, in case I said something she didn't or vice versa. I read books. I watch TV. I am not a dummy. The detective escorted me to my '87 Trans Am. He stood next to me while I fumbled with my keys.

"Listen," I said, "you go easy on my friend. She's a good kid and this is a big shock to her."

Nailor smiled, but his eyes reached into mine, questioning. "Ms. Lavotini, if your friend's telling it like it really is, she's got nothing to worry about. From us, that is."

"What do you mean by that exactly?"

Detective Nailor stared at me for a moment. Behind him the neon lights of the Blue Marlin flickered and went out. It was dawn on the Redneck Riviera and the sun was starting to rise.

"This wasn't some random robbery. That man was killed somewhere else and brought to Ms. Curtis's apartment. I'd say someone's sending your friend a message."

I wanted to ask him more, but I stopped because I realized he didn't know any more. Detective Nailor was as new to the scene as I was, only I knew about Arlo and Nailor didn't. I shrugged my shoulders and slid into the driver's seat.

Nailor pushed the door closed, then leaned his hands on the open window and peered inside.

"I'll be in touch," he said.

"I'm sure you will," I answered.

I took off in a cloud of exhaust, revving my engine and laying tracks out of the Blue Marlin. It was six A.M. on a spring beach morning, my friend had lost a dog and gained a dead man, and suddenly I was very, very tired.

Four

I was dreaming. Me and Fluffy, my Chihuahua, were riding in the front car of the roller coaster at Disney World. Fluffy was holding her tiny front paws up in the air and yelping with excitement. Her lips were pulled back in what can only be described as a grin of pure joy. Then we shot into a tunnel, and the sound of the roller-coaster wheels on the tracks was intensified a million times. We covered our eyes, but the noise continued. It was so loud, it woke me up.

The sound of thunder in a tunnel continued, and now Fluffy, who had been sleeping on the pillow beside me, woke up and started barking furiously.

"What in the hell?" I grabbed my purple chenille robe and hopped off the bed. The trailer park was not known for tranquillity, but this was ridiculous. I ran over to the window, pushed up a few miniblind slats, and peered out into the bright sunlight. My trailer was currently surrounded by at least a hundred bikers—okay, maybe ten bikers, but they didn't have baffles on their tailpipes, so it sounded like a hundred. Only a few of them wore helmets, those spiky ones that look like World War I German helmets. The rest had bandannas tied around their heads. All of them had long hair and beards.

"These friends of yours?" I asked Fluffy.

Fluffy smiled and I took that for a "maybe." As the bikers didn't show any signs of leaving, I decided it might be best for me to meet them head-on. I stepped into my high-heeled slippers, the ones with the pink feather stuff across the top, and went to the door.

It was boiling outside, one of those late April afternoons in Florida when the temperature spikes up and the heat shimmers off the roofs of the metal trailers. The Lively Oaks Trailer Park is arranged in such a way as to make all the trailers line up like cemetery crosses. There are no oak trees, as the name implies, only sandy patches of ground interspersed with weedy grass. Everybody could see everyone else's trailer, and I was sure they were all watching mine right now.

I stepped out onto the stoop, feeling like the Statue of Liberty; all I needed was a cup of coffee to hold up like a torch. I waited to see what was going to jump off next. The bikers were staring at me, making gestures to one another and snickering. The guy closest to my steps seemed to be the one in charge of this little mission. Unlike the others, he had hair that was fairly short, and a dull brown, but he had a mustache, a Fu Manchu, that dripped off the sides of his jaw. He was big, a beefy kind of man, but I didn't think much of that was fat. His bike glimmered in the mid-afternoon sun, and black leather fringe hung off the handlebars, like a kid's trike.

All the bikers wore leather vests with some kind of emblem on the back, so I figured they belonged to one of the local clubs, the Warlocks or the Pagans or something. That worried me a little bit, but I tried not to show it. At a signal from the front man, the bikers began turning off their engines, one at a time, until at last there was relative silence.

"Are you Sierra?" the big guy asked. He was wearing leather gloves with the fingers cut off, leather chaps, and scuffed biker boots. I was figuring that after a few more minutes in the sun, he was going to smell pretty ripe.

"Who wants to know?" I answered.

"Denise sent me," the big guy said. Then I recognized

him. He'd been into the Tiffany a couple of times to pick up Denise after work. She'd told me she was seeing someone new.

"And you are?" I asked, still not moving.

"Frankie." The big guy smiled, and I noticed a dragon tattoo on his arm. FRANKIE, it said in big letters underneath it. He saw me staring and laughed.

"So I don't get wasted some night and forget," he said.

"I'm assuming you was wasted when you did that."

The others snickered again, and Frankie silenced them with a look.

"Denise wanted me to come by and tell you she's okay. The cops kept her talking for most of the morning, but she cut out of there around lunchtime. I told her to get some sleep and I'd come check up on you."

Pretty friendly for a biker, I was thinking.

"Where is she?" I asked. Inside I could hear Fluffy hurling herself at the door in an attempt to get out. I stepped back and turned the knob. Fluffy tore outside, barking and growling. She raced down off the stoop and lit right into the guy next to Frankie. Her teeth sank into his boot, and before I could move, the guy kicked Fluffy into the air. She landed with a thud on the concrete parking pad.

"You fucking douche bag!" I screamed. Fluffy stood up slowly, shaking her five-pound body. I was off the steps and over to her side. Frankie was off of his bike and in between me and his friend.

"Bitch," the other guy said, "I'm gonna skin that dog and tack its head to your door if it tries that again."

He was starting to move, but Frankie stood right in front of him. "It's a fucking mouse dog, you goddamn idiot," he said calmly. "It's teeth won't even cut through your pants."

The others laughed.

"Hey, Rambo," one yelled, "you afraid of a mouse?" The others thought this was hilarious. Rambo, however, didn't think anything was funny. His face reddened and his eyes took on a wild glare, like maybe he was inches from losing control.

My heart was pounding and I couldn't move. I wanted to get up in his face. I wanted to hurt him, but I was also weighing the odds of surviving. Whatever was going to happen wasn't going to come from me—not then, at least.

"Back off, man," Rambo said to Frankie. Frankie didn't move.

"We don't have time to waste on some pissant dog," said Frankie. "We've gotta get back to the clubhouse. We got something to take care of."

The others were starting up their bikes and turning around. Frankie stepped back, still watching Rambo. Rambo started his bike, pulled a wheelie, and was gone, roaring down the trailer park street and out onto the road. Frankie turned to me.

"Is your dog all right?" he asked.

I was hopped up on adrenaline, my heart was pounding, and my ears were ringing. I wanted to hurt somebody, anybody, and Frankie was the closest. I stood up and launched myself at him, all in one movement. I slammed into the side of his nose with the heel of my hand, almost catching him unaware.

Just as quickly, he grabbed my arm and twisted it painfully behind my back. We stood there like that, him maintaining pressure on my arm until I was almost bent double, and me trying to move.

"I'll let you go when you calm down," he said. He didn't sound angry, just matter-of-fact. Beside us, drops of blood began dotting the grass. His nose was bleeding and inside I felt good.

Behind us, across the narrow trailer park street, I heard a screen door slam. Then I heard Raydean, my next-door neighbor.

"Son," she said softly, "if you don't want to meet your maker right now, today, I suggest you unhand that young woman and take a giant step backward."

Raydean stood on her trailer steps aiming a shotgun at Frankie. Raydean had leaned her frizzy gray-haired head along the left side of the gun and was eyeing Frankie down the barrel. Raydean was dressed in her pink flowered housedress, her knee-high nylon hose rolled down to her ankles, her white saggy legs and arms rippling when she moved ever so slightly to keep Frankie in her sights.

Frankie slowly let go of my arm and I straightened up all the way. Fluffy was standing where I'd left her, growling. Raydean followed Frankie through the sight of the gun.

"Sugar," she called to me sweetly, "you want I should blow his testicles to kingdom come now?"

Raydean was a sweetheart, but she was also batshit. Raydean was fine as long as she made her trip to the mental-health center every three weeks for an injection of Prolixin. If she missed that appointment, within two weeks she'd be seeing little folks who weren't there and calling the cops to say that the Flemish were invading the complex. This would soon be followed by Raydean shooting out the window at invisible soldiers, then being carted off by the cops to the state hospital. So I wasn't real sure if Raydean thought Frankie was Flemish, or if she had an accurate read of the situation.

Frankie didn't know any of this, but he still looked plenty nervous.

"How's about this, Raydean," I said, eyeing Frankie and praying he didn't try to run. "How's about we let him go this time, but if he ever tries anything like this again, then you can shoot him."

Raydean thought for a moment, lowered her gun slightly, and looked at me. "He ain't one of them Flemish, is he?"

"Nah, Raydean," I answered. "He's a biker." This seemed to satisfy her.

"Go on, then, son," she said.

Frankie moved slowly to his bike and climbed on. I

took a few steps toward him, careful not to aggravate Raydean. The adrenaline rush had gone.

"I'm sorry I lashed out at you," I began.

Frankie looked a mess. Blood was still running down his face and had stained his shirt.

"It's all right," he said. "Shit happens. Rambo's an asshole." He sighed and wiped his nose with the back of his hand. "Denise's in Room 320 at the Blue Marlin, but don't call till after six. She needs to sleep." He turned the key in the bike's ignition and pressed the electric start button. The Harley roared to life. In an instant he was gone.

I turned around to Raydean, but she, too, was gone. Fluffy stood in the middle of the driveway, staring after Frankie. She wasn't smiling.

Five

They call the beachfront in Panama City the Miracle Strip. In the two years I'd lived there, I hadn't latched on to what the miracle was. Maybe it was a miracle that any one town could attract so many young rednecks. More likely, the Chamber of Commerce wanted the tourists to think that this particular stretch of beach was the best the Panhandle had to offer. I'd given up trying to figure it. I was now sitting on the far western edge of the Miracle Strip, enjoying a piña colada on the deck that runs across the back of Sharky's.

It's hard to miss Sharky's Beach Club. It is a faded gray, thatched-hut sort of joint that juts out along the edge of Front Beach Road, its sign screaming to passersby. And if that's not enough to grab your attention, there's always the giant shark hanging out in front of the entrance.

I was looking at the sunset and the people wandering up and down the beach in front of the back deck bar. A couple of young guys in white shorts and shirts were lowering the blue beach umbrellas and hauling equipment up to a nearby hotel for the night. This was the time of day I liked best in Panama City, the brief lull in the action, when sunburned nymphets napped and tired men showered, preparing for another round of partying.

It was hard to believe that less than ten miles away, at the Blue Marlin, life had turned ugly just before dawn.

Now the sun was sinking and people went on about the business of excess, oblivious to the rest of the world.

"I got here as soon as I could." Denise had slipped onto the stool next to me and I hadn't even heard her coming. She was wearing dark glasses and her thick red hair was pulled into a severe topknot. Her face was pale, despite the makeup she'd carefully applied. The only color on her at all were her huge gold and amethyst earrings.

"I thought we oughta talk before we go in tonight," I said.

I had an agenda. Denise and I had hung around with each other for a year, and what really did I know about her? Everybody got to know Arlo, but who really knew Denise?

"I thought about it, Sierra. I'm gonna try and reason with them. I don't have a hundred thousand dollars, anybody oughta know that. Maybe somebody thinks I'm somebody else." Denise shook her head and shrugged like it was all a mystery, but her hands shook when she reached for an ashtray.

"Are you?" I asked.

"Am I what?"

"Are you somebody else?"

Denise looked irritated.

"What the hell kind of question is that?" she asked. She fumbled in her oversized black leather bag for her cigarettes. I signaled the bartender for another piña colada.

"Well, I see it like this, Denise. I've known you since you moved here a year ago, and what do I really know?" I paused as my piña colada appeared. "You're twenty-eight, grew up in Miami, got divorced about a year ago, and now you got a dead guy lying in your place and your dog's gone. So I'm thinking: How well do I know you?"

A cool breeze was blowing in off the Gulf. Denise turned her head away, shielding her face as she tried and failed to light her cigarette. Exasperated, she flung the lighter on the counter and turned back around.

"Man, you and the cops." Her tone was bitter. "Everybody wants my fucking history. There's no way to get a break and start over, is there?"

"Cops is one thing, Denise, but I thought we were friends."

Denise pulled off her dark glasses. Her eyes were red and swollen.

"We are." She sighed. "But I don't know what kind of friends we'll be when I tell you about me."

"Denise, everybody's got something they don't want anybody else to see, something they're ashamed of. You're not so different from the rest of us."

"I know that. It's just . . . Well, all right," she said, apparently making up her mind to get it over with. "Here goes. I was married to this guy, Leon, for five years." She looked over at me and I nodded. "At first everything was wonderful. He was so good-looking. He always had money and nice things. The part of Miami where I grew up, nobody had nothing. He treated me like I was a queen, for a while. Then I really saw what he was like, how he made his money. That's when I started getting scared. He was a real bad person, Sierra."

"He hit you or what?" I asked.

"Oh yeah," she said matter-of-factly, "that was part of it, but he was connected."

"Connected—like to the mob, right?"

"Right," she said, "and he was kind of on the low end of things." She stopped, fooling with her cigarette lighter again.

"And?" I prodded.

"And well, he was a pretty big dope dealer. He started to make me help him—you know, make connections, hold the money sometimes. He got popped three years ago and that's when I decided it was safe to leave him."

"What do you mean 'safe to leave him'?" I asked.

"Well, he would've beat the living shit out of me if I'd left and he could get to me, but with him in prison, I could go. He was mad, but at that point he thought he was looking at a lot of time, so he signed the papers. I moved here and decided to start over."

Denise sat back and tried to act like that was that. I thought not.

"What did you mean he thought he was looking at a lot of time? Isn't he still in prison?" Denise's lower lip trembled ever so slightly.

"No," she whispered. "He got a new attorney and he got some kind of appeal process going. He's out until the new trial. He's been out a month."

No friggin wonder the girl was scared. Her ex gets out of jail, her dog gets snatched, and a dead guy ends up on her doorstep.

"So you think Leon's messing with you?" I asked.

"Wouldn't you?" She looked at me like I was stupid or something.

"Did you tell the cops?"

"Sierra, he'd kill me if I did that!" Denise was gathering up her things.

"Denise, I hate to break it to you, but isn't that what he's leading up to here?"

Denise slapped a five-dollar bill down on the bar and anchored it with her empty glass. "I can't think about this anymore, Sierra," she said. "I'm tired and I've gotta go to work. For all I know, Leon's got a new squeeze and doesn't even know where I live. Frankie'll look out for me. He hates Leon."

"Frankie knows Leon?" I could imagine that relationship.

"No." She shook her head. "Only by reputation. Look, I gotta go. I'll see you at the club later. I've gotta get changed and get over there."

"What about Arlo?" I protested.

Denise's eyes welled up with tears. "I don't know, honey. Frankie said he'd nose around, see if he heard anything." She smiled. "He told me he met your neighbor."

"He don't know how close he came to meeting Jesus, too," I said.

Six

I wasn't in a Little Bo Peep kind of mood. As an exotic dancer, I am a creative artist. If doing a particular act doesn't feel right, I do not invalidate my inner child. Never force art. So I was rummaging through my old metal locker, looking for a costume that suited my mood, when Bruno poked his head in the dressing room.

"Hey, Sierra," he rumbled like a pit bull, "some guy's out here, says he's looking for you." What could I expect from a steroid-impaired bouncer?

"Of course some guy's looking for me." I sighed. "Some guy is always looking for me, Bruno. It's your job to make sure they don't find me."

Bruno favored me with his wounded-dog look. "No, Sierra, what I'm saying is, I think he's the heat and he wants to talk to you, professional-like." Bruno watched too many cop shows on TV.

I straightened up from the wardrobe and glanced at myself in the wall-length dressing-room mirror. Everything was in order.

"All right, Bruno, here's the deal. Lead the gentleman to a table, pat him down, tell him sit, and I'll be along presently."

Bruno looked shocked. "Sierra," he said, "you can't pat down a cop."

"Jesus, Bruno," I said, "I know that. I was being sarcastic. Tell him take a load off and I'll be there in a minute." Bruno withdrew and went off to deal with the visitor. I took a moment to figure out what I wanted to say.

I was leaning in close to the mirror, wearing my naughty French maid costume and carefully applying lipstick, when Marla walked in. Marla is the other headliner at the Tiffany. She is not what I would describe as an artist. I would, instead, say that she is a prima donna, or your basic pain in the ass. Marla is about six feet tall in her stocking feet, and stacked. Vincent Gambuzzo is particularly fond of her because she kisses up to him and doesn't give him any crap when he pulls his power trips. She makes up for it by torturing the rest of us.

"Vincent isn't gonna like it, you having an officer of the law pay you a visit at the club. It doesn't look right." She was standing in front of the mirror at the other end of the room, adjusting her bra straps and peering at a spec of green that was stuck between her two front teeth.

I turned and walked toward her. Marla didn't like that. She was afraid of me, on account of a few other little occurrences in which things didn't work out so well for her.

"Marla," I said pleasantly, "what wouldn't look right would be if your teeth was to be so far down your throat, you'd have to fart to talk." I smiled.

Marla tossed her long black hair over her shoulders and tried to look bold. It didn't work.

"Don't touch me," she cautioned. "I'll tell Vincent."

"Telling Vincent could be difficult if you wasn't able to speak clearly," I said. I sailed past her and out of the dressing room.

Detective John Nailor was not uncomfortable. I was trying my best to rattle him, but it wasn't working. Bruno had placed him at one of the tables in the back and was hovering nervously, gesturing and making strange facial movements to indicate that this was the man who had asked to see me.

I sauntered up in my black silk maid costume, with the flouncy white apron and the tiny lace cap. I towered over him in my black patent-leather stilettos and fishnet stockings. Then I pulled out a chair and straddled it backward, leaned my arms over the back, and waited to see what he was going do.

He did nothing for a full minute. He carefully placed his drink back on the table and then casually inspected the merchandise, like he did it every day of his life. For all I knew, this could be standard operating procedure for him. He didn't wear a wedding band. In fact, he was so slow and methodical in his inspection that my plan backfired and I felt myself getting nervous.

"Time is money, Detective," I said. "My boss, Mr. Gambuzzo, don't like the help sitting around shooting the shit with the customers. If you don't get down to brass tacks quick, I'm gonna end up having to do a table dance and charging you for it."

He smiled, but it was an I-dare-you. Without breaking eye contact, he reached into his suit coat pocket and pulled out a small notepad. Out of the corner of my eye, I could see Denise wiping down the bar and watching us.

"Why were you and Ms. Curtis going back to her apartment at three-thirty in the morning?" The old double check, I thought.

"Detective, in this business, three-thirty is not late; it's quitting time. You gotta unwind before you can sleep. We were just going back for some girl talk."

Nailor looked over at Denise for a moment, then turned back to his notepad.

"There was no sign of forced entry into Ms. Curtis's apartment, Ms. Lavotini. Now, what do you make of that?" He looked puzzled and earnest, like I should believe he cared what a stripper thought about a crime.

"Jeez, Detective, I don't know. Maybe I should come clean with you and tell you that me and Denise were really coming back to her place to leave a dead body, then call you so you'd think we were innocent. Whoops," I said sarcastically, "our little ruse failed." I leaned back and stared at him. Behind us, Denise, Bruno, and Vincent were huddled together.

"How well do you know Ms. Curtis?" he asked. The guy wouldn't rattle.

"Well enough," I answered.

"Really?"

"Really."

Vincent Gambuzzo was making his way toward our table. Detective Nailor folded his notepad shut and put it back inside his jacket pocket.

"Then you know she spent the two years before she moved here doing time in a federal correctional institution."

I didn't have time to answer, which was good since I couldn't. Vincent Gambuzzo took that moment to step up to the table.

"Sierra," he said, all swagger, "you're on in five minutes. That is," he said, turning toward Nailor, "unless you have further business with this gentleman?" Vincent did not like having a cop in the house because it made the customers nervous.

"No," I answered, "I'm guessing we're through."

Detective Nailor smiled his I-dare-you and reached for his empty Coke glass.

"If it's not too much trouble," he said, holding the glass out toward Vincent, "I'll take another one of these."

Vincent's face turned a lovely shade of scarlet, and he looked like he wanted to choke John Nailor, but he didn't.

"Of course, Detective," he answered, stressing the word *Detective* so nobody would doubt that Vincent Gambuzzo knew the heat was in the house. "Why don't you stick around and watch Sierra. She's got a hell of an act."

"Oh, I know that already," Nailor answered.

I stood up and propped one of my legs on the chair.

"You ain't seen nothing yet, Detective," I said.

I left him there. This was going to be quite an evening.

The house lights went down. The music started and I was ready. If John Nailor wanted to dare Sierra Lavotini, I'd give him something to remember. I strutted out onto the stage and walked right down front.

I reached behind my back and started slowly undoing my apron strings. As I did, I looked out into the audience, looking at John Nailor's table. It was empty. The Coke glass sat waiting for the barmaid to collect it. The detective was walking away, his back to me and his hand lightly resting on the shoulder of a woman. She turned once and glanced back as they were leaving. She was a knockout—chestnut-brown skin, huge dark eyes, and a figure that would have given any girl at the club a run for her money. Who the hell was that? I wondered.

I couldn't keep my mind on my work, and that was a first. Usually I take the time to center myself by meditating before I go on, but in my rush to show up Panama City's finest, I'd forgotten. Now I was caught in the middle of a routine, unfocused and unable to concentrate. I remembered what Nailor said before he left. Why hadn't Denise told me she'd done time? I looked over at her, but her back was turned. She was avoiding me. I peeled down a stocking and twirled it over my head mechanically. Denise wasn't going to get off so easy when I got ahold of her.

Seven

*D*enise had the key in her car door when I stepped up behind her.

"I would like to think that you were an honest person," I began, "but in the past twenty-four hours, I am not so sure."

When she turned around, I could see she was crying.

"That idiot cop told you about me, didn't he?" she said, sobbing.

"Well, didn't you think he would?" I asked. She hung her head, big fat tears dropped like rain. The parking lot was dark and almost empty. The customers had all left and only the cleanup crew remained inside.

"I don't know what I thought," she sniffed. "I guess I wasn't thinking. I needed help and I didn't think you'd help me if you knew."

"That is lame," I said. "You know me better than that. Now, what gives?"

Denise sagged against her car. A week ago I would've told you she was a great kid, fun to be around, a real hell-raiser. Sure, she had her walls, those places where you just didn't go with her. You could see it in her. Her eyes would kind of glaze over when you asked a question, and she'd switch the subject or call Arlo over to be a distraction. But hell, we work in a strip club. Even though the Tiffany is the top of the line, we're still life's outcasts. We all have walls. We've all got secrets. You think I tell people I read books and wish I could maybe be a writer or an artist? No way. They'd eat me alive. So I talk tough and I don't take nothing off nobody. Everybody works the Tiffany for a reason. It ain't like being a nun. No higher power called us. We needed money, we saw the way, and we grabbed it like an uptown bus.

"I don't tell anybody I did time," Denise said. "What if Vincent found out and fired me? You don't think I held my breath every time he wanted to talk to me? I know sooner or later he'll find out and that will be that. But I needed a job."

"Get real, Denise," I said. "Half the girls at the Tiffany have been arrested for one thing or another. It comes with the life."

Denise shook her head. "The Tiffany is a nice place. Vincent pays good. He don't do trash; he's trying to have a classy place. I knew he wouldn't hire me if he knew." She shook her head in disgust. "Don't you think that I applied at a hundred other places first? I was honest with them, and what did it get me? Not a job, that's for sure."

I let it go. For all I knew, she was right. Vincent Gambuzzo didn't have to hire a bartender with a record. Dancers were another story. If they were talented, you didn't ask too many questions. After all, good T and A brings in the money, pure character ain't worth shit.

"So, what'd you do time for?" I asked.

"Possession with intent to distribute," she answered softly.

I was puzzled. "Why'd you pull time for that? You're a first offender."

Denise laughed bitterly. "Yeah, but I was married to Leon Corvase. They made such a big deal of who I was married to at the trial that I didn't stand a chance. Leon got twenty-five years for trafficking and it was his first offense." She rolled her eyes.

I couldn't figure it. To my way of thinking, Denise was a victim here. Obviously, the courts thought otherwise.

Denise was rummaging through the backseat of her car.

"What are you doing?" I asked.

"Looking for this," she said, her voice muffled by the car's interior. She backed out, holding a bottle of tequila. "Want some?"

"When have I ever turned down tequila?" I answered. Denise knew me too well. She hunkered down on the bumper of her old VW and twisted off the cap. I walked over and sat down next to her. It'd been a long night.

"Hey," I asked, taking a big swig off the bottle, "who was the looker who left with Nailor?"

Denise took too big a swallow and choked. I leaned over and clapped her on the back a couple of times. I know they say it doesn't help, but it helped me to beat on her a little.

"Ease up," she sputtered, regaining her composure and handing me the bottle. "You don't know?"

"Would I be asking you if I did?" I was feeling warm and relaxed. Maybe the evening had some promise after all.

"That's some special agent, visiting from South Florida and working with Nailor. I think her name is Carla Terrance. Don't be fooled by her looks. She asked some of the questions last night at the station. She's a real ball-buster. I think she was pissed 'cause Nailor got her out of bed or something."

I took another hit of tequila and passed the bottle back.

"You think they got a thing or what?" I asked. Stupid question, but we all get stupid when we drink. Denise wiped her mouth with the back of her hand and laughed.

"I doubt it," she answered. "Why? You interested?"

"Hey, watch your mouth," I said, taking a swipe at her head. "You know he ain't my type. Speaking of types," I said, switching the subject, "what's with you and Frankie? Is this serious?"

Denise looked embarrassed. "I don't know, Sierra. There's something about him."

I laughed. "Yeah, like what? He has to tattoo his name on his damn arm to remember who he is? Is that what turns you on?"

Denise didn't like that. "He was drunk that night, Sierra. He wishes he hadn't done it, too." She paused and took another swig. I didn't know about her, but I was feeling a distinct buzz. "All I know is, he ain't like Leon. He's kind and gentle to me. And he loves Arlo."

At the mention of Arlo's name, Denise started to cry. For a minute she sat there, drinking and crying. There was something about Denise, something childlike and vulnerable. It made you want to help her, make it all better. Maybe Frankie saw that in her, I sure hoped so, 'cause girls like Denise, with their wide-open hearts, get stomped on all the time. I hoped Frankie treated her right and kept her away from his friends. I hoped it didn't last long, either. That kind of life was not the thing for someone like Denise. Maybe she thought she could tame him, but she was wrong. I've been down that road too many times to think she'd be his magic charm.

"Arlo's gone, Sierra," Denise wailed. Suddenly she was drunk. "He's never coming back. Only one ever really loved me, and he's gone." She leaned her head against my shoulder, and maybe that's what saved her, because as she moved a bullet tore through the back window of her VW, shattering the glass and scaring the living shit out of me.

Denise screamed and I pulled her roughly to the ground. Gravel bit into my knees and the palms of my hands as I crawled around to the other side of the car. The shot had come from the direction of Thomas Drive. Denise was still screaming.

"Shut up, Denise," I hissed. "Your mouth makes you a target."

I poked my head up cautiously. A long white sedan with tinted windows blocked the front entrance of the club. The left rear window was lowered several inches. I pulled my head down quickly. Another shot was fired and went wide. Whoever was shooting was having trouble finding us. Denise was shaking like a leaf.

"Okay," I whispered, looking behind us at my black Trans Am. "Here's the deal. We're going to stay low, crawl to my car, and try and get the hell out of here."

"How?" Denise wailed.

"We'll drive out the exit."

Denise didn't look so sure. "I think I'm gonna be sick," she moaned.

"Suit yourself," I whispered. "Puke and get your brains blown out or put your ass in gear and get out alive. It makes no nevermind to me."

Denise started moving with me right behind her. I heard another bullet ping off something a few feet away from where we'd been. We reached the car and I crawled across the passenger seat and slid behind the wheel. Denise climbed in behind me.

We sat, panting, while I fumbled for my keys. The side door to the Tiffany suddenly flung wide and Bruno emerged out into the driveway. He was holding a shotgun.

"Hey!" he yelled, the sound echoing off the stucco walls of the Tiffany. "What the fuck are you doing?" He was using the door as a shield, aiming the gun around the side at the white sedan. He fired and the sedan took off. As the car sped away, I saw something—a gray paw, a white-and-black muzzle—at the window. Arlo. I started my car and raced out the exit drive.

"Sierra!" Denise screamed. "What are you doing?" I gunned the accelerator and we bounced the curb and took off down Thomas Drive. Ahead of me, the white car shot down a side street, past the Signal Hill Golf Course, headed east through the back streets and away from the beach.

"I thought I saw something. Besides, you think I'm gonna let some chickenshit shoot at me and then run?"

Denise was grabbing for anything to hold on to.

"Yes. I do. That's called saving our asses!" she yelled. "This is called suicide."

She was right. If this was Denise's ex-husband, or one of his associates, then I was insane to chase him. On the other hand, what if Arlo was in that car? All right, so I wasn't thinking clearly. I didn't have a plan for what we'd do if it was Arlo, but at that moment, nothing was going to stop me from chasing that car.

We played tag, whipping around cars, ignoring red lights, and tearing toward Hathaway Bridge, the bridge that separates Panama City Beach from Panama City. The white car tore past the state patrol station and Gulf Coast Community College. The driver tried to lose me when he hit Harrison Avenue. He suddenly made a series of turns, whipping through the residential and business section of Panama City. Denise was yelling at me, but I didn't pay attention. It was me and the Trans Am, chirping tires, taking corners too tight, and making it anyway. The car cut past Patterson Elementary School in an effort to avoid the police station and the fairgrounds. Whoever was driving sure knew his way around PC. We came out in Parker, zooming down Business 98 and suddenly crossing Dupont Bridge.

We were flying out 98, doing in excess of eighty-five miles per hour. We'd passed Tyndall Air Force Base and were now headed for Mexico Beach. I couldn't believe a cop hadn't spotted us. The road was flat, surrounded on either side by scrubby pines. At four in the morning there isn't much traffic between the air force base and Mexico Beach. We passed a couple of cars like they were standing still. Denise had a death grip on the sides of her seat.

"Sierra, let them go. If it's Leon's people, you don't want to mess with them."

"I can't," I answered, watching the road up ahead. The adrenaline pumping through me had long since chased out the tequila buzz. "Denise, I think Arlo's in there."

Denise leaned forward, peering at the car in front of us. "Arlo? Oh no!"

We were coming up on a big truck, filled with pine logs and moving slowly. The white car whipped around it. I edged up behind the truck and pulled out. I was almost able to see the rear plate. The white car pulled in front of the truck and jammed on its brakes. The truck driver reacted, not seeing me, and pulled sharply to the left. We were airborne before I could blink. The last thing I heard was Denise screaming.

Eight

Someone was singing, softly, under her breath, but I could make out the words.

We are standing outside and we're hungry as sin.
Won't you open your doors up and welcome us in.
Hallelujah, I'm a bum. Hallelujah, bum again.
Hallelujah, give us a handout to revive us again.

Someone shifted a chair. There was the sound of metal on metal. My eyes were closed, but I could feel bright white light seeping through.

"Come on, Catfish," the voice whispered. "Wake up. I brought someone to see you."

There was a faint whimper, then a cold wet nose pushed at my fingers. Fluffy. I struggled to wake up, to pull my eyelids open. It felt like moving steel doors, but slowly I opened my eyes, wanting to cover them with my hand but unable to move.

"Ah, there you are." I heard a strong, familiar, satisfied voice. A substantial form hovered over me. Pat.

"Pat," I whispered through cracked lips. "Fluffy?"

Fluffy's small body wiggled next to me, licking my neck and chin. Where the hell was I, and what was my friend Pat doing here?

"Fluffy insisted." Pat's gruff voice broke the silence.

"I didn't have the heart to leave her home, not after all she's been through." She sounded irritated.

"What's going on?" I tried to remember and found I couldn't.

"According to the paper, which is the only way I knew anything, you were driving—racing, actually—and wrecked your car. Two other people were injured, your passenger and a truck driver. The truck driver—" She stopped, apparently thinking she'd said enough.

My eyes slowly brought Pat into focus. Her brilliant white hair was stark against her tanned, lined skin, and her bright blue eyes were clouded with concern. Pat was a charter fishing boat captain, my landlady, and my friend. I think she looked at me like the daughter she never had, and that suited me fine at this particular moment. Any other time, we'd be arguing. I usually tried to reassure her that I was a competent adult while she debated the point. Right now she'd be winning.

Things began coming back to me like outtakes from a bad movie. I looked around and confirmed that I'd landed myself in the hospital. Then I looked down at my body, checking to make sure I'd arrived all in one piece. There was a bandage on my right forearm and I hurt all over, but nothing was missing, everything worked.

"Pat," I said, struggling to sit up, "I wasn't racing. The people in the car I was chasing had tried to shoot me and Denise. They pulled in front of the truck and slammed on their brakes. The truck driver didn't see me when he swerved to avoid hitting their car." Pat was staring at me, a concerned look on her face. I couldn't tell her about Arlo. What if she got responsible on me and decided to tell the cops?

"The paper didn't say anything about a white car. It said you were trying to pass a truck and lost control of your car." Pat didn't believe in sugar-coating life.

"Ask Denise," I protested. "Ask the truck driver."

Fluffy sensed my anxiety and started to growl deep in her throat. Pat wiped her weathered hands on her faded jeans and looked uncomfortable.

"I can't ask the truck driver, Catfish, he's in a coma and they don't know if he'll make it." My heart started beating in my throat. I had to get out of here.

"What about Denise? How is she?"

Pat frowned. "The girl riding with you?"

I nodded.

"She was treated and released, just cuts and bruises." Good, I thought, then she'll be here soon and we'll get this taken care of.

Pat stood up and grabbed an oversized tote bag. She looked worn out. Her gnarled fingers were red and swollen and she moved slowly. I couldn't see how she kept taking people out fishing five days a week. She had a mate, but still, it was a demanding job.

"Pat, how long have I been here?"

She frowned. "Two days," she answered. "You had a concussion or maybe a hairline fracture. They said when the swelling went down, you'd wake up."

"Well, I've gotta get out of here, so where did they put my clothes?" I was trying to swing my feet over the side of the bed when she gently pushed me back. My head exploded and sparks of light flashed around me. I was in agony.

"You're not going anywhere until they release you." Pat's no-nonsense voice cut through my headache. "Your clothes were a mess, what's left of them. I'll bring you fresh ones tomorrow. Now," she said, smoothing the covers, "I need to get Fluffy out of here before someone comes in and catches us." She scooped Fluffy out of the covers and plopped her unceremoniously into the tote bag. Fluffy growled once, then subsided. She knew the score.

"Pat, really," I began, "someone did try to shoot at us. I didn't want them to get away." My voice sounded like a bullfrog croaking and my body was on fire. Pat sat on the edge of my bed and took my hand in hers.

"Catfish, even if that were true, you almost killed yourself and two others." She shook her head, worry lines etched around her eyes. "You're in a lot of trouble. If that truck driver dies, you won't be coming home from the hospital. You'll be headed straight to jail."

My brain was banging against my skull, trying to get out, and I couldn't pull myself together. What was going on, and how had I landed myself in such a fix?

As if to echo my thoughts, the heavy door to the room creaked slowly open. It was my worst personal nightmare. Detective Nailor and his friend Special Agent Carla Terrance stood framed by the doorway and they didn't look happy.

Pat stood up abruptly, jiggling the bed and sending my headache racing through my body. She was gone before I could say good-bye, but on her way past the two detectives, I heard Fluffy growl.

I didn't need a mirror to know I looked like hell. I could see my reflection in Detective Nailor's eyes. He looked shocked. Carla Terrance was staring at me like I was some vaguely interesting yet disgusting lab specimen.

"Ms. Lavotini," Nailor began, his tone all business, "this is Special Agent Terrance."

I nodded. She didn't move, just continued to stare at me.

"We have some questions we'd like to ask about your accident," he said, going again for his suit coat pocket and the notepad.

"I thought you were homicide," I said.

"Let's say I'm interested," he answered. "Now, why don't you tell me what happened?" He wandered in closer, pulling a chair up by the bed. Terrance hadn't moved from the doorway and she hadn't stopped staring.

I went over it all, everything I could remember. I might as well have told it to the wall, because Nailor didn't say a word.

"You can ask Denise," I said, aware that my voice sounded thin and weak. "You can ask Bruno, at the club."

Nailor glanced over at Terrance. "We've got someone interviewing Bruno," he said, "but there's a little problem with your friend Denise." They were both looking at me now, like I somehow knew something that I hadn't told them. Maybe I was being paranoid.

"What do you mean, problem with Denise?"

"She seems to be missing," Nailor said. "She seems to have walked out of the hospital and vanished into thin air. No one has seen or heard from her in two days."

There was a moment when time seemed to freeze. I couldn't comprehend what he was saying. Denise couldn't be gone. The hairs on the back of my neck stood up and goosebumps ran down my arms.

Nine

*T*he nospital and I reached
the mutual conclusion that it was time for me to go. From
their side of things, I had no insurance and, hence, might
not be good for the tab. From my way of seeing it, hospitals are bad places to hang around. You go in for one
problem, and if you stay too long, they start finding other
stuff. A person could die in one of those places.

Pat came and got me in her faded blue 1957 Chevy
pickup. Raydean was riding shotgun, so to speak. After
the two of them had gently deposited me in the front seat,
Raydean climbed up and looked back at the concrete-
and-glass hospital.

"They run them electrical shocks through you in
there?" she asked. Obviously, this was Raydean's experience of hospitals.

"Nope," I muttered, "they were more into the emotional kind of shocks."

Raydean grinned wisely. "I know the kind you mean.
They set you in a bunch of chairs and some young social
worker starts off talking about how your mother is the
cause of your problems. Shit"—she spat tobacco juice
out the window—"it's them Flemish is what the problem
is. Didn't nobody ever wonder how a human could survive in all that cold?" Raydean was due for her Prolixin,
that was for sure. Pat and I looked over Raydean's frizzled head and made eye contact.

"We're on our way there after we drop you," she said.

"On our way where?" asked Raydean, peering anxiously at Pat.

"To pick up your medicine," Pat answered calmly.

"They ain't human," Raydean answered. I wasn't sure if she meant the Flemish or the mental-health center staff. "Aliens is what they is."

My head was pounding as we drove through the blinding sunlight toward the edge of town and the Lively Oaks. I couldn't wait to see the trailer, to fall into my bed and sleep for a week.

"Sierra," Pat was saying, "somebody called from your work while I was over feeding Fluffy last night. They said not to worry, folks'd be taking turns staying and taking care of you until you're on your feet." Not if I can help it, I thought.

Pat pulled into the drive and cut off the engine. Someone's shiny red Corvette stood on the concrete pad. None of the dancers I knew could afford that car; besides, none of us would have been caught dead driving a Corvette. My friend Archie, a sociology professor down at the community college, says men who drive those cars have small penises. I couldn't believe it when he said that, but he said the Corvette looks like a guy's thing, and it's full of power, so it's kind of a wishful-thinking car. I wondered who was wishing on a star in my trailer.

Pat was holding my arm like I was going to break. We weren't even to the steps yet and I could smell something wonderful. Inside Fluffy was barking her tiny head off, but the sound was almost drowned out by another, more hideous, noise. Longhair music.

I hate longhair music, especially opera. Nothing's worse to me than a bunch of people all wailing as loud as they can about somebody killing themselves. Whoever was inside my trailer had the music turned up as loud as it could go and was wailing along with it. My head started pounding in time to the music.

Raydean opened the door and stepped inside. The music stopped almost instantly, as did Fluffy's barking.

"I know what you were doing!" Raydean screamed. "You were calling the mother ship!"

Pat and I hurried up the steps but it was too late. Raydean was off, communicating with the extraterrestrials, and Vincent Gambuzzo was caught wearing one of my aprons over his black silk suit, holding a baking dish containing perfectly done lasagna, and wearing two red oven mitts like gloves. For the first time ever, I saw fear in his face. Raydean had grabbed a butcher knife and had him backed against the oven.

"Raydean!" I shouted. "It's all right. He's my boss."

Raydean hesitated and cut her eyes over at me. Pat took the opportunity to move up behind her and grab the arm that held the knife. Raydean started to struggle, but Pat was much stronger.

"Raydean," she said calmly, "Sierra ain't up to this. Leave the nice man be, and let's us go on."

Raydean pouted, or else still had quite a wad in her jaw. I sighed and looked over at Vincent. The pan with the lasagna shook ever so slightly.

"Beware the Ides of March," Raydean said cryptically. Pat led her gently from the kitchen and out the door.

Vincent slowly backed away from the oven and put down the lasagna.

"I'm sure you're tired," he said, trying to act like Raydean hadn't shook him. He looked ridiculous in my apron, but I didn't say anything. I was tired.

"If you want to go lie down, I'll bring you something to eat in a little while." He looked embarrassed. "It's my mother's lasagna," he said, nodding toward the pan. "She swears by it, an old family recipe."

"Vincent," I said, suddenly wanting to cry, "that's

decent, thanks." I headed toward my room with Fluffy at my heels. "There's no place like home, Fluffy," I said.

Whatever the deal was with Denise and Arlo, I'd done as much as I could. It was time for somebody else to take over and leave me out. When I found her, that was just what I was going to say. That is, once I knew she was all right.

Fluffy leaped up on the bed and stood on her pillow watching me undress. I had to move slow, pulling each arm gently out of my blouse, careful not to disturb the stitches on my right forearm or jar the wrenched shoulder on my left side. I was covered with bruises and scrapes. I stood for a moment and stared at my reflection in the mirror on the back of my closet door. My long blond hair needed attention, but it hurt to lift my arms to brush it. My usually tan, thin body looked pale and scrawny, and my legs were covered with black-and-blue splotches. I wouldn't be dancing for a couple of weeks.

"So how're we gonna pay the bills, eh, Fluff?" Fluffy growled deep in her tiny throat. She was worried about her dog chow. "Hey, I always take care of you, don't I?" Fluffy eyed me cautiously. "Have I ever left you hanging?" Fluffy barked and I took that for agreement. We'd get by, but it'd be lean for a while.

I slipped into my SAVE THE EARTH nightshirt and crawled in between the covers. They'd given me another painkiller before I left the hospital, and I could feel it drifting up behind my eyes and pulling me down. I fell asleep and had the strangest dream. Denise and I were riding on her Harley, with Arlo on the handlebars. Frankie and Rambo were passing us on their bikes, going in the opposite direction. Rambo was leering at me but Frankie was screaming, his mouth wide open and blood trailing behind him. His eyes were fixed and filled with terror. Denise tried to reach for him as he flew past, but I pulled her hand away, forcing her to stay on the road.

* * *

I woke up to the sound of Vincent rumbling through the trailer, coming down my tiny hallway. When he reached my closed door, I could hear him shifting a tray filled with dishes.

"Sierra?"

"Come in," I answered, hitching the covers up to my armpits.

Vincent stood in the doorway. The apron had vanished and he carried a tray. Fluffy was gone from her pillow, outside I assumed.

"What time is it?" I asked. Vincent set the tray down on the edge of the bed and consulted his gold Rolex watch.

"Four-fifteen," he answered. I pushed up further in bed and motioned toward the one chair in my room, an old cane-bottomed piece I'd found at a garage sale. It was taking a risk, but I figured it could hold Vincent.

"Take a load off," I said. Vincent looked uncertain but did as I asked. The chair groaned. I held my breath and waited. Nothing broke.

"Vincent, I appreciate what you did here. You didn't have to do that. It isn't like we've been the best of friends or nothing." I paused, trying to think of what to say next and how to say it. Vincent took that problem right out of my hands.

"Sierra," he began, "don't think I don't know how you and the others talk about me. I got my ways of knowing what's going on." I didn't doubt that; he probably had tape recorders stuck in the dressing room. "But you girls gotta understand, the Tiffany means a lot to me. I gotta be tough to keep you guys in line. That don't mean I'm gonna sit by and let one of you get hurt. And you being Moose Lavotini's daughter . . ." His voice trailed off and he gave me a look of significance.

I felt bad, because I wasn't going to correct his belief that I was Big Moose's daughter. I needed that hold, and

I wasn't going to give it up just because he was here making me lasagna. For all I knew, he was trying to get in good with Big Moose. So I laid back against the pillows.

"But I need to know what's going on, Sierra," Vincent said. "Don't think I don't know something's up."

"What are you talking about, Vincent?" I asked innocently, stuffing lasagna in my mouth. Vincent's mother's recipe was a killer.

"Arlo hasn't been to work with Denise in five days. She's walking around crying her eyes out and you're whispering to her every opportunity you get. Then some dead guy turns up at her place. Someone shoots at you two in the parking lot, thereby making it my business, and now Denise ain't been to work or called in for three days."

"And all that means what to you, Vincent?" I was avoiding looking at him. Instead, I stared at his mother's lasagna.

"Don't act dumb with me, Sierra," Vincent snarled, back to his nasty disagreeable self. "I want to know what's going on with you two. I got rights here, you know."

Fluffy picked that moment to go off. She came scampering through the doggie door and down the hallway, barking to alert me that we had company and they weren't friends of hers.

"Better see who that is," I said to Vincent. He didn't like it. He wanted to stay and hear me answer his question, but Fluffy upped the ante by barking louder and jumping all over him.

"Get off me, you mutt," Vincent growled. He stood up and looked out the window. "It's that cop that came to see you at the club. He's got some woman with him."

"That's Agent Terrance." I sighed, my heart suddenly picking up the pace and forcing the lasagna to stick in my throat. "Look, you put them in the living room and tell them I'll be right there." I'd be damned if they'd catch me looking like hell again. If I was going to jail, then I'd go in style.

Most people don't know much about double-wides and trailer parks. Some people have the preconceived notion that trailers are flimsy and trashy, that those of us who reside therein don't have taste. That couldn't be further from the truth. My trailer is real nice. It isn't new, not by any stretch of the imagination, but it's bright and filled with sunlight from the bay windows in the kitchen and the living room.

If you come in off the parking pad, then you'd come in through the kitchen. In the eat-in area I've got a round, high-topped table and four barstool chairs that I got from a club that was going out of business. The kitchen cabinets are a light maple and the walls are white. I've got all kinds of doodads that I collect at flea markets and the like. I keep them on the pass-through bookshelves that divide the kitchen from the living room.

The living room is filled mostly with plants and my stereo. I've got a futon sofa and a couple of armchairs, but it's where I practice my routines, so I keep it clear in the middle. I keep my book collection on shelves I made out of boards and bricks. I've got a complete collection of McMurtry novels, J. D. MacDonald's Travis McGee series, some Eudora Welty, and some old psychology books, just for a better understanding of my fellowman.

After storms and usually in the winter, I go down to St. Andrews Park and collect shells. I keep them all lined up across the bay-window ledge. That's where I found Detective Nailor, inspecting my shell collection. Special Agent Terrance was writing something down on a notepad and ignoring Vincent.

Nailor smiled when I walked slowly into the living room. I ached all over from getting dressed and putting on makeup. For only a moment, he didn't smile like a cop, he smiled the way a man smiles at a woman. I don't think Special Agent Terrance saw him, but behind me I heard her notebook snap shut. Nailor looked at her for a moment, then back at me.

"Your story checked out with the truck driver," he said. "He woke up yesterday and we saw him this morning. Also, we recovered spent bullet casings from the parking lot of the Tiffany, and Bruno backed up your story."

I was about to heave a sigh of relief when Terrance decided to get in on the act.

"That doesn't mean we couldn't make a case against you for reckless driving, driving while intoxicated, and reckless endangerment," she said, her voice a husky rasp.

"Then why don't you?" I said, spinning to face her. Vincent had wandered over to the kitchen and he coughed like he was voicing the opinion that I should quit while I was ahead. Something about Terrance irritated me and I couldn't put my finger on it.

Special Agent Terrance took a step closer. I didn't back off. If I hadn't hurt so bad, I might have considered adding the charge of assaulting an officer to her list of possibilities, but as it was, I was doing well just remaining upright.

"Where is Denise Curtis?" she snapped.

"You tell me," I answered. Vincent coughed loudly. Terrance looked past me and over at Nailor.

"I didn't come all this way to have some two-bit stripper give me a hard time," she said. "I say we take her in. Screw doing things the nice way."

Nailor looked concerned, like maybe Terrance was going a little too far. He looked over at me and shrugged.

"Ms. Lavotini," he said, "you are going to force this to turn ugly. I don't think any of us wants that to happen." I wasn't so sure Terrance agreed with that. She looked like she'd like nothing better than a good fight with anyone in the room.

"Put it together for yourself," he continued. "Your friend finds somebody dead in her apartment. You and your friend get shot at. What does that say, Ms. Lavotini?" He didn't wait for my answer. "It says Ms. Curtis has pissed somebody off, and maybe they're pissed at you now, too."

I'd like to say that I'd already thought of that, but I hadn't. Maybe Denise had got herself disposed of, and now whoever it was would come after me. Maybe they would think I knew more than I did. I didn't want to consider that possibility.

"Why were you chasing a car that had fired shots at you?" Terrance asked.

"I was doing my job as a model citizen," I said. "I thought I could catch the license plate number and turn it over to you."

Underneath her dark complexion, Terrance burned a bright red. Nailor must've known she was about to blow.

"Ms. Lavotini, I'm asking you to remember what I said about this turning ugly."

"All right," I said. "I thought I saw Denise's missing dog in the car and I was going after him." When you can't dazzle them with bullshit, hand them the truth.

Even Nailor looked disgusted now. Terrance snapped shut her notebook and shoved it in her purse.

"I'm telling you the truth. Someone snatched Denise's dog, Arlo. They left her a note saying that when she gave them a hundred large, she could have him back."

"What the hell kind of dog was it?" Terrance demanded.

"A mutt," I answered.

Nailor shook his head, like I was a slow learner. Terrance was still inches from my face.

"Who in the hell would think a mutt dog was worth a hundred thousand dollars?" she asked. "There isn't a dog in the world worth that much money."

Fluffy, who until this moment had been lying quietly on the arm of the futon, stood up, looked over at Carla Terrance, and proceeded to break loud, stinky wind.

The interview was over. Nailor and Terrance left the trailer in one hell of a hurry. Denise's search for Arlo meant nothing to the cops. They considered me an unreliable and hostile witness and they considered Fluffy a menace to society.

Ten

I woke up at two A.M. because there was a strange noise in my trailer. Little clicks and gentle taps. I looked over on the pillow and found that Fluffy was gone again. I'd come into my room hours ago to lie down, but instead had slept through dinner and into the night. I heard voices now, low and muffled. Who was in my trailer?

Someone laughed and said, "Hit me." I pulled on my purple chenille robe and ventured out of my room, creeping slowly down the hall. I paused at the entrance to the living room. A card table and four folding chairs were now arranged in the middle of the floor. A lamp had been dragged out from its place by the wall and positioned near the table. Bruno, Raydean, Pat, and Vincent sat around the table, embroiled in a game of seven-card stud.

Bruno was dealing, an unlit cigar clenched between his teeth. From where I stood, it appeared that Raydean and Vincent had folded, leaving Bruno and Pat. Pat drew her last card slowly toward her, picking it up gently and placing it in her hand. She let the slight corner of a smile edge out, then quickly pulled it back into a frown. Bruno watched her and rearranged his hand.

"How many d'you want?" he asked.

Pat pretended to study her hand, the slight grin slipping

loose again. "None." She reached for two more chips and slid them toward the pot.

Bruno shifted in his seat. "I fold," he muttered. "Let's see what you have. I know it was something 'cause of how you were grinning."

"Was I?" She looked flustered. "I can't see how." She inspected her cards, like maybe they'd changed and no one had told her. I felt sorry for Bruno; he was being played like a fiddle. "All I had was this." She laid down her cards, face up. A pair of threes and a busted flush. Nothing.

"And all this for me," she said, raking the pot toward her. "How about that?"

"Hit me!" Raydean exclaimed. "Hit me, big man. I love this game!" Raydean leaned over toward Vincent, who recoiled as if afraid. "What you say they call this game?"

"Poker, Raydean," I said. "Deal me in, Vincent."

Vincent was up like he'd been stung, grabbing a chair and pushing it in between his seat and Raydean's.

"Sierra, don't they want you to stay in bed?" Pat had moved from cardsharp to mother.

"I've been in bed all day. This'll keep my mind off things," I said, pulling my chair closer to the table. "What're you guys all doing over here at two in the morning, anyway?" Vincent looked about half shot and Pat had to have a boat going out in three hours.

"I told them I didn't need company," Bruno huffed. He probably thought his manhood was in question. "If there's any trouble, I got Bruce." Bruno edged his suit coat open to show the gun butt protruding from his shoulder holster. "I ain't never needed no backup at the club and they all know it."

This was something. An elderly charter boat captain, a threehundred-pound nightclub owner, and a crazy person, all keeping watch over the professional bodyguard who was watching me.

"You guys are something," I said, looking around the table. "Who's watching the club?" I asked Vincent.

"Ralph," Bruno answered for him, "and I called Big Ed in to cover the door. It's taken care of." Vincent glared at him.

"And don't you have to work in a couple of hours?" I asked Pat.

"Not tomorrow," she answered, bristling, "it's Friday. I don't go out on Fridays. And the issue here, Sierra, is your safety. We're all concerned. I thought I could help out, that's all." Oh great, now I'd hurt her feelings.

Raydean was the only one without a clue. She leaned over close to me and patted my arm gently, her expression blissful and loving.

"Hit me, big man," she whispered, and began dealing out the cards. Her expression suddenly changed, and she became intent and focused on her job. She glared around the table. "Five-card stud," she growled, "deuces wild. Luck be a lady." I wasn't sure if her medicine had kicked in or if she'd decided we were all aliens.

We played until the sun came up. I couldn't tell you who went home a winner. Vincent had been the first to leave. The urge to run over to the Tiffany to check the night's take was too much for him and he left around four A.M. Raydean passed out on the futon around six A.M., and Pat wandered off to her trailer in time to catch the *Today* show. Bruno wouldn't leave. He sat at the table, playing solitaire and watching out the bay window in the living room.

"Bruno," I said finally, "the cops were blowing smoke. Nobody is looking to hurt me. I am fine."

Bruno shook his head and kept on playing. He wasn't much for heavy conversation. I struggled to make coffee, hoping something would keep me going. It was going to be a long day. See, I'd been playing cards, but I'd also been formulating a plan. The plan didn't involve Bruno watching my every move. If I was going to find Denise, I needed a little room to maneuver.

The way I saw it, the cops didn't care about her. I hadn't seen her boyfriend Frankie around, so chances were, he wasn't busting his hump with concern. That left me. And Sierra Lavotini don't run out on nobody, especially when I'm figuring they're in trouble. If Denise's ex had decided he had to have her back or possibly pay her back for leaving him, then somebody had to do something.

I waited for the coffee to finish brewing, then poured a cup and faced Bruno. He was bent over his cards, and like a concentrating child, a tiny piece of his tongue protruded from his mouth. Bruno had a flattop, military haircut, and as he leaned closer into his game, I could see shiny white skin gleaming under his dull brown hair.

"You know, Bruno," I said, yawning, "I could do with a little lie-down. I think I'll wander back to my room for a while." He grunted and I escaped.

Fluffy watched me come into the room and close the door. She knew something was up and she wasn't going to miss out on the action.

"Don't worry," I said, "these are just the preliminaries." I pulled the phone across the bed and dialed. "Let's call your uncle Al. He won't give us the runaround, eh, Fluff?" Fluffy sighed and rearranged herself on the pillow. "Yeah, I know," I said, "pray his girlfriend already left for work."

Of my four brothers, Al was the least likely to ask questions. He was twenty-three and in love; that combination was going to keep him too preoccupied to pry into my affairs. Al was also the only one of my brothers not to follow my old man into the fire-fighting business. He had it into his head to be a cop. This meant he caught hell from his brothers and was always looking to try and prove that cops were as valuable as firemen.

The ringing stopped and my brother's sleepy voice came on the line. "Hello?"

"So you baggin' work today or what?" I asked.

"Sierra?" Al's voice sounded thick with sleep, deep and raspy. "Sierra, where are you?"

"Still in Florida. Where else?"

Al stretched and moaned into the phone. "What time is it?"

"Jesus, Al, it's nine already. What's with you?"

"Nine? Only nine?" He sighed and I could hear him struggle to sit up. "I'm working nights. I must've drifted off. How you doin'?" Now he was with me.

"Fine, Al. I'm doing fine. I called to see how you were doin'."

I looked over at Fluffy. She was smiling. She knew a lie when she heard one.

Al yawned again. "We're doin' fine, Sierra. Me and Rose is getting along pretty good. I'm thinking she could be the one, you know what I'm sayin'?"

God, yes I knew. Al had been after Rosie since high school, but she never gave him a look until he was one of Philly's finest, then she was all over him. I knew her type from way back. Cheerleader, popular, always with an eye looking over her shoulder for the next best thing. But you couldn't tell a guy, not even your own brother. You just had to stand back like a bystander and watch the head-on collision. Then, when Rosie moved on to her next best thing, our family would pick up the pieces.

He went on about how wonderful it was to be in lust, until I finally sensed he was winding down. Now I could lead the conversation where I wanted it to go.

"So, are you keeping Philly safe?" I asked. That launched him for another few minutes on Philly politics, how don't nobody respect cops, not even his own family. Ya da, ya da, ya da.

"So do you guys ever hear about a Leon Corvase?" I asked.

"Why're you asking about that scumbag?" Al's voice sharpened and he sounded like he'd moved closer to the receiver. "Sierra, that ain't no kind of guy to be associating with. He's got an organization out of West Palm. He's like this huge dope dealer, Sierra." There was a brief pause, like Al was facing his worst fears about me and finding them entirely possible. "Sierra, you ain't dating that cheese ball, are you?"

That's one reason I live in Florida. None of my family can come careening into my business like a Greyhound bus and assume the worst. They've got all these assumptions about dancers, and for the most part, they're right. But I am not just any dancer. I am capable of making a smart decision.

"No," I huffed, "don't be an idiot. I've got this friend and she knows him." Al didn't need to know everything.

"Well, you better tell your friend he's bad news. Tell her don't be fooled by his money and his looks." I knew Al wasn't so sure there was any friend. He was thinking it might be me.

"I never met the guy, Al. I'm trying to help my friend. She seems real taken with him. I guess he must have a big mansion in Miami or something." I paused, hoping Al would take the bait.

"Nah," he said, "that's out these days, Sierra. You ain't nothing if you don't have some mile-long boat with a crew. Corvase's got that, and a go-fast boat and a bunch of other crap. They couldn't touch all that stuff when he got popped a few years back. He had it all buried in paper so's he wouldn't lose none of it. He named his boat the *Mirage,* like now you see it, now you don't. I'm tellin' you, Sierra, stay the fuck away from him."

I had what I needed. "Calm yourself, Al. I was only curious about who my girlfriend was all hung up with. You know I'm smarter than that."

Al grunted, like maybe he wasn't so sure. He lectured me a little about responsibility and my future, like he'd forgotten that I was his big sister, not vice versa. But that's family for you. Truth be told, if Al knew a quarter of what I was up to, he'd have my brothers and Pop on a plane headed for Florida. Made me wonder where Denise's family was. Why weren't they wondering where their baby was?

"I don't get it, Fluff," I said after I'd hung up. Fluffy cocked her head and pricked up her long pointy ears. "Maybe her family doesn't know she's lost. Maybe she went back home." Fluffy didn't have an opinion. "Fluff, if she was your friend and didn't nobody else seem to care, you'd look for her, wouldn't you?" Fluffy seemed to nod, or maybe she was looking for fleas. Whatever, I took it for agreement.

"Then I'm gonna go look for her." Fluffy wasn't smiling. "What harm can it do? I'll act like I'm a long-lost friend of Denise's and don't know she's divorced. How could anybody have a problem with that?" Fluffy growled deep in her chest.

"I know," I answered, "but it's the best I can come up with on short notice. I'll do better before I see her ex."

Fluffy got down off her pillow and trotted across the bed to me. She lowered her head and nudged at my hand, wanting me to pet her. Her nose was cold and wet. When I scratched her behind the ears, she rolled over, wanting me to rub her tummy. I couldn't leave town without getting someone to take care of Fluff, and I couldn't do that without answering a lot of questions. This could take some doing, or else Fluffy was going on a road trip.

Eleven

*I*n order to go on a road trip, one must have a car and be physically able to drive said car. I was stealing 0 for 2 on that count. I spent the better part of the day trying to come up with options and drifting off to sleep. I couldn't help myself. Every time I had to take a pain pill, I became a zombie. If I didn't take something for the pain, then I couldn't think straight. It was a vicious circle.

I woke up from my third nap of the day with a pain pill hangover and an answer to my transportation troubles. Raydean had a car. She didn't drive much anymore, which for Panama City was a blessing. However, she kept the car, an old Plymouth Fury, serviced and ready to go, in case the Flemish took over the town and it became necessary to evacuate. Raydean would see nothing odd or unusual about me asking to borrow it for a few days. She wouldn't ask questions and she wouldn't remember the answers even if I told her.

Bruno, or whoever was now my "attendant," stood between me and freedom. I could hear voices out in the living room. It might be easier to slip over to Raydean's than try and make arrangements with people in my house. One person would pay attention to me, but two might not watch me so closely.

I eased my way down the hallway, trying to identify my visitors, but the talking had stopped when I'd opened my bedroom door. They had to have been talking about me. That made sense. Just as abruptly, the voices resumed, this time louder, staged for my benefit.

"Anyway," the female voice said, "I thought she might like this. Be sure you keep it refrigerated. It's got whipped cream and coconut milk in it."

Marla. What in the hell was she doing bringing me food? We hated each other. What we had was more than a professional rivalry; it was personal. I burst into the living room as Marla was opening the door to leave. She stopped, turning to face me with her best choke-and-die smile pasted in place.

"Sierra," she cooed, "I was telling Vincent here how concerned we all are down at the club." Vincent was looking very uncomfortable. "I baked you a cake. Thought you might like something sweet." Her tone was all Southern honey, but her smile didn't quite touch her eyes. "See you, Vincent. You think over what we talked about, y'hear?"

She was gone, her sharp heels clicking down the steps and across the concrete to her car. A moment later I heard her tiny Miata start up and zoom away toward the trailer park exit. Vincent stood in the middle of the kitchen, his pudgy hands wrapped around the mile-high coconut layer cake. I could tell by looking at it that Marla aimed to kill me by cholesterol poisoning. I'd gain ten pounds just staring at the cake.

"What was that about?" I asked Vincent. He wouldn't look at me. He watched Fluffy trotting into the room, her nose working overtime to figure out who the visitor with the cheap perfume had been.

"She was bringing you a cake." Vincent wasn't wearing his dark glasses and now I understood why he needed them. His left eye started twitching, a dead giveaway that he was lying.

"You know what I'm talking about," I said. "What is she wanting you to think about, and why did you two shut up when I came out of the bedroom?" Fluffy growled once in Vincent's direction, then hopped up on the futon, where she could keep her eye on him.

Vincent fumbled nervously with his black silk tie, thinking. He was trying to figure what was gonna be worse, telling me the truth or lying. He took up a few moments by opening the refrigerator door and sliding the cake onto one of the nearly empty shelves next to the gourmet dog food I buy Fluffy.

"She was concerned about you being out for a few weeks," he rumbled, his back to me.

"Bullshit," I answered.

"She wanted me to take your name off the front marquee and put hers in larger type." He sighed. "You know how it is with you two, never a dull moment." He tried to laugh nervously, but choked.

"For Christ's sake, I'm only gonna be out two weeks and she's acting like I'm history. Hell, if I use body makeup, I'll be back before then, one week tops."

Vincent was looking at his watch.

"What? You got someplace you need to be?" I asked. Maybe I was going to get some privacy after all.

"What?" Vincent seemed distracted. "Oh, yeah. I gotta get back to the club. Big Ed's supposed to come over for a while, but he's late. I told the girls I wanted to see them before they started their shift, kinda go over the lineup, what with you bein' out and all."

"Vincent, this is only for a few days, you know?" I was starting to get nervous. After all, until the accident, me and Vincent hadn't been exactly bosom buddies. In our business, if you blink, if you look away for an instant, you're liable to be replaced by some nymphet with 40DDs looking to undercut you by twenty bucks for the opportunity. The Tiffany was not supposed to be that way. We were supposed to go by talent, not physical largesse, but you never knew. Maybe Vincent was talking out of two sides of his mouth.

"Don't worry about Marla, Sierra," Vincent said,

pulling his dark glasses out of his suit coat pocket. "She's just trying to get ahead. You're still top bill and you still got a job. Take whatever time you need." The glasses were back in place, and if he was twitching, I couldn't tell. Somehow I wasn't reassured.

"Vincent, if you gotta get back, go on ahead. I've gotta run over to Raydean's trailer for a sec anyway." Vincent wasn't sure, but I pushed it. "Go on," I said, heading for the door. "I've got Fluffy and I'll be right across the street."

Vincent took the bait. "You're sure?"

"Absolutely," I said. The coast was clear and I was gone.

Raydean's trailer was a minefield of booby traps and bird feeders. Raydean, in her saner moments, was an avid bird-watcher. She surrounded her trailer with bright red hummingbird feeders and assorted birdbaths and bird-houses. One had to be careful, however, in admiring her jungle of avian paraphernalia because Raydean had care-fully placed trip wires and other handmade alarms throughout her yard. If an unlucky mailman stumbled or erred from the exact path to the door, sirens would sound and Raydean would appear, shotgun in hand.

The whole neighborhood took great pains to avoid going anywhere near Raydean's trailer. Even the worst of the trailer park children weren't bold enough to risk Ray-dean's sanity. If she hadn't been such a god-awful shot, due to cataracts, it would have been truly dangerous. As it was, it was risky business at the best of times. Only the initiated few—me, Pat, the mailman, and the van driver from the mental-health center's day program—knew the narrow path to Raydean's door.

It involved following the sidewalk exactly to the door, then avoiding the bottom step to her stoop and walking on the left-hand side of the stairs. Once on the top step, you didn't ring the doorbell. Raydean had somehow wired the buzzer so that it gave a nasty shock to the uninitiated. You had to knock on the door, three short raps followed by two, then one. I pitied the poor Flemish.

Raydean shuffled to the door, peered through the tiny diamond-shaped window, and began undoing her system of locks. She opened the door a crack, peered past me, and then stepped back to let me in. In the background, Raydean's parakeets, Dolly and Porter, sang noisily.

"Hey, Sugar," Raydean rasped, "you get tired of sittin' around with them fat boys? Can't say as I blame you none. That one with the dark glasses, it'd do to keep an eye on him. He looks to be the nervous type."

Raydean's housedress was a washed-out floral, the pockets stuffed with tissues and a crossword puzzle book. I looked past her into the crowded living room. Raydean was a fan of plastic see-through slipcovers, something I thought had gone out in the sixties. She'd covered her sofa, her armchairs, and even her recliner in plastic. The rest of the room was heavy with the kind of ceramics they probably had you do during art therapy at the mental-health center, little figurines and Christmas trees that plugged in and lit up. Plastic plants hung suspended from macramé holders, drooping with accumulated dust. Time stood still for Raydean. She was lost somewhere in a time warp that encompassed only the sixties and the seventies.

I had to sit down at the Formica-topped table in the kitchen and accept a cup of tepid tea in a Melamite cup that screamed *See Rock City* before I could finally broach the subject of Raydean's aging Plymouth Fury.

"Raydean," I said, pushing the sticky-sweet tea to one side, "you know I wrecked my Trans Am when I had my accident." Raydean nodded slowly. "And now I'm stuck without wheels and I'd rent a car, but my insurance don't cover that."

"It's the global economy what done that, Sugar," Raydean said, nodding wisely. "Blame that NAFTA crap." I ignored her and plowed ahead.

"Anyway, I was wondering if maybe I could borrow your car for a day or two." I didn't look up, afraid that she might jump in with a political comment if I gave her an opening. "See, I'm worried about Denise. She's my friend, and you know how it is when your friends are in trouble, you gotta do what you can to help. I need to see if I can find her."

Raydean stood up and walked to her front-hall closet. I gripped the edge of the table, ready to run in case I'd said the wrong thing and she was heading for her shotgun. Instead she turned around clutching her purse and staring back at me.

"Well, Sugar, what're you waiting for?" she asked serenely. "Let's get a move on."

"Oh, Raydean, no. I didn't mean you should trouble yourself. I'll just drive down to Fort Lauderdale and take a look-see. You don't need to come. I know you have things to do. I'll go."

Raydean didn't seem to be listening. She was pouring food into the parakeets' dish and muttering to herself. She disappeared into the bedroom in the back, leaving me still sitting at the tiny kitchen table. How was I going to get out of this one?

Raydean reappeared, clutching a shopping bag with straw handles.

"Now, Sugar," she said firmly, "I don't let no one go off in my car without me riding along. I need to be with my support system." Apparently she meant the car. She walked to the door, held it open, and looked back at me, her eyebrows arched into sideways question marks.

And so it was that at five o'clock Friday afternoon, Raydean, Fluffy, and I set out in Raydean's ancient Plymouth Fury. Destination: Fort Lauderdale. It wasn't the way I'd planned it, but lately nothing seemed to follow my designs. In the meantime, I'd put the pedal to the metal, drift along down I-95, and hope for the best.

Twelve

$\mathcal{O}$ne winter, when I was about ten, Pop won the raffle down at the Sons of Italy Social Club. You gotta understand, Pop never won nothing in his life. He bought them raffle tickets for the same reasons everybody else did: It was expected. It was for a good cause. People like Pop, they don't win stuff. They gotta most times come by it the hard way.

So when Pop won, he came whooping into the row house around suppertime. I don't think I ever saw him so happy, before or since. I was sitting at the kitchen table doing my homework, while Mom kept an eagle eye on me and cooked the ravioli. My brothers was all doing likewise, only the older two were mainly goofing on each other and trying to get the other one in trouble. When Pop came in like that, early for him, on a frigid November night, and yelling, well, you can see how we thought something was wrong.

We kids all sat there and watched. He picked up Mom and swung her around. You could tell he hadn't done that in a long time, if ever, because she looked so surprised, and maybe even a little fearful. Pop took no notice. He was waving a piece of paper and yelling.

"I won, Evie, I won! We're goin' to Florida for Christmas!"

By the time she had him calmed down enough to show her the papers, we kids were all getting the gist of the idea. We were going to the Land of Oranges. We were going to the place where mythical palm trees swayed and college girls in bikinis posed next to boys with long hair and surfboards. We were going where no snow falls even in the coldest winter.

Mom don't like a fuss. She don't like people knowing what's on the inside, but even she was excited. I could tell, because for the next few weeks until we left for Fort Lauderdale, she hummed and smiled. A couple of times I even caught her and Pop dancing in the kitchen after us kids were supposed to be in bed.

We drove to Fort Lauderdale. Pop, like a maniac, wouldn't hardly let us stop to pee. Mom loaded up the station wagon with her "essentials"—noodles, olive oil, sandwiches on thick Italian bread, salamis and hard cheese—in case they didn't have the "good" stuff in Florida. We thought Florida was almost a foreign country, and my oldest brother, Jimmy, said they might not even speak good English like we did on account of how everyone had moved there from Cuba.

It was romantic and exotic, just the thought of being somewhere totally different from Philadelphia. Florida was going to be all the things Philly wasn't: clean, pulsating with rhythms and music. Philly was like an old black-and-white movie. Florida breathed in Technicolor.

I wasn't disappointed. None of us was disappointed. There's a picture that Pop had a stranger take. It was all of us—Mom, Pop, my four brothers, and me—standing at the Bahia Mar Marina in front of the *Jungle Queen,* the biggest walking goofballs you ever wanna see. Pop, his black socks halfway up his white hairy calves, plaid madras shorts, and a Hawaiian shirt. Mom and me in our huge straw hats and our gigantic sunglasses. My brothers, all with Phillies baseball caps and cutoff blue-jean shorts because they didn't have swimsuits. All of us grinning like idiots. What a picture! And yet we all have a copy of that picture somewhere in our homes, somewhere where we can pull it out and stare at it, remembering that for that one week we, the Lavotinis from nowhere, were golden and nothing could touch us.

I was thinking about that picture at five A.M. when we hit the outskirts of Fort Lauderdale. Raydean was asleep, her head leaning against the passenger-side window, little snorts of sleepy breath escaping her pursed lips. Fluffy had curled into a ball between us, her head resting on Raydean's purse. It was just me seeing Fort Lauderdale in the pink and purple haze of dawn, like Pop must've seen it almost twenty years ago. Only now there was high-rises and development everywhere. Cars raced down the highway, even in the early dawn. There were parts of town where tourists weren't to wander for fear of losing their lives, and the tiny mom-and-pop hotels were all gone.

I drove down I-95 trying to figure what our next move was gonna be. I had sixty bucks and a credit card, a Chihuahua and an elderly maniac. My options felt limited. My eyes were red-rimmed and I knew I wasn't thinking clearly. I pulled into a service station, across from the airport, that advertised hot coffee and hot dogs, thinking maybe more caffeine and some protein would improve my chances of developing a plan. Raydean shot up in her seat when I came to a stop in the parking lot, instantly vigilant.

"Where are we, Buttercup?"

Her hair was smushed flat on one side and her skin was pockmarked with indentations from the window and door lock. I doubt if she knew what planet we were on, let alone what part of Florida. Fluffy was starting to stir, pushing her tiny paws out and stretching.

"We're in Fort Lauderdale," I answered. "I'm gonna get a cup of coffee and try and figure out where to stay. You want anything?"

Raydean was staring out the window, her eyes focusing on a jumbo jet that roared off the runway.

"Let's stay there," she said, pointing toward the Airport Hilton. "Then I can watch the planes taking off, monitor the activity."

Fluffy was awake now, staring in the direction Raydean was pointing, her lips curving into a smile. I looked over at the Hilton and sighed. A cup of coffee and a hot dog there, let alone a room, would just about bankrupt me. I was going to have to break it to Raydean that this was not a vacation and I was not the Queen of England.

"Raydean, that place is expensive. It's gotta be over a hundred dollars a night. We're kind of on a tight budget. I've only got sixty bucks cash and a credit card that's almost maxed out." I sighed and felt for the door handle. "I'll get us coffee and a hot dog."

"I'd really rather have a nice glass of tea and one of them mints they stick on your pillow," Raydean said petulantly.

She fiddled with the handle of her ancient leather purse. I counted to ten, slowly. I am in her car, I reminded myself; I will be grateful and patient. Every bone and muscle in my body screamed with impatience. My stitches were starting to itch. Maybe this was a stupid idea.

"There," Raydean said. "This oughta do it. A hundred dollars a night? Sign me up. Them Flemish cain't touch me in a place like that. It's a documented fact they don't like airports—too many metal detectors and magnetic fields. We'll be safe. Let's go."

I turned back to face Raydean, all set to tell her how it was going to be. Instead I found myself staring at a crumpled pile of bills—large bills—that spilled out of her purse and into her lap.

"Raydean," I breathed, "where'd you get money?"

"Life is full of assumptions," she answered in her cryptic way. "Just 'cause I live in a mobile home and entertain funny notions now and then don't mean I cain't have a few dollars put back."

"But where—"

She didn't let me finish. "I was married once," she answered. "Most of it come from him when he died, the rest come from my family. I share that information"— she glared sternly at me—"on a need-to-know basis. When the big day comes and you people see how right I was, I will be prepared. Now, hit it sister."

The Airport Hilton is down a drive lined with palm trees and little grass-covered hills that hide the fact that the airport is directly behind the hotel. When you pull up in front of the hotel, men dressed in white shirts and shorts with flawlessly groomed hair and smiling faces rush your car. They open the car doors and usher you out like you were visiting royalty and your car was a limo, even when in fact it's a rusting lemon and you look like roadkill.

"May I take your luggage?" our little guy asked.

"No," I barked defensively, "we'll get it later." Raydean, holding Fluffy in her arms, still wearing her faded housedress and rolled-down knee-high stockings, sailed into the brass-and-marble lobby, leaving me to trot behind her. People were staring.

I kept a pace or two back, smoothing my hair and hoping my bruises were somehow more attractive in the glow of wealthy surroundings. Raydean had rested her purse on the reservations desk and was entering into a conversation with a young woman whose nametag proclaimed her to be Maria from Panama.

"Honey, we're gonna need a room with two double beds and a view of the airport."

Maria looked uncertain. She was sizing Raydean up and finding her not to be Hilton material. I figured it was time to take over. I moved up beside Raydean.

"Mother, let me take care of the arrangements."

Raydean frowned slightly and took a step back.

"Me and Fluffy'll go take a seat in one of them upholstered chairs. Be sure they know I like mints. Take what you need from my purse, Sugar."

I turned to Maria, who was watching Raydean's retreat to the lounge with growing horror. In a moment I felt certain she'd be calling for her supervisor and maybe security to have us escorted back to our car and off of their fine premises.

"Maria," I began, deepening my voice into what I hoped was a wealthier range, "my mother is a little, shall we say, eccentric? Her doctor at the Mayo Clinic feels it may be early-onset Alzheimer's. I mean, why else would a woman of her means dress like a bag lady?" Maria shifted her gaze to me.

I laughed softly. "She's got this delusion that we're only inches from the poorhouse. Daddy insisted that we take our vacation, but the annual board meeting with the shareholders was this week, and in his position, he couldn't leave. So here I am, escorting Mother."

Maria looked like she might believe me, so I reached into Raydean's purse and extracted a fifty.

"I'd appreciate it if you'd arrange a few extra mints for Mother's pillow. We do so try to humor her." I let my face look sad. "One never knows, does one?"

Maria shook her head dolefully. "I can't believe it," she whispered in a thick Hispanic accent. "I can give you Room 510." She reached into a drawer for the room key and began scrawling the room number inside the key holder.

"Maria, Mother wishes to pay cash. We'll only be here one night. I'll give you three hundred now, to cover the room and expenses. Of course you'll want a credit card to guarantee . . ." Maria took my card and made an impression.

We were in, and I could finally get Raydean off my back long enough to figure out how I was going to find Leon Corvase. I walked slowly toward Raydean, aware that every spare eye in the hotel lobby was watching us.

"Come, dear," I said sweetly. "Your room is ready."

Raydean stood up, still clutching Fluffy, and managed to look confused, not unlike the Alzheimer's patient I'd portrayed her to be.

"They ain't no Flemish here, is there?" she asked in a loud, querulous tone. I led her smoothly toward the bank of elevators. Behind the safety of the reservations counter, Maria was whispering to one of her counterparts, gesturing toward Raydean and shaking her head sadly. One never knows, I thought.

"Poor dear," I whispered as we passed the bell captain.

"Cold as a witch's tit in here," Raydean said as the elevator doors closed behind us.

Thirteen

Upper-class hotels cater to the forgetful. They leave little shower caps and shampoos on the counter in the bathroom. They stick hotel stationery and postcards in the desk. The really ritzy ones even let you wear their bathrobes on account of how rich people might not remember to pack said item because they were too busy making an important deal. The gift shops in these hotels are better stocked than most department stores. The Hilton was no exception.

After a few hours' sleep, I left Raydean still snoring and headed down to the gift shop. On the sale rack I found a little white bikini with gold nautical braid and a short white minidress that would do for most of the places I had in mind to visit. The girl behind the cash register couldn't have been more than twenty-two. She had streaked blond hair, a deep tan, and looked like she spent most of her time waiting to be noticed by Mr. Right. She took my money without hardly glancing up from her soap opera magazine. She would have returned to reading up on *All My Children,* had I not interrupted her.

"Excuse me," I said.

She looked up, focusing on my face for the first time. Her face had assumed that well-trained, courteous "I live to serve" expression. The magazine was quietly folded and surreptitiously placed on the shelf behind her. Her name tag was visible now. *Tanya from Florida,* it read.

"Tanya," I said, "you live around here, don't you?" Stupid question—of course she did—but it started the conversation.

"Yes," she said cautiously.

"I was wondering, where are the good clubs in town?"

She sized me up for a moment and seemed to decide I was in her generation.

"Well," she said slowly, "there's Septembers or Yesterdays, or Shooters if you like to watch the boats." We were getting where I wanted to go now.

"Yeah," I said, laughing, "I like big boats, especially big boats with rich men."

Tanya actually laughed back. "Who doesn't?" She seemed to think for a moment. "If you want to meet those guys, you oughta cruise the marinas."

I looked like the idea had never occurred to me and that she was a genius.

"Wow," I breathed, "like where? I mean, where are the big boats?"

Tanya was proud to be an expert. She had forgotten all about the soap operas.

"There's two where I'd go," she said. "Pier 66 and Bahia Mar. Bahia Mar's got this little place out by the pool—Skipper's, I think it's called. You can sit outside, eat lunch, and do all the sight-seeing you want."

I couldn't believe it. The Bahia Mar, home of the *Jungle Queen,* now the home of the Whopper. In my mind the Bahia Mar was forever frozen in a time when the only people with huge boats were old, not fast and illegal. I walked out of the gift shop, my bag of clothing clutched to my chest, thinking. I'm not usually the type to have doubts about my actions, but suddenly I had a king-sized case. And I was frightened. Denise might be dead; in fact, that seemed like a likely assumption. The mob doesn't do divorce well, especially when the spouse knows all about its illegal activities. But if there was even a minuscule chance that Denise was alive, I had to know and I had to get her help. I had to step into the pit and dance with the viper. I'm a pretty good dancer, but from all I knew so far, Leon Corvase was a great viper.

I tiptoed back into our darkened room, trying to make as little noise as possible. Raydean still slept. Fluffy opened an eye, and when she saw it was me, she jumped down off my bed and followed me into the bathroom.

"I'll take you," I whispered, "but let's pray Raydean sleeps through it all." Fluffy smiled; I knew she felt the same way I did. Raydean was a loose cannon. I struggled to pull the dress over my head. The stiffness was wearing off a little, but it hurt to wiggle into a tight skirt. Fluffy balanced precariously on the edge of the toilet and took a few sips while I slathered on makeup. After a careful inspection, I decided that I looked almost normal, especially with dark glasses.

"All right now, tiptoe," I cautioned Fluff. I pulled the door open slowly and walked out. Raydean sat in a chair, purse clutched in her lap, a determined expression on her face. She was humming "Fly Me to the Moon." I didn't even attempt to dissuade her, as it would have been a wasted effort.

"Ready?" I sighed.

"As I'll ever be," she answered.

Raydean almost made it out of the hotel without incident, but the gift shop caught her eye. She made a beeline inside, cornered Tanya, and demanded peanuts and a Coke. Tanya hustled up off her stool and busied herself pleasing Raydean.

"What's this here?" Raydean demanded. She had picked up a grotesque plastic puppet head, the kind you stick your fingers into and wiggle to make silly faces.

"I got to have me one of them. And fetch me up one of them large pencils, too." Tanya quickly picked up a two-foot-long pencil that was covered in pink flamingos and had a bright red tassel. "Sugar," Raydean said suddenly, "what y'all people need here is a good stock of Vienna sausages and some Moon Pies. Civilize this place."

Tanya's eyes were wide. "Yes, ma'am," she murmured.

Tanya didn't notice me until she was giving Raydean her change.

"All set?" I asked Raydean. Raydean nodded, pouring some of the peanuts into her Coke. "Well, let's cruise, then. Maybe we can find you a nice rich one." I heard Tanya behind us, choking, as we headed off toward the hotel lobby.

Once the valet had brought Raydean's car around and we had pulled out into the flow of traffic, I could think. Fort Lauderdale was probably like most cities. It appeared large, but was actually divided into areas and neighborhoods that functioned almost like small towns. There had to be a limited area where Leon Corvase could be found.

He had a large fast boat, an upscale, illegal lifestyle, and a need to keep a low profile. In Philadelphia, that meant private-party rooms in the best restaurants and clubs. It had to mean the same thing here. Leon would hang with the big-league party boys, and keep his boat in an expensive but discrete marina. I knew the boat name from my brother; it was the *Mirage*. A piece of cake, right? Sooner or later, I'd run into him, or more likely, word would reach him that a blonde, a Chihuahua, and an old lady were driving around town asking after him.

We were on the 17th Street Causeway, just over the bridge. Raydean and Fluffy had their noses pressed to the glass, staring at all the boats. We hit A1A and the ocean broke open in front of us. It was no longer the way I'd remembered it as a child. Now there was a fancy brick walkway and a low white wall that curved and undulated like the Great Wall of China, only tailored to midgets.

The palm trees were still as I remembered, and the lifeguard stations, but the old Lauderdale was gone. In its place was the smell of money and privilege. The funky little bars that visiting college students called home were interspersed among fancy clothing and jewelry shops. I had the sense that soon even the bars and beach-supply stores would vanish and be replaced by art galleries and home furnishing meccas. There wasn't much room here for the regular guy and his wide-eyed family, let alone for a nostalgic stripper.

I almost missed the *Jungle Queen* and Bahia Mar. The big gaudy boat blended in with the rest of its surroundings and somehow seemed small. When I was little, the smokestacks of the big paddlewheel touched the sky. The bright red and gold paint had seemed brighter, truer than the fire-engine red of Pop's hook and ladder. Now it seemed faded, a poor relation among the gleaming white cabin cruisers that rimmed the Bahia Mar.

We parked amid Cadillacs and BMWs. Raydean had produced yet another floral housedress from her Piggly Wiggly sack of clothing and God knows what else. Her hair was no longer smushed flat on one side. It stuck out at random all over her head. We were going to be noticed, no doubt about that.

Fluffy was walking on the end of the rhinestone leash that I keep in my purse for important show-off occasions, and when leash laws are in danger of being enforced. Fluffy fit in here—at least that's how she carried herself. She pranced like this cousin of mine did in my brother Tony's wedding. My aunt Angie thought my cousin was a big disgrace, calling attention away from the bride. But my cousin was taking her moment, letting the world know that she was fine with herself.

That's how Fluffy took the dock at Bahia Mar Marina. She looked from side to side, taking her time, looking to see who was around and who was watching. The damn dog had more self-confidence in her toenails than my aunt Angie ever mustered in her life.

Raydean was oblivious to everything but the big boats. She walked along, her clunky shoes catching now and then in the thick wooden slats of the dock. She looked like a drunk.

When Fluffy screamed, and that's really what it was, I was unprepared. The high-pitched yelp of pain and panic caught at my chest, sending my heart racing. At first I must've been in denial, 'cause I looked around for another dog, then instantly knew. It was Fluffy.

I looked down and saw blood spurting from her foot. Fluffy had fallen and was continuing to scream. I knelt at her side, trying to get to the foot, but in her pain she snapped at me, catching the side of my hand and drawing blood. She wouldn't let me near. The side of her paw welled with blood and in the center I could see a large fish hook. I started to make a grab for her again, but someone placed a firm hand on my shoulder, pulling me back.

A man stooped down beside us. He was tall and thin, with salt-and-pepper gray hair that had a white streak across the front. His nose was long and narrow, like maybe he was part Indian. He was tanned, like most of the water people, and wore tan chino shorts and a too-white sport shirt.

"Wait," he said. His voice was calm and in charge. "Like this." He reached around behind us and grabbed a pair of heavy leather gloves from the top of a chest next to one of the boats.

"I'll hold her. You try and calm her down. Then we can get the hook out."

He reached for Fluffy and she bit him. He barely flinched, just held her while we both spoke softly.

"It's okay, girl," he murmured.

"Baby, Mama's here," I said, not knowing what to do next.

"All right," the man said. "I'm going to put her on this chest and hold her. You're going to have to push the hook through her paw and out."

I felt my stomach turn over and my skin prickled. I couldn't do that to her.

"Let me take her to a vet," I said, backing off a little.

The man looked up at me and I saw his eyes were a clear, strong gray. He looked like I'd somehow disappointed him or, worse, let Fluffy down.

"You can do that," he said slowly, "but then she'd be stuck with this hook in her foot for another hour or so, and her paw would probably be bleeding longer."

I looked at Fluffy. She was whimpering, her eyes liquid with pain.

"All right," I said. "What do I do?"

"What's your name?" he asked.

"Sierra Lavotini," I said, my voice shaking.

"Sierra, you can do this," he said, his voice reassuring. "It happens all the time to fishermen. She'll feel better as soon as it's over."

I wasn't so sure.

"With one motion," he said, "push the barb through and out. Then pull the rest of the hook through. I'll hold her as still as I can." Fluffy, sensing something was about to happen, struggled against the man whose name I'd never asked.

"Easy, sweetheart," the man cooed. "Go, Sierra," he said, his tone changing to a no-nonsense command.

"Easy, Fluff," I breathed, and reached for her paw. Behind me I could hear shuffling feet and the intake of a collective breath. We had drawn a small crowd of Bahia Mar's patrons, all queued up like rubberneckers at a car accident, unable to pass and unwilling to look away.

Fluffy looked at me, her eyes trusting and full of the pain from the fish hook. I tried to find the switch I use in emergencies, the one that shuts down the emotions and makes me feel removed from the situation. Fluffy was my baby. No, I couldn't think like that. I grasped her paw firmly.

"I love you, Fluffy," I whispered. Then I took a sharp breath, held it, and pushed the barb through Fluffy's little paw. She screamed again, and tears poured down my face.

"Easy, Sierra," my helper cautioned. "Take this." He handed me a clean white handkerchief from his back pocket. "Wrap it around her paw, tight, so it stems the blood flow, but not too tight."

I wound the handkerchief around Fluffy's tender paw and took her from the man's lap. Fluffy was only whimpering now, no longer screaming. The man leaned over and carefully picked up the bloody hook, examining it.

"It looks pretty new," he said. "Probably made a clean wound, but you never know. Now's the time to get on to the vet. There's an emergency clinic out on Tamiami Trail. You can walk right in with her."

"Thank you," I said, my voice shaky.

"You'd better get going," he said, the gray eyes watching. "I'll help you get her to the car. I think you can manage to get her there by yourself, if she'll lie still for you."

"Oh, I'm not alone," I said, turning to look for Raydean. She was gone. The people who had stood watching were wandering away, sensing that Fluffy was going to be all right and embarrassed to be caught openly gaping.

"Well, she was right here," I said, bewildered. This was not what I needed. We had to get Fluffy to the emergency clinic.

"What does she look like?" my companion asked.

As the onlookers scattered, I saw Raydean sitting alone on a bench at the end of the dock, leaning forward. She had her head in her hands, rocking.

"There she is," I said, starting to move forward.

"Your mother?" he asked.

"No, a friend of mine. We came down looking for another friend of mine. She used to live here. Denise Curtis—er, Corvase. You don't know her, do you?"

The man thought for a moment. "Denise Corvase," he murmured. He shook his head. "Can't seem to place her. Friend of yours, you say?"

"Yeah. She kind of disappeared on me. I thought she might be having some trouble with her—" I broke off, aware that I was babbling far too much. "Well, I was wondering if she was here. She used to live on a boat called the *Mirage*. Ever hear of that?" I asked.

My new friend thought again, his face furrowed. "Sorry," he added. "But I'll ask around. You staying nearby?"

We were almost up to Raydean, and she wasn't looking so good. I needed to get her in the car and do damage control. Fluffy's injury had probably scared Raydean out of whatever fragile balance she had.

"I'm staying at the Airport Hilton," I said quickly. "It's Sierra Lavotini. Just leave me a message. And thank you for what you done for Fluffy." Raydean was crying softly as we walked up to her.

"Will she be all right?" he asked.

"Sure," I said, looking up at him. "We'll be fine. Thanks for everything."

He took the cue and left, walking slowly back down the dock. I walked over to Raydean and placed my hand on her shaking shoulder.

"Honey, are you okay? Fluffy's going to be fine. We just need to take her on to the vet and she'll be right as rain." Fluffy whimpered as if to contradict me. Raydean slowly raised her head. Her face was puffy and red from crying.

"This is not a safe place," she whispered. "I want to go home."

Raydean shook as I led her to the car. Every now and then, she'd look over furtively at Fluffy. I didn't know what she was thinking, but I was even more concerned with getting Fluffy to the vet.

We pulled out of the marina and were headed toward the emergency clinic before Raydean spoke again. She sat with Fluffy perched gingerly on her lap, staring at the wounded paw.

"Sierra, why're we here, anyway?" Her voice had slipped into a little girl's hesitant whispery tones, not at all Raydean.

"We're looking for Denise, honey," I said softly. "She used to live on a boat called the *Mirage*. I thought—"

Raydean yelled out "Mirage" so loudly, I swerved. A passing car blew its horn as I came too close.

"It's a mirage," she was saying. "It was a big mirage." She was shaking so hard I thought Fluffy would slip off her lap.

"What's a big mirage?" I asked, trying to humor her.

"That boat, where Fluffy hurt her paw. Did you not see?" she asked, her old Raydean voice returned. "That boat was the *Mirage*. Said it was out of Boca Raton."

Fourteen

*I*t was dark when I finally had time to consider life's ironies. Fluffy was resting comfortably on a pillow in the hotel room. Sitting beside her, pillows behind her and Moon Pies at her side, Raydean was watching the Braves on cable. I'd had my hands full all day. We'd waited for hours at the emergency clinic, just so a vet could wrap Fluffy's little paw, lecture me on dog safety, and charge me a hundred bucks.

Raydean had lapsed in and out of some state where it seemed hard to get her to respond. It'd been hell to get her to eat supper. She seemed to eye every restaurant suspiciously, refusing to eat anything but prepackaged food from the grocery store. I'd finally convinced her that we couldn't leave for home until tomorrow because I was tired. I had no idea how to break it to her that we needed to return to the Bahia Mar tomorrow.

I slipped into my new white bikini and used my shirt for a cover-up. Maybe some laps in the pool would loosen me up. That was the ticket, laps and a frozen piña colada. Raydean waved absently as I left for the pool. Fluffy slept on unaware.

The pool at the Airport Hilton was surrounded by white lounge chairs and lush tropical greenery. Like most of your upscale hotels, it featured a poolside bar and a disinterested bartender. The pool was warm, and lit by soft yellow lights. I had the place to myself.

I couldn't tell you how long I swam. I let myself sink into the repetition of stroke after stroke. At some point I realized I was angry. I was pushing myself through the chlorinated water, pushing against everything that seemed to overpower and control me. I pushed away the tears that I'd wanted to shed all day. I pushed away my frustration at being so close to the *Mirage* and being so stupid. That man had to have known the *Mirage* or Leon Corvase. Hell, he could've worked on the boat for all I knew. Like a stupid schoolgirl, I'd let my emotions ride me.

I swam on and on, cursing silently, hurting my sore muscles as punishment, until I was too limp to move. I hauled my water-puckered body up onto the edge of the pool, doing it the hard way. I walked over to my table and dried off with a harsh white pool towel. Now I could have the piña colada. Now I could stop beating myself up and figure the rest of my plan.

I sat, panting, drinking my slushy drink. Somewhere nearby someone lit a cigarette. In my younger, careless days, I'd smoked. Years later, my nose still caught the whiff of a freshly lit cigarette and reached out to inhale. There was something about that first pungent whisp of smoke.

"You saved me the trouble of calling your room."

The voice, deep, resonant, and steely calm, cut through the darkness and took me back to the morning. He stepped from the shadows and walked up to my table, casually pulling out one of the chairs and sitting down. He was wearing white linen trousers, Italian tassel loafers without socks, and a pale pink Izod shirt. Unless my sense of smell was off, he was also wearing Paco Rabon cologne. The white streak in his hair was more prominent in the dark, and his eyes seemed clearer, perhaps more colorless than they had that morning. He carefully set his cigarettes and ornate silver-and-turquoise lighter down on the glass table.

"Mr. Corvase," I said, my voice a calm lie, "I wondered if you'd come in person or send along a messenger." Inside, I shuddered. I looked over at the bar, hoping for a witness, but it was deserted. The steel shutter had been pulled tight and locked. It was me, alone with Denise's ex.

"You were looking for Denise," he said casually. His cigarette glowed orange in the darkness. A few feet away, in the hotel restaurant, patrons ate their dinners by candlelight, looking out at the pool but unable to see me. My table was hidden from view by a bougainvillea. Leon Corvase stretched, his muscles taut, like a large cat.

"That's funny," he went on. "I've been looking for Denise, too." He leaned closer to me. "Maybe we can help each other out." He smiled and his eyes were hooded. "Two people, looking to help Denise stay safe."

I pushed air into my lungs. "I wasn't aware that you were concerned for Denise's safety," I said. "I was thinking it was maybe the opposite way around."

He laughed but let it die in his throat. "And so you were going to come all the way down here, with your midget dog and your crazy old lady, to save my wife from me?"

"Something like that," I answered.

He laughed again, this time letting the sound echo through the empty pool terrace.

"Either you have an inflated idea of your own capabilities or you've seriously underestimated mine." The thick lidded eyes widened for a moment, glaring, but the smile never left his lips. He reached across the table in one flash of movement and gripped my wrist. "I need to find Denise," he whispered harshly. "She has something that belongs to me."

"And what would that be?" I asked, not letting him know that his grasp was tight, painful.

"She knows," he answered. His mood suddenly changed, and he became the man from the dock, the one who'd cared for Fluffy. "Sierra, I don't want to hurt

Denise." His eyes were sorrowful pools. "In some ways your friend Denise is a child. She lashes out when she's hurt. That's what she's doing now." His grip relaxed momentarily, then tightened until I gasped. "You tell her I think she's being very stupid. She knows I won't tolerate stupidity, even from her."

It was like he'd forgotten I was there. His eyes burned past me, his fingers bit into my wrist. He was thinking about Denise. A door from the hotel swung open and a woman laughed as she stepped out onto the concrete walkway. A man's voice teased as the couple walked toward the pool. Leon snapped back into awareness and stared at me.

"Sierra, I'm sorry," he murmured. "She brings out the worst in me. We do that to each other."

For a moment he seemed wistful. I thought about Denise, sitting on the barstool, telling me about how Leon beat her and threatened her. The Denise I knew didn't love Leon. She feared him. I looked over at Leon. Was this his way of throwing me off track? For all I knew, Denise was locked away some-where or dead. But a sneaking little voice was beginning to gnaw away at me. What if Denise really did have something that belonged to Leon? What if she was conning me and Leon both?

Leon watched the couple wandering by the edge of the pool, then he leaned very close to me.

"Sierra," he said, "I'm going to give you a number to call if you hear from Denise. Call collect."

"Oh yeah, right." I sneered. "Like I'd tell you if I heard from her."

Leon's voice was pure menace. "I'll know if she contacts you. I'll find out eventually. You can circumvent a lot of pain to yourself and your family if you get in touch with me as soon as she calls."

I opened my mouth to speak, but he gripped my wrist, flipping my hand over to expose my palm. In his other hand, he held his glowing cigarette, bringing it so close to my skin that I could feel the heat.

"Don't try to fool me," he said. "You're afraid of me, and that's a good thing. That's self-preservation."

"I'm not afraid of you," I said loudly. The couple by the pool looked in our direction. They were too far away to hear what I'd said, but close enough to catch the tone.

"Then you've made a serious mistake," he whispered. He stood up and dropped a thin white business card on the table. A phone number was printed on it, nothing else. In an instant he had vanished, walking back through the darkness, toward the hotel lobby. A car started and pulled away. Leon Corvase was gone.

I was shaking too badly to move. I sat massaging my wrist and waiting for my knees to feel strong enough to support my legs. My gut was telling me that Leon Corvase wanted to find Denise as badly as I did. But then, my gut told me to come to Fort Lauderdale and look for Denise. Some instinct. I'd only caused more trouble for myself and Denise. On top of it, I had a mobster dope dealer threatening my "family," Raydean and Fluffy. Some help to Denise I was turning out to be.

Raydean didn't ask questions when I came back up to the room and told her I'd decided that she was right, we needed to go back home to Panama City. She nodded, half hearing me, half watching her beloved Braves. Maddux had given up three runs, and Raydean was yelling at the manager, Bobby Cox.

"Hell, you knock-kneed tree toad," she ranted at the TV, "I could do better than you. Can't you see the boy's tired? Hell, he's thrown ninety pitches already. Take him out!" Moon Pie wrappers littered the bed where Raydean and Fluffy lay. Fluffy was sitting up next to Raydean, her eyes bulging and her tiny body quivering. Either Fluffy felt as Raydean did about Bobby Cox, or Raydean had O.D.'d Fluffy on sugar. I voted for the latter.

When I emerged from the bathroom, ready for bed, I found Raydean and Fluffy sound asleep, Greg Maddux still on the mound for Atlanta, and Bobby Cox phoning the dugout. I pulled back the covers on the other double bed and crawled between the sheets. I aimed the remote at the TV and sent Bobby and the Braves to the showers. Tomorrow meant a long, hot drive home, but even that was preferable to Leon Corvase and Fort Lauderdale.

Fifteen

"You coulda left a note, Sierra." Bruno was angry. He stood on my doorstep, his bull neck pulsing with emotion and steroids. "We were all worried sick about you, and Big Ed took it personal when you disappeared on his watch. He felt responsible, Sierra. You coulda thought about what you were putting us through."

I hung my head and looked at Bruno's pointy-toed cowboy boots. He was right. I'd rushed off, like it was some big game and I was the leader. I wasn't used to accounting for myself, not since I'd left Philly.

"Aw, Bruno, I'm sorry," I muttered. I felt like I was in front of Sister Mary Margaret, my second-grade teacher. "I guess I got ahead of myself."

Bruno softened a bit. "Well, it's all right," he said. "Now that we know you're okay." He shifted from one foot to the other, looking uncomfortable. "Marla ain't gonna be so happy you're lookin' good again."

We were getting to the heart of the message. Marla. I could feel my heart starting to race and my stomach tighten. Marla hadn't been sitting still while I'd been gone, I was sure of that.

"What about Marla?" I asked.

"She's got this new act," he began. "She's doing a tribute to our men in uniform."

"Aw, that's lame," I said. "Marla's done that before.

She's trying to suck in all the boys at Tyndall. Those boys can't afford the Tiffany. A few'll come in, but the rest'll end up down at the Golden Nugget."

Bruno shook his head. "Nah, Sierra," he said, "this time it's different. She got Big Ed to rig up this apparatus that makes her fly."

Immediately I started to picture Marla, her big boobs hanging like watermelons as she careened out over the audience, singing in her squeaky off-key voice "God Bless America." Big Ed, nice guy that he was, couldn't have rigged any device that could make Marla fly gracefully across the runway. It was impossible. Even if he had, Marla didn't have the natural wherewithal to pull it off.

"No big deal, Bruno," I scoffed.

"No, Sierra, it is a big deal. She made it all fancy, with a silver sequin costume made up to look like a B-52 bomber. She even got silver wings on her arms. The guys love it, especially when she grabs her tits and yells, 'Bombs away, boys!' I'm telling you, honey, they're flocking like bees. Vincent said the door was up five hundred bucks last night." Bruno didn't look any too happy.

"So? That's great, isn't it?" Bruno didn't need to see me sweat.

"No, it's not great. Them Air Force boys get to drinking, then they start fighting. Then I gotta break it all up. It's a pain in the ass, Sierra. The Tiffany don't cater to that crowd. If she keeps this up, the regulars will stop coming in."

"Bruno, take it easy," I said. "I'm coming back tomorrow."

"You are?" He looked uncertain. "How're you gonna do that?"

"Bruno, I'm fine, really. Tell Vincent I said to make sure my spot's open because I'll be there."

I'll admit I was feeling a little nervous, but Marla was

going to eventually screw it up, it was her nature. She wouldn't need my help to topple, but nonetheless, I shouldn't take chances. I'd been out long enough. It was time to make my return, and it better start off with a bang.

Sixteen

The house lights dropped. The spots panned the audience briefly, more a product of Rusty's ineptitude than intention, then crossed together to form a slender pool of light in center stage. The fog machine I'd rented for my big comeback belched a low gray cloud across the runway.

Out in the house, the crowd was noisier than usual. Marla's fans were ready for action and stoking their libidos with alcohol. I stood behind the curtain, waiting. The music began. Tracy Chapman's throaty voice undulated over the crowd, signaling that the headliner was about to make her appearance.

I stepped out of the fog wearing a strapless black velvet sheath. The skirt was slit to my thigh on either side, and five-inch stiletto heels stretched my legs to infinity. I wore black satin gloves up to my elbows and a rhinestone dog collar necklace, and I had piled my blond hair high up on my head. If you can't dazzle them with silver sequins and B-52s, give them the real thing.

I moved forward, stepping out of the fog and onto the runway, letting the music guide my movements. I swayed, slowly, running my satin-sheathed fingers up my torso, bringing them up until they cradled my breasts, pushing them forward like an offering. The room had come to a complete standstill and the only sound was Tracy Chapman's smoky voice, echoing through the night.

I slowly stripped off each glove, tossing them to the quiet servicemen who knelt almost reverentially in front of the runway. Then I reached back to undo the zipper of my gown, letting it fall in a puddle around my high heels. There was a collective sigh, and I knew every man in the room was mine.

Instead of going for the thigh-high black fishnets, I let my hands wander slowly up my neck, up until I reached the pin holding up my hair. Men were slowly moving toward the stage, as if drawn like lemmings by an unstoppable force. Their eyes were pleading. Take it down, they begged silently. Men are such babies, I thought.

Habit led me to glance over at the bar, looking for Denise. Frankie and Rambo were sitting there watching. Rambo stuck his boot out when he saw me looking and made a kicking motion. I ignored the asshole and turned my attention to behind the bar, where a newcomer stood wiping it down. Mechanically, I reached for one of the hooks holding up a fishnet stocking. Fucking Vincent, I thought. That was loyalty for you. Denise had been gone what, a week? Already he'd replaced her.

Now her replacement was watching me. He stood behind the bar, a tall, lanky man in a Stetson. His face was thin and full of angles. Vincent must've hired a token cowboy. The bartender smiled, a slow, easy, knowing grin, and I looked away. Smart-ass cowboy.

I ran my stocking between my legs and tossed it out to a businessman at one of the front tables. He caught it, grinned, and walked up to the edge of the runway holding a twenty-dollar bill. The room was heating up. I saw Bruno and Big Ed move protectively forward as I started to unhook my bra. The airmen were in for a surprise if they tried getting out of hand. There was always one, but Bruno'd snarl at him and it'd be over before it really started.

Rusty, the stage manager, was standing by the fog machine, waiting for the grand finale. I tossed my bra in his direction and strutted forward down the runway. This is always my favorite part, right close to the end, when the tension and the testosterone are mounting and I'm the one in charge.

I reached the end of the runway and stood there, massaging the tips of my nipples until they stood up stiff and hard. There wasn't a dry seat in the house. Then with one hand I snatched at my breakaway panties, and with the other I dropped the little smoke bomb my friend Ernie at the magic shop had given me. There was a moan from the audience and I'd disappeared.

Vincent was backstage when I walked off. He handed me my silk kimono and he was smiling.

"You came back in a big way," he said. He wasn't gonna be pissed that I'd disappeared on him. His headliner was back and the bucks were rolling in. Out in the house I could hear the dull roar of the crowd, still clamoring for more Sierra.

"So, who's the asshole in the cowboy hat you got out front?" I asked.

Vincent didn't flinch. "That's Lyle. He's from Texas."

"No, I wouldn't have guessed."

Vincent knew we were going to have a problem. His dark glasses could hide his twitching eye, but they couldn't hide the way he clenched his jaw.

"What about Denise?" I asked. "We just going to forget about her and hire Roy Rogers?"

We were drawing a little audience. The girls getting ready to go on couldn't quite pretend they weren't listening. Rusty stood just behind Vincent, to his left. He was openly listening, forgetting all about the next act.

"Sierra," Vincent huffed, "I run a business. That girl's been gone a week. She ain't called. The police ain't worried about her. It's the general opinion that Denise don't want to be found. What else can I do? I covered for her with the backups as long as I could, but I need someone here full time to cover her shift."

I didn't answer him. I whirled around and headed off for the dressing room. Why did I think anybody around here gave a shit, anyway? I knew Vincent was only doing what he had to do, but still it felt wrong, unfair.

Marla was waiting in the dressing room. She was carefully applying silver glitter eyeshadow and trying to act nonchalant. She was wearing part of her costume, a silver sequined bodice with an American flag on her chest. Matching silver shoes lay beside her chair and the wings leaned against the side of her dressing table.

"You're back," she said in a strangled, little-girl tone. "I'm glad."

"No you're not," I said pointedly, "but nice try." Marla straightened up and eyed me nervously.

"Sierra," she said, all sugar and spice, "let's us try to get along. We're all one big family—"

"Marla, cut the crap. I'm not in your family and you damn sure ain't in mine. Face facts. You spent the week I've been gone trying to worm your way to the top and take my slot." She wouldn't look me in the eye. "I expected no less from you. But I'm back now," I said as I walked slowly toward her, enjoying the fear in her eyes, "so any ideas you had about taking my place are hereby made history. Got that?"

Marla was trying hard not to blink, not to back down, but her south Alabama breeding didn't hold her up. She swallowed hard and would have answered me, had not Rusty interrupted us.

"Sierra, the new guy, Lyle, told me he found some of Denise's stuff behind the bar. He was wondering what to do with it. I figured you might want it, maybe you'll be seeing her."

I stared at him, completely forgetting Marla. Rusty stood holding the dressing-room door open. He was trying to act like it didn't faze him, seeing girls running around half dressed, but he was one of those guys who never quite get used to it. Rusty was fair-skinned and red-headed. His feelings had a way of creeping up his neck and staining his face, no matter how much facial hair he tried to grow. Rusty was a boy and wouldn't be a man even in old age.

"Where is it?" I asked. I hadn't even considered the possibility that Denise had left something behind at the club.

"Lyle's got it behind the bar. Says it's a makeup bag or something like that." Marla was using the distraction to edge her way toward Rusty and out the door. I let her go. Life had suddenly slipped back into focus. I had Denise and Arlo to think of. This was no time for a catfight.

Lyle was an efficient bartender. He combined an economy of motion with an easy patter of small talk. I watched him reach into the cooler for a beer and a frosted mug with one hand, while neatly placing a napkin in front of a customer and saying something that made the man in front of him laugh. He was a man's man, but not one of those with a point to prove. He was easy and confident with his masculinity.

I stood at the edge of the waitress station, watching him finish with the customer and waiting. I knew he saw me because he reached under the bar and picked up Denise's floral makeup bag before he turned around and walked toward me.

"You must be Sierra," he said in a soft Texan drawl. He glanced up at me quickly, then looked away, almost as if he were shy.

"No flies on you, cowboy." I took the bag he offered, my fingers lightly grazing his. "This all?" I asked.

Lyle shoved his tan felt Stetson a little further back on his head and stared into my eyes. With my heels on, we were even. Maybe he had an inch or so on me, but I could look almost straight back at him. His face was tanned and lines played around his eyes and mouth. He looked like the genuine article, but why would a real cowboy tend bar?

"It is, Sierra, less'n you'd do me a favor and let me buy you a drink after closing."

I looked back at him, then over his shoulder at the customers lining the bar. They were all watching, and despite the volume of the music, I had the feeling they all knew what was going on and what Lyle was asking. They were rooting for Lyle.

Lyle looked at me, his gaze unwavering, expectant, and earnest. What I liked about the way he asked was that he was straightforward. No gimmicks. It wasn't going to make or break his day if I said no. Shit. Why the hell not, I thought, I say yes to one guy and simultaneously fulfill the fantasies of ten others. It wasn't like I exactly had an overload of male company in my life. And it was only a drink, for pity's sake. Why the hell not? I said yes and the whole bar ordered another round.

To his credit, Lyle didn't try to act like this was a goal and he'd just scored. He merely nodded politely, said he'd see me later, and went back to his job. I went backstage clutching Denise's bag and feeling like maybe the tide was turning.

Don't misunderstand me. I am not a princess and I do not feel like any man who gets to spend time with me has been granted some royal privilege. Quite the contrary. But in my line of work, men overlook the personality inside and deal only with the package. I can understand that. I created my image. It earns me a good living, but the drawback, and sometimes the blessing, is that I don't meet too many men who go beyond the exotic dancer to the self-actualized inner being.

I dated a therapist one time who told me this was a defense mechanism. "Well, who doesn't know that?" I said. "Sometimes being a little lonely, with money to spare, is better than life with an alcoholic asshole who beats you."

My therapist boyfriend said, "Let's talk about the alcoholic asshole who beat you."

"Hey, Sigmund, when I need a therapist, I'll pay one,"

I said, and quit dating him. Like I was saying, who needs complications and assholes? Just give me a man who doesn't feel you're an engine that needs to be tuned up or overhauled. This once, let me find a guy who doesn't only want to get laid and own you.

I was ready to hop up onstage and start lecturing when I remembered Denise's bag and the real reason for traveling out and meeting Lyle in the first place. I took a detour into the dancers' rest rooms and decided to have a look-see in private.

I sat down on the commode in one of the stalls and unzipped the bag. Denise had crammed her few essentials into a small space. A lipstick in a cheap gold case spilled out onto the floor and rolled across the cracked ceramic tile. Mascara, powder, and various other cosmetics crowded to the top of the bag. I emptied them out hastily into my lap, hoping to find something, anything, that might lead me to Denise.

At the bottom of the bag, I found the only remaining tokens of Denise's life in Panama City, a picture of Arlo sitting on the back of Denise's Harley and a Blue Marlin Motel key. I figured the key was Denise's spare, hidden in her bag in case her other one got lost. I cradled the picture of Arlo, staring at his little gray face. His dark dog eyes seemed to stare back at me. Where are you guys? I wondered.

I packed the makeup back into Denise's bag, keeping the key and the picture. Denise had been gone for a week. If she'd really left town, then her stuff would be gone from the motel efficiency. Her Harley wouldn't be parked out in front of her room and her car would have vanished, too. But if someone had snatched her, then maybe her stuff would still be around. Maybe there'd be something in her apartment that would help me prove she'd been kidnapped, because no matter what anyone else said, I was sure Denise had left against her will.

Seventeen

*H*e caught me as I was leaving. I almost didn't recognize him without the hat. He stood there outside the supply closet, holding a case of liquor and looking at me with his big dark eyes. It was going on three A.M. I'd done my last set, removed my stage makeup, and scurried into my clothes. I had one thing on my mind and Lyle had another on his.

In my rush to get to the Blue Marlin, I'd forgotten Lyle and the promised drink. I turned back around and faced him. I could have blown him off and continued on my way, but a promise was a promise. Sierra Lavotini keeps her word. Truth was, I wanted a drink before tackling Denise's room. And truth was, too, Lyle was growing on me. I liked the way his hair fell over his forehead into his eyes when he wasn't wearing his Stetson. I liked the way his forearms rippled and pulled taut when he hefted the case of bottles.

"I didn't forget," I began, shifting my dance bag up on my shoulder.

"No?" He didn't believe me, but he was playing along.

"No," I said firmly. "I was going to toss my stuff in the car so I wouldn't forget later. I'll be right back."

He favored me with one of his half-amused lopsided grins. "If this is not a good time, Sierra—" he began. I cut him off.

"Lyle, really, this is a great time. How about a vodka gimlet?" He nodded and headed off toward the bar. I watched him walk away. He had a nice ass for a cowboy.

The vodka gimlet was waiting when I returned. It was perfect, heavy on the vodka, light on the lime. Lyle leaned back against the wall behind the bar and watched me take the first sip. He was drinking a Corona, a wedge of lime squeezed down the long neck of the bottle. An empty shot glass stood next to a bottle of tequila and a salt shaker.

I sat and waited for the preliminaries, because they always come: "I liked your act" and "How'd a girl like you . . ." But Lyle didn't say any of the expected.

"I hear tell you didn't exactly cotton to me taking over your friend's job," he said, his voice a long, dry drawl.

"It don't have a thing to do with you, I guess," I said. "It was just a shock to walk in after only a week and see you."

Lyle laughed. "Believe me," he said, "it was a shock to look up onstage and see you walking out of the fog and not the B-52s of Miss Marla Angelica." He grinned. "It was a very welcome surprise, I might add."

I took another sip of my gimlet and looked Lyle over.

"You got something against our men in blue?" I asked. I was going to enjoy this. The vodka was warming its way down my body and I felt like sitting for a while.

"No," Lyle said slowly, "I don't object to a military salute, but I'm not a glitter-and-sequin man, personally. I like a woman who knows she's a woman, with the right equipment, and ain't afraid to use it. I like," Lyle said, leaning forward, "simplicity and sophistication."

Something other than vodka was spreading like a brushfire through my body. This had the makings of a long evening. I looked down and realized that my glass was empty. Just as quickly, Lyle replaced it with another gimlet. He poured a shot of tequila, licked the *V* between his thumb and forefinger, salted it, and licked again. He tossed back the tequila with one short move, then bit into a wedge of lime. We sat quietly for a few moments, long enough for me to realize he'd switched the bar music to country.

"Why'd your friend quit?" he asked after a while.

"She didn't quit," I answered impatiently. What had Vincent told him, anyway? "She's missing."

Lyle straightened up and looked like maybe he hadn't heard me right. "Missing?"

"Yeah, but nobody else thinks so. Vincent and the others think she took off."

Lyle looked concerned. He moved closer to the bar and touched my hand lightly. To my surprise I found myself crying—not big crying, just tears leaking and running down my cheeks.

"Man," he said, sighing, "I can see now why you were so upset to see me here. How'd she disappear?"

I thought about it before I spoke. I tried to figure his angle. Did he want to know because he was really concerned or was this the come-on before the usual come-on? I somehow didn't think so. I figured that if Lyle wanted to sleep with me, he'd ask.

So I told him the whole story. I told him about Arlo and Denise and the dead body in her apartment. I told him about Frankie the Biker and Leon Corvase. I told him how Denise had dropped out of sight after the accident and how I knew she'd never run off without Arlo. I told him I didn't think she'd run out on me either, but that part I wasn't so sure about.

Lyle listened. He leaned back against the wall, arms folded against his chest, a serious, intent look on his face. He didn't ask questions. He didn't look away. He let it all drain out until I had nothing left to say. I swallowed the last of my gimlet and sat there, feeling empty.

"So you've got her key," Lyle said. "When are you going to use it?"

I pushed back from the bar and reached for my purse, feeling through the leather pocket to make sure the key was still there.

"I was planning on going there later tonight."

Lyle took my empty glass and, instead of refilling it, dunked it in the soapy water behind the bar. I guess it was his way of saying two is enough. He was closing down for the night. He leaned over and switched off the music.

"Let's go," he said. "I'll follow you." He reached for his hat and started out from behind the bar.

"Wait a minute," I said. I wasn't so sure this was the way I'd planned it.

Lyle stopped, his slow smile warming his face.

"You're right," he said. "I was inviting myself along. But," he said, looking at his watch, "it's going on four A.M. I just thought it might be a little hairy, doing it all by yourself, without a lookout. I mean, if someone snatched your friend, maybe he's watching her place, or hanging around nearby." He looked apologetic. "I was thinking you could use a little muscle, if'n it came to that."

He had a point. Leon Corvase had made me a little cautious. Maybe he was having Denise's place watched. If he hadn't snatched her, he'd be looking for her. I made a snap judgment.

"You can come," I said, "but you have to stay outside and watch from there." Then, belatedly: "I'd appreciate having someone cover my back."

Lyle stayed right behind my rental car the whole way over. He drove a big pickup, with some kind of shiny chrome wind-scoop deal on the roof of the cab. It looked like an out-of-place cowcatcher. His truck was bright red with gold curlicues detailing the lines along the truck's sides. I got to worrying that having Lyle's pickup in the parking lot of the Blue Marlin would be like taking a mobile billboard advertising my presence.

Apparently, Lyle thought the same thing, because

when I turned into the Marlin, he drove past, turning into the lot of a hotel further down the street and doubling back on foot. I eased my car up to Denise's door and looked around. I'd seen her VW still in the lot of the Tiffany, its rear window shot out and bullet holes in the fenders. But her Harley was missing from the motel lot. Denise was picky about that bike, said it was an antique. She kept a canvas cover over it to protect the canary-yellow paint job, and she always parked it right outside her door. It wouldn't be like her to go off without her bike.

When Lyle strolled up, I took the key out of my purse.

"You can wait in my car," I said softly.

He nodded and slipped behind the wheel of my Rent-A-Wreck. Something clanked against the metal door frame as he slid into the seat. He leaned down and grabbed an object off the ground.

"What is that?" I asked, staring at the small gun in his hand.

"It's a gun, Sierra," he said. "I don't plan to use it, but you've been messing with some violent people and this is a precaution."

"Listen," I hissed, "don't go running the Lone Ranger routine on me here. I was fine about doing this by myself. I want it quiet, low-key, and over with as soon as possible. You just sit here, all right?" Lyle glared back at me. "And, for Christ's sake, keep that gun in your boot or wherever it was."

I didn't wait to hear a rebuttal. I marched to the door of Denise's room and stuck the key in the lock. It wouldn't go all the way in. I pulled it out and started to turn it around and try the lock again when I caught the door number on the key: 320. That's right, I remembered, she had moved after the dead man landed in her apartment. Her new apartment was three doors down. I gave Lyle a brief glance and moved down to 320.

This time the key slid in easily. I stepped into the tiny

apartment, closed the door behind me, and switched on the lights. Denise's belongings were piled in a clump by the dresser. It looked like she'd grabbed what she could from the other apartment and moved in without unpacking. There were clothes strewn across the bed, which was unmade, and trash littering the floor. She'd propped a few pictures up against the lamp. One was of her and Frankie sitting on Frankie's bike. Arlo sat on the ground beside them. A family portrait.

"Yeah, where are you now, asshole?" I asked the smiling biker. "You show a lot of concern here, buddy." Denise seemed to have really bad taste in men.

I picked up the other pictures and inspected them. They were Arlo shots. Arlo in the Tiffany, sitting up at the bar like Denise trained him to do. And Arlo as a puppy, sleeping.

I wandered into the tiny kitchen and looked in the sink. Dishes and pots, the food dried to form hard craters and crevices, threatened to spill over the sink's edges. Denise had made spaghetti and spilled the sauce from the sink to the refrigerator. Swipes and blotches of dried red sauce were everywhere. What a slob.

Out of curiosity, I walked over to the refrigerator and pulled open the door. The smell hit me almost before I could take in what I was seeing. Someone had removed all the shelves. Leon Corvase stared back at me, an empty, fish-eyed stare. He was wedged against the rear wall of the refrigerator, blood crusting over his chest and face. Blood had congealed in a mass around his body. As I stood, paralyzed, holding on to the door, Leon started to move. His body slid down, pushing its way out of the refrigerator and onto the kitchen floor.

I moved then, jumping back out of the way, and seeing for the first time the real truth of Denise's kitchen. The spaghetti sauce was in reality dried blood. Leon Corvase had fought and died in this little room, for surely he had fought. His body was battered, his chest was soaked through with blood. Blood had dried on the countertop, in splatters on the mottled tile floor, and in smears on the refrigerator and the door leading off of the kitchen and into what I felt sure was the bathroom.

My heart was choking me, stuffing itself into my throat. I felt cold, even in the stuffy apartment. I had to get out of here, but I knew I had to look in the bathroom first. What if Denise was in there? What if the person who killed Leon had killed Denise, too?

I inched toward the door, my hands shaking and icy. I reached out and shoved it open. The bathroom was empty; only a few bloodstains remained on the sink. My breath was frozen in my lungs, my stomach heaved, and I had to leave. I turned, seeing the room as if for the first time. Arlo's tiny face stared out from his picture, staring at Leon Corvase's battered body, a two-dimensional dog smile plastered across his face.

Eighteen

*L*yle knew it had gone wrong. He stepped out of the car when he saw me lock Denise's door and start moving toward him.

"Sierra," he said, walking quickly to meet me on the sidewalk. "You look awful. What's wrong?"

I was off-balance, lurching into him, trembling uncontrollably. I was going to be sick, I knew I was, but I couldn't, not now.

"You've gotta call the police," I said.

"Is it Denise?" he asked. The lines deepened around his face. "Is she in there?"

"No, but her ex-husband is. He's dead, Lyle." My voice rose sharply. "He won't be needin' no ambulance, Lyle. He's cold, Lyle." I was laughing, like it suddenly struck me funny, but my brain was screaming to me, "Shut up." I couldn't stop.

Lyle was all business. He grabbed my shoulders, shook me once, and stared into my eyes to see if he'd had an effect. I stopped laughing, leaned past him, and hurled my cookies into the gutter.

"I'll call the police," he said. "Are you okay to wait here?"

I must've looked uncertain because Lyle reached past me, opened the car door, and gently deposited me in the front seat.

"Lock the doors. Wait until I get back or the police

drive up. Don't leave the car." He spoke gently and slowly, like I was a wild horse and he was trying to coax me into compliance. I didn't need persuasion. I nodded, closed the door, and locked it.

Lyle took off past the darkened motel office, down the street. He headed toward his pickup truck and whatever phone he could find at five in the morning. I sat as still as I could, willing my body to stop trembling, wishing my heart would leave my throat and return to my chest. What in the hell was going on?

There were no sirens this time. The police arrived with the whoosh of tires, the slight squeal of brakes, and the faint squawk of their radio. There wasn't any traffic to speak of so early in the morning and no need to draw a crowd. I watched them pull up in front of Room 320 and thought, It's all happening again. Even the cops were the same.

I unlocked the door and stepped out into the early-morning light. There was a glimmer of recognition in the young patrol officer's eyes when he spotted me. He gestured to his partner, who picked up the radio mike and started talking. Probably calling Detective Nailor, I thought dully.

"Miss Lavotini, wasn't it?" The officer stood in front of me, his uniform starched and pressed, his blond hair regulation cut. "Someone called in a body at this location. This isn't a joke, is it?"

"Is that what I look like to you, Officer?" I asked. "Do I look like the type of girl who has nothing better to do at five o'clock in the morning than call in a phony report, then wait around for you to get here?" I answered my own question. "I think not."

The kid scowled, scribbled something on his notepad, and turned back to his partner. "Ready?" he asked him. "You wait here," he said to me, bristling with self-importance.

"I wouldn't dream of going anywhere," I muttered. I leaned back against the Rent-A-Wreck and prepared to wait for Detective Nailor. More police cars arrived, the mobile crime scene van pulled up, and at last, behind everyone else, the familiar brown sedan of Detective Nailor.

Carla Terrance was the first out of the car. She looked fresh and crisp, as if she'd been sitting at the station, waiting for a five A.M. phone call. She barely glanced at me, just walked over to the edge of the crime scene tape, spoke to the first officer on the scene, and then ducked carefully under the yellow ribbon and went inside.

John Nailor didn't look fresh at all. His clothes were rumpled, like they'd been tossed on the floor, then just as carelessly put back on. He didn't wear a tie, and his face was unshaven. He saw me but didn't approach me just yet. Instead he walked over to Room 320 and darted under the tape. He was inside for less than five minutes, then emerged pulling a latex glove off his hand. He headed straight for me.

"Ms. Lavotini," he began, his voice dark and serious, "I'm going to have to ask you to accompany me to the station." His eyes were bloodshot and unhappy.

I wasn't surprised. Same witness, same crime scene, twice within little more than a week? I'd be taking me down to the station to talk, too, if I were him. It looked suspicious, sure, but he couldn't be thinking I had anything to do with Corvase's murder, could he? It seemed that he was reading my thoughts.

"I don't know what your part is in all this," he said, "but it's time you got honest." He took my arm, as if to escort me to his car, but I pulled back.

"I can drive my own car. I'll follow you."

He shook his head, like I didn't get it. "I'll see that an officer returns you to your vehicle when we're finished." His voice was stiff and formal. There wasn't an option.

"All right," I said. "If that's how you want it, so be it."

I felt strangely sad and I wasn't sure why. I guess I thought he knew me better. Stupid thought, I know. How could a cop see me as anything other than my stereotype?

We rode the three miles to the police station without speaking. Now and then, Nailor's radio crackled as the dispatcher moved officers around to respond to calls. A few times he reached for the mike and spoke softly in the ten-code that only police personnel understand. I stared out the window and watched Fifteenth Street slip by. The morning traffic hadn't begun to build and we had the road to ourselves.

When he pulled into the parking lot of the squat, sprawling police department, I could feel my stomach tense up. Nailor picked up the mike, spoke briefly, then turned off the car. I got out and followed him down the sidewalk to a tinted glass door. Here goes, I thought.

The Panama City Police Department was nothing like I expected. It wasn't like a precinct house on television. We entered through the back door without fanfare and wandered through a maze of dimly lit beige corridors. John Nailor's name was on his door in plain black letters. His office was no larger than the tiny bathroom in my trailer.

He motioned me into a utilitarian black chair and then squeezed himself behind his desk. I looked around the room, gathering information. No family pictures in frames. No personal items in evidence with the exception of training diplomas and police mugs and badges. There was a corkboard next to his desk, but the only thing displayed there was a Most Wanted poster and a few newspaper funnies. His office was all business, just like the man who occupied it.

At least he offered me coffee. We sat clutching thick paper cups and staring each other down. It was almost six A.M. and I was whipped. Nailor looked as exhausted as I felt, but I knew this wasn't going to be a short morning. He was too tenacious for that. He intended to wring every drop of information he could out of my sleep-deprived brain.

He looked across at me and for a moment I could imagine what he must have looked like as a kid. His ears were too large and his dark, straight, short hair only served to frame them and make them all the more obvious. As a kid, he would've looked kind of goofy and serious. As an adult, he just looked vulnerable. I mean, how dangerous is a man with big ears? He looked earnest, like it would hurt him personally if you weren't straight with him. He didn't look like he was expecting you to lie. I had the curious urge to reach across the desk and stroke the side of his tired face. It was the little boy still trapped inside him that lured me.

"Sierra," he said, his voice soft in the tiny room, "I've been sitting here trying to put myself in your place." Despite the warmth of his voice, I felt myself tense up. Nailor stretched back a little in his chair.

"Your friend Denise comes to you one night and says someone's stolen her dog and wants one hundred thousand dollars to get him back." The detective shook his head, like this alone would have been enough to let him know something was wrong with the picture. "Then she invites you back to her hotel room and you find a dead man. Then someone shoots at you and your friend. You allegedly chase the car that fired the shots because you think you see her dog and 'cause that's the kind of friend you are." I started to interrupt, but he held his hand up to stop me.

"Then," he continued, "you land in the hospital. Your friend disappears. And now we've got the body of her ex-husband dead in your buddy Denise's refrigerator."

Listening to him, I could see it like he saw it. He didn't think Denise had been taken by her ex. He thought Denise was a liar and probably a murderer. He thought I was too dumb to see through Denise. John Nailor laid his hands, palms up, on the scarred wooden desk. His eyes were sad.

"I need your help, Sierra," he said. "I think you're a loyal friend, but I think Denise has taken advantage of you." He pulled his hands back into his lap and leaned forward. "Sierra, Denise spent the last two years before she came to Panama City in a federal prison. She was a partner in her husband's dope operation. She conned and manipulated people for a living. Don't hold on to some misguided sense of loyalty."

I was so confused. The way he laid it out, I'd be a fool to believe anything Denise ever told me. But in my heart I saw little Arlo, his dark, liquid eyes staring back at me. Could a sociopath own such a good dog? Then this other voice in my head started wondering if Arlo had a sense about Denise and had run off.

"Detective," I said finally, "I'm tired. I've been up almost twenty-four hours, so pardon me if my brain ain't all it could be, but do not mistake me for a bimbo." Deep inside I felt the Lavotini temper begin to well up.

"I may not have your training and education. I may not have a career in the limelight of society, but I am a good judge of character. I have solid, true friends. I stick with them, and they stick with me. So when I tell you that my friend Denise Curtis is on the straight, I don't need to be patronized or talked to like I'm some kind of idiot." I took a deep breath. "I will tell you again everything I know, and then I am going home to bed."

I didn't care what John Nailor thought anymore. I didn't look for the little boy in him. I didn't even look him in the eye. I stared instead at the desk. I told him everything that had happened in Fort Lauderdale and everything leading up to finding Leon Corvase's bloody body. When I finished I took a deep breath and looked straight at Detective Nailor.

"Unless I need to call a lawyer," I said calmly, "I'm leaving. I don't want a ride back to my car. I'll walk." I pushed my chair back and prepared to stand. It was a great exit, spoiled by Carla Terrance.

She pushed open the door and blocked my path, then glared past me at John Nailor.

"You're not letting her leave, are you?" she demanded.

Nailor stood up and motioned toward the door. "Excuse us a moment," he said to me. An angry red flush began working its way across his face as he moved toward Carla. I could tell he didn't like her tone of voice in front of me. The door had barely closed when I heard the rumble of furious voices. I stood up and silently crept to the door. When I pressed my ear against the crack by the door frame, I could hear quite nicely.

"This is an open investigation," Carla was saying. "I have my interests to protect. If you get in the way, so help me, I'll go to your chief and then I'll call my boss in Miami."

"Don't threaten me," Nailor said, his voice a quiet inferno. "We've got no reason to keep her. Your personal feelings are getting in the way here." I plastered myself as close to the door as I could, rooting for Nailor.

Carla tore back at him like a wildcat. "Personal," she spat. "Don't get personal! Don't flatter yourself, John. I'm here because I have to be; it's my investigation. Don't you think I would have done anything to stay away from you?"

Bad blood, I thought. This was getting good. There was a moment of silence and then Nailor's voice again.

"Carla, I didn't want to work with you any more than you wanted to work with me, but I like to think we're both professional enough to bury our feelings and do our jobs."

"You sanctimonious shit," she hissed. "Don't lecture me about professionalism. Do you think the DEA would've taken me on as a special agent if I weren't one of the best?" This was getting worse by the moment, I thought. These two hated each other. "That was always the problem with us, John. You couldn't handle a little competition."

"No, Carla, that wasn't the problem. The issue was your insecurity. I was proud of you. I backed you all the way, but you never believed it. I gave our relationship everything I had, but it was never enough."

Relationship? But they broke off as a third voice interrupted.

"Is there a problem here?" The deep male voice didn't wait for an answer. "I knew it was a mistake putting you two together, but there was no option. If I was mistaken about the caliber of your abilities, then . . ."

Carla and John rushed to reassure him there wasn't a problem.

"Then I don't want any more of this bickering," the gruff voice continued. "I got a call from the lab. You got two blood types at the scene. The medical examiner hasn't set time of death yet, says she has to run a few more tests. They'll do the autopsy this afternoon. I want you there, Nailor. And Nailor?"

"Yeah, Chief?"

"Pull the others off whatever they're working on. This takes precedence. I want this one wrapped up in a hurry, before we have some kind of media zoo."

Heavy footsteps moved off down the hallway and there was silence for a few moments.

"Well, at least find out her blood type," Carla said.

"I can get that from the hospital," Nailor answered. "Let's wait for all the forensics to come back and focus on where she was at the time of death."

I couldn't hear Carla's answer. I scampered back to my chair right before Nailor walked into the room. His face was a dusky red and his eyes were even more blood-shot than before.

"I'll give you a ride back to your vehicle," he said.

"I meant it, I'll walk," I answered.

He sighed, frustrated. "Don't be ridiculous. It's three miles and you've been up all night." He walked to the door and held it open for me. Three miles in stilettos is a hell of a statement, no matter who you are or how accustomed you are to wearing spike heels. I took the ride.

He didn't say a word the whole way back to the Blue Marlin, but I could tell he was stewing. When we pulled into the lot, the mobile crime scene unit from Pensacola stood parked in front of the motel pool. Technicians moved with calm efficiency in and out of Room 320. John Nailor pulled next to my Rent-A-Wreck and parked. I reached for the door handle and turned to look at him. He wasn't looking at me. His attention had turned to the crime scene.

"By the way, it's type O," I said in his direction. "Me and approximately forty-five percent of the rest of the world."

He whipped his head toward me. "What?" He looked irritated.

"I'm type O. I thought maybe you could tell that to your partner and she'd climb down off your ass." He looked surprised, like he couldn't imagine for a moment how I knew. "Relationships are a real bitch, Detective," I said as I opened the door. "The way I see it, you can't win for losin'. People are just like magnets, Nailor, they're always drawing the worst out of each other."

Nailor frowned. "I thought magnets repelled each other," he said. "Only opposites are drawn together."

"The trouble with you, Nailor," I said, "is that you think too much."

I closed the door before he could answer. Poor dummy, he was probably clueless. He was probably one of those poor guys who thinks all you gotta do is lay your earnest card on the table and it's clear sailing from there.

The only way a relationship makes it is if both parties happen to stare into the mirror in the morning and say, "Hey, I'm no bargain either." I couldn't see Carla Terrance looking in the mirror and admitting she wasn't a bargain. That was the problem with their whole relationship, as far as I could see—Carla was too insecure to admit she wasn't perfect and Nailor was too busy being earnest to realize Carla was afraid. Of course, that and a buck won't buy you a cup of coffee in Panama City. It certainly wouldn't help Leon Corvase or his ex-wife. Leon was an ice cube and Denise was missing. I hoped Denise hadn't decided to take matters into her own hands.

Nineteen

*F*luffy and I worked the kinks out of our relationship years ago. She didn't hold it against me if I stayed out too late, as long as I left her some food and made sure the miniature doggy door was in working order. When I straggled in and headed back to the bedroom, Fluff was waiting, her head nestled on the pillow, a welcoming smile on her face.

"You know, Fluff," I said, stripping off my clothes and reaching for a nightshirt, "you're about the one true thing, you know what I'm saying?" Fluffy seemed to nod reassuringly.

"I mean it, girl," I said, crawling under the covers next to her. "Who else can I rely on, day or night?" Fluffy sighed, content in her place within my universe. "That guy that pulled the hook out of your paw?" She watched me, her features impassive. "He's dead." She licked my cheek. "Denise? Who knows where the hell she is? Then there's this new bartender, Lyle. He goes off to call the cops and never comes back. What kind of reliability factor does he have, eh? I'm thinking he rates a zero. I'm telling you, Fluff, it's me and you against the rest of the idiots."

Fluffy moaned in disgust and I felt my eyelids filling with sand, making it hard to hold them open.

"Oh, I know, girl," I murmured. "Raydean and Pat, but honey, Raydean's a lost ball in high weeds and Pat's too old to worry about us all the time. We should be taking care of them. The guys at the club, well, there ain't no free lunches, Fluffy. That's all I can say." Fluffy had fallen asleep, her warm dog breath brushing softly against the crook of my neck.

I couldn't have slept more than two hours, although my clock said I'd slept well into the afternoon. Someone banged incessantly at the kitchen door, sending Fluffy into a frenzy and irritating the hell out of me.

"Hold on," I yelled out impatiently. "I'm coming." Fluffy ran past me to the door sniffing and yelping. Apparently, she knew my visitor and approved.

"Fluffy, tell your mama to come on," Pat's voice groused through the door. "Any type of decent person'd be up already."

When I opened the door, Pat almost fell through in her hurry to get to me. She smelled of fish and sweat and salt-water. Obviously, she'd come straight from the boat without stopping to shower or change. Her blue eyes glittered with emotion and her stark white hair framed her face in a windswept halo. Unflappable Pat was rattled and that worried me instantly. Whatever was bugging her had to be important.

"Sierra, I don't know what you've been up to, Sugar, but you've certainly stepped in it." Pat paused and looked me over, waiting for me to react.

I headed for the coffeemaker, deliberately taking my time. I wasn't going to give Pat the feeling that I was in any kind of trouble. She'd been through enough with me. I was going to manage whatever it was without involving her. I glanced over at Fluffy. She was licking Pat's leg and sniffing warily. Maybe Pat's smell reminded her of Fort Lauderdale and fishhooks. Whatever it was wasn't making Fluff any too happy.

"Pat, what do you mean, 'stepped in it'?" I filled the coffee carafe and carefully poured the water into the machine.

"Catfish, I've got kids older than you, meaner than you, and, I'm starting to think, smarter than you. Don't play innocent with me." She was glaring at me. I could feel her eyes boring into my back. "A detective from the Panama City Police Department was waiting for me when I docked the TCB this afternoon. He wanted to ask me a bunch of questions about you."

With that comment, my heart started racing and my stomach began to churn. Why were they talking to Pat about me?

"Oh yeah," I said, playing it cool, "Detective Nailor. He's on some personal vendetta and thinks I know where Denise is. Don't worry, he's harmless."

Pat shook her head. "It wasn't him or that woman he had with him at the hospital. I never saw this guy before. He was a young fella, about mid-twenties, flattop haircut, well built, kinda cute, actually."

Who in the hell was that? I let my mind race back over the crime scene and the police department. I hadn't seen any other detectives.

"Well, who was he?" I asked. In spite of myself, I could hear my voice rise an octave with anxiety.

Pat drew a white business card with the Panama City Police Department insignia on the top right side. "Dennis Donlevy. He was real nice, said he was checking on some background information for a homicide investigation. Asked me what kind of tenant you were. Did you pay your rent on time and in cash or by check. Did I notice any unusual activity in the park, especially around your trailer." It was Pat's turn to play cool. She laid the information out like she'd been pleasantly chatting with the guy. She had to know it was eating at my guts.

"Oh, that's all," I said, nodding. "They just want to check me out. Standard operating procedure when you investigate homicides. No big deal."

Pat's frustration finally showed. "Damn it, Sierra. When were you going to tell me you'd found another dead body? And come to think of it, when were you going to come around again after your little Fort Lauderdale escapade?" Her face reddened with anger and her hands flailed uncontrollably at her sides. "You know, Catfish, I'm trying to be your friend here, but you make it hard sometimes. You've got that wall you put up, like you're expecting the worst from the world. Just run off to Fort Lauderdale, don't say thank you or kiss my ass or nothing."

"I didn't want to bother you any more than I already had," I said. Next to me, on the counter, the coffeemaker hissed. Strong, black coffee began dripping into the pot.

"Bother me?" Pat sputtered. "You scared me and your friends half out of our minds. Now you've got the cops investigating your background, trying to figure out where you've been when and if you're the kind of person who'd kill or help kill two people." Pat shook her head again. "How can I defend you when I don't even know what's going on?"

It was beyond my control. I could feel myself shutting down. The thick wall slowly moved into place, and as much as I wanted to give Pat everything she needed, I couldn't. Sometimes the world wanted more than I was ready to risk.

"Pat," I finally said, breaking the long silence that lay between us, "you're right. I should have called or come over. I just really didn't want to put any more on you." But the words had a hollow, mechanical ring to them and Pat saw right through me.

"I don't know if that's the case, or if you were just plum self-centered. Either way, I'm disappointed in you. It's time to step up and be responsible, Sierra. I'm not your mother, I'm your friend." Pat didn't wait for me to respond. She turned and walked out of the door, leaving me to stare after her.

If it all wasn't bad enough, when I went to the window to see if Pat had really left or was maybe still in the front yard waiting for me to do the right thing, I saw an unmarked white police sedan parked a little way down the drive from my trailer. I was being watched. Detective Nailor hadn't been as secure in my story as I'd thought.

"What'd I tell you, Fluffy?" I asked. "It really is you and me against the world." Fluffy seemed to scowl. "All right," I said, sighing, "you're right, I could've played this hand better. I could be more responsible. But Fluff, don't you ever get that deer-in-the-headlights feeling? You know you oughta be doing something, but you can't quite get up the energy to make it happen."

Fluffy'd had enough of my thought process. She sighed back at me loudly and walked out of the kitchen, headed back to the bedroom and her trusty pillow.

"No matter where you go, Fluff, there you are," I called after her. She didn't answer. Her sharp nails clicked across the parquet hallway. She was in no mood for my theories.

Detective Nailor waited to make his appearance until I'd arrived at the club and was minutes from doing my act. He could have used the back-door entrance, could have been low-key, but I was learning that wasn't his way. He enjoyed seeing Vincent and Bruno look uncomfortable. He counted on throwing me off stride. Why else stroll in the main entrance, sit down near the front of the house, and ask to see me?

I was ready for him this time. I figured that since the police had gone to enough trouble to put me under surveillance, Nailor would have to show up sooner or later. It was obvious that the cops weren't done with me. So be it, I thought. I sauntered through the back hallway and stepped out into the house.

Nailor had a low tumbler filled with soda sitting in front of him and a slight scowl on his face. He was watching one of the new girls go through her paces. The whole club seemed tense, sensing the presence of law enforcement on the premises. Vincent was particularly bothered by the return of the heat. He slowed as he passed me on his way to his office, where he would watch Nailor through his two-way mirror.

"Lose him, Sierra," he growled. Easier said than done, I thought. I strolled up to Nailor's table and pulled out a chair. I stared at him, waiting for him to look up. When he did, I sank down slowly, straddling the back of the chair.

"I'm flattered, Detective. If you wanted to make sure you caught my act, you could've called and asked when I went on. You didn't need to send your boys to follow me."

Nailor stared back. His eyes wandered slowly down my body, taking in the black sequined bustier and the gold glitter I'd sprinkled in my cleavage.

"You're not taking this seriously, Sierra," he said.

"You're right, John," I said, deliberately using his first name. Two could play this game. "I can't take it serious when you guys are spending all your time following me around and not listening to me about Denise. I got nothing to hide, John. Look all you want."

Nailor turned his head and watched Marie lose her bra. His eyes took in every detail, but he watched like a scientist tracking the movements of a brightly colored fish. He wasn't turned on, he was gathering his thoughts.

"Ms. Lavotini, maybe you don't know how the police work a homicide in this town." He moved slightly closer, his eyes burning into mine. "When a homicide occurs in Panama City, like it does about eight times a year, everything comes to a halt. All available investigators are pulled in. We form a task force. We go to work on every lead, every suspect."

I tried to look unafraid as he went on.

"You're the key to this investigation right now, Sierra. That means we're going to check out every aspect of your life. We'll talk to your friends, your family, your coworkers. When we're finished we'll know you better than you know yourself, Sierra." He leaned very close to me, his breath a whisper of mint and Coke. "Are you sure your life can take that kind of scrutiny?"

I wanted to scream. I wanted to lose it and tear his eyes out. It took every ounce of self-control I had not to slap him.

Nailor smiled slightly. "You know how well I know you, Sierra?" he said softly. "I know you well enough to know you want to hit me right now. You can taste it. That's how you handle a tough time. I hear you even bloodied a biker's nose the other week."

My ears were ringing, and blood was rushing into my head, staining my face and chest.

"Maybe Leon Corvase pushed you over the edge, Sierra. Maybe you took him out. I don't think so, but we'll know for sure in a few hours." He pushed his chair back slowly and stood up, staring down at me. He leaned over, his knuckles whitening as he rested his weight on his hands.

"Every time you see me, Sierra, I'll know a little bit more about you. If there's anything you want to tell me first, anything about you that you don't want me to find out the hard way, then you'd better hope you find me before I have to come find you." He flipped his business card on the table. "It's always easier when you do the talking, Sierra."

He was gone before I could trust myself to look up. Son of a bitch. Who in the hell did he think he was?

I sat motionless for a moment, trying to pull it back together. Come on, I told myself, this was police bullshit. He's not really going to track down your entire life. I moved to Panama City to get away from my past, not to have it dredged up and carried back to Florida. What could they really find out? I didn't have a criminal record. On the other hand, I watched *60 Minutes* and those other news shows. They were always talking about how much people could find out about their fellowman. All you needed these days was a computer and you could know what brand of toilet tissue your subject used in 1968.

"Sierra, you all right?"

A voice crashed in on my thoughts, bringing me back to the Tiffany. Lyle. I looked up and scowled.

"So what happened to you last night, Cowboy? It would've been nice for you to at least stop back by and make sure I hadn't been killed by the same guys that whacked Denise's ex."

Lyle looked uncomfortable. He squirmed in his snake-skin boots and fiddled with the brim of his hat.

"Well, it's kinda like this," he said. "I would sorta like to avoid the police."

"You would sorta like to avoid the police? Now, what in the hell does that mean, Lyle?"

Lyle looked around anxiously, searching the faces at the nearby tables, hoping my voice wasn't carrying. I didn't care who heard us. He'd left me alone with a dead body and the police to deal with. I was going to have an explanation.

"If you don't mind," he said, "is this something we could discuss later? You're due up in a minute and Mr. Gambuzzo's gonna have my tail if I don't get back to the bar. Besides which, it ain't exactly the time or place for me to be talking about this."

It was the longest speech I'd heard Lyle make. Of course he wouldn't want to be involved with the cops. Why should I be surprised? Everybody I ran into these days didn't want to be involved with the cops. After my little tête-à-tête with Detective Nailor, I could understand the common reluctance.

"Sure," I said, "tell me all about it later." That's what I was, the understanding dancer, always ready to hear somebody's explanation of how whatever'd happened wasn't their fault. They always meant to call, they always wanted to be there for you, but somehow fate intervened and whisked the opportunity to be reliable away. Lyle must've sensed my skepticism.

"Sierra, I'm serious about wanting to talk later. How about after we close?"

I looked up at the big brown cowboy eyes and thought he looked sincere, but what kind of judge am I? Fluffy was sincere. Arlo was sincere. Men are dogs, true, but that don't make them sincere.

"I don't know, Lyle. I gotta get backstage. You gotta bar full of thirsty customers. Let me see how I feel after work, all right?"

I didn't wait for the answer. As far as I was concerned, nothing mattered right now. Humankind was closing in too quickly on me and I needed space. No better way to escape than to dance. At least when I danced, the rest of the world sat below me, looking up, and I was untouchable.

Vincent just had to get in the last word. He waylaid me as I wandered toward the back of the house, stepping outside his office and motioning me into the inner sanctum.

"Sierra," he growled, "you got a problem." Damn, did everybody have to crawl my ass at the same time?

"Vincent, I don't got any problems that I can't handle."

"Be that as it may," he huffed, "the cops are coming around, there's an unmarked car with two detectives in it sitting in my parking lot, and you're getting your panties in a wad over this Denise deal." I started to interrupt but he kept going. "I know she's your friend and you can't find her, but Sierra, did you ever think maybe she don't want to be found?" Vincent didn't really ask the question to hear my answer.

"I don't have to tell you how it is in this business. There's lots about that girl you probably didn't know and may never know. The Tiffany can't have cops watching the door. It's bad for business. So bottom line, you get them off you or you gotta go."

"Vincent, don't blow smoke. I'm your top act. I could go to the Show and Tail tomorrow and you'd be out a headliner." What was this?

"Sierra, a headliner don't mean squat if the house is empty. You got until the weekend to lose the heat. Much as I don't want to lose you, business is business." Vincent wasn't going to back down. He stood behind his battered metal desk, his glasses reflecting the sequins in my costume, his jaw twitching, and his mind made up. The cops backed off me or I was out of work and with the cops on my tail, nobody'd hire me.

I was too mad to talk to Vincent, and it wouldn't have done any good, anyway. After all, he was right. Law enforcement and exotic dancing didn't mix, not with customers and not with dancers. I had to get Nailor and his task force of overeager detectives off my back. If I didn't, then Fluffy and I would be out on the streets, unemployed and unemployable. There was only one way to fix the situation. If I couldn't find out where Denise was, I had to find out who killed Leon Corvase.

Twenty

I wasn't really thinking; instead I drifted, flitting from thought to memory. My body was moving, becoming the music and, in the process, twisting the minds and wills of every man in the club. An old Bonnie Raitt tune, "Love Me Like a Man," boomed through the club. The lights, strobed in reds and blues, pulsated, throbbing along with the tensions of sexually frustrated men.

My old man found out I was dancing shortly after I turned nineteen. I'd moved out of the house that summer, and in with one of the other dancers from this little joint where I worked in Upper Darby, Pennsylvania. I'd moved so my parents wouldn't find out what I was doing for a living. I was sure there'd be hell to pay when they found out, and I was trying to postpone the inevitable.

Upper Darby's a close-in suburb of Philadelphia, full of blue-collar workers. I started off dancing there in a club that was only a step up from a biker bar. I figured nobody my parents knew would come in and see me, but of course, I was wrong. Word got back to Pop before I'd been there two months. Thank God, he had the decency not to show up at the club. Instead he arrived, unannounced, at my apartment one afternoon.

I opened the door, saw him standing there, and knew he'd found out. He looked at me like he'd never seen me before, and then he started crying. Silently, tears streamed down his lined cheeks. I'd never seen my pop cry, and it sucked the youthful feeling of invincibility right out of my body.

"Why, Sierra?" he asked. It wasn't anger, just disappointment. That tore at me worse than anything.

"Pop," I said, drawing him into the apartment and closing the door, "it's not like you think."

"No, that's not what I'm asking," he said. "I'm asking why you didn't tell me. Why you thought you needed to sneak off in the dark and hide what you're doing. That's what makes it wrong, honey. That's what says you're ashamed."

He had me crying then. I sat at my kitchen table with him, the two of us crying, and tried to explain to my pop why I did what I did.

"Pop, you and Ma raised us to do our best, to do what made us feel good inside. Johnny and the others knew, right from the get-go, what they wanted to be when they grew up. They wanted to be firemen, like you, or a cop. I didn't know, Pop. I just knew it couldn't be like anything I'd ever heard about."

Pop was listening hard, like maybe he thought he should make up for not hearing me before in my life, like maybe he'd gone wrong with me by not listening when I was a kid.

"You know I didn't like school. I did okay, but it didn't come easy. I got more of an education from reading. And none of those jobs I tried after high school lasted. I couldn't hack it, doing the same thing day after day for no money. I needed to do something exciting, where I was in charge."

Pop was nodding and I knew why: He felt the same way. That's why he fought fires. That's why I started them.

"Then why didn't you tell us, Sierra?"

"One night, me and a bunch of the girls were out at a club, for a bachelorette party. It was one of those clubs where guys and women both strip and they had an amateur night. I'd had a couple of drinks, sure, but they dared me and I thought, Why not?"

Pop chuckled. It was just like me, impulsively answering a dare.

"Pop, I was a little nervous at first, but then when the music started and all those men were staring at me, I felt this energy flowing all through my body. The more I danced, the more I saw what I could do. It was awesome, Pop. All those guys, stuffing money in my garter belt, and I made them do that."

I looked to see how he was taking it, but his face was neutral and I couldn't tell what he was thinking.

"I won the contest that night, Pop. I came home with two hundred dollars in prize money and one hundred in tips—from one dance. I knew what I wanted to do then, Pop. I wanted to be the best in the business. I wanted to make a bunch of money and then, when it was time to retire from dancing, I'd have a nest egg. I could run my own business if I wanted."

"Then why didn't you tell your ma and me?" Pop asked in exasperation.

"And risk you not understanding, or worse, demanding I quit? I was going to tell you sometime, but I wanted to be working in a better club first. Pop," I said, "I'm a good girl, really I am. I don't use drugs. I'm not doing anything illegal. I just love what I do, finally."

Pop shook his head and reached for my hand. "Honey, don't you think that's all your ma and I want for you? Yeah, I gotta admit I was angry when I heard, but part of that's 'cause I heard from a friend and not from you. How you think I felt, hearing my daughter was taking her clothes off in some club in Upper Darby, no less?"

"I'm sorry, Pop."

"You should be sorry for that, Sierra. That ain't no way to show respect for your parents. But you should never be sorry for doing something you feel is right.

Your ma and me, we raised youse guys to hold your heads up and be proud of yourselves. If you want to be the best dancer there ever was, then do it, but don't you never apologize to nobody."

Pop stood up and put his hand on my head. "I love you, honey, and I'm proud of you, no matter what you think. I'm going home now. I'm not going to tell your mother about this talk because it would hurt her to know you was afraid to come to her. But I expect you home for dinner on Sunday. I expect you to walk in and look your ma in the eye and tell her what's what. That's all I'm asking of you, Sierra. Hold your head up and respect your mother. God gave you a talent, and that ain't nothin' to be ashamed of, honey."

He left and I showed up for dinner on Sunday. My brother Johnny was the only one to try and give me any grief. I asked him did he think he could strut down a runway, get naked, and walk off with two hundred dollars? He was concerned about his friends finding out.

"So what you're saying, Johnny, is that you're afraid of what they'll think of you." Johnny sputtered and denied it, but I cut him no slack. "I'm no different naked than I am with clothes on, Johnny. I'm the same person. I haven't lowered myself. I'm not ashamed of my body. It earns me a decent living. If my dancing makes you insecure, then that's your problem."

Nobody else gave me any grief. When they saw that I hadn't changed and I was still the same old Sierra, everyone lightened up. My brothers even referred some of their friends to my club for bachelor parties. Ma took to helping me craft some of my costumes.

"There," she'd say, holding up a G-string, "this'll bring in the tips." In a way, my sheltered, stay-at-home mother was getting her own kicks out of seeing me be successful.

It was a nice couple of years, back then. I worked my way into some better clubs, made some more money, and enjoyed myself. That was before it all got so complicated and long before I made the move to Panama City. I guess I'd been naive to think that geography cured complications. Life in Panama City was turning out to be far more complicated than life in Philadelphia.

I finished my dance and my shift on autopilot, barely aware of the applause and catcalls. I wanted out of the Tiffany. I needed to think. I didn't need to hear some sorry excuse from Lyle about why he ran out on me. I just needed to be alone, to think. I knew now that nothing would be right again until I'd gotten to the bottom of Leon Corvase's murder and brought some control back into my life. That fact was underscored as I walked to my car in the parking lot. The unmarked white sedan had been replaced by a brown Ford. I was still under surveillance.

"Piss on it," I said to no one, my voice filling the almost-empty lot. "I'm headed back to my trailer, if it makes it any easier for you," I yelled across the lot. "Maybe you'd like to lead this time." The detective sitting in the car ignored me.

I slid behind the wheel of the Rent-A-Wreck, turned the key in the ignition, and said a prayer of thanksgiving when it started. At least tomorrow I could go used-car shopping, maybe find another Trans Am. I attempted to chirp the tires as I took off, like I would've done in the old Trans Am, but all the rental did was belch black exhaust. I pulled out of the lot and onto Thomas Drive followed by my trusty police dog.

"Sierra," a voice said in the darkness. My heart took off and I gasped. "Don't be afraid. It's me, Frankie."

The voice came from the backseat, somewhere near the floorboards.

"About time you surfaced," I said. "Where's Denise?"

"We'll talk about that in a couple of minutes," he said. "First you gotta lose your boyfriend back there."

"How do you know?"

"Sierra, don't be stupid. I had to wait four hours to find a time to sneak into your car. I've been trying to get ahold of you for two days. You got cops glued to you like dogs got fleas. Of course you got a tail. Now let's lose him."

I was feeling some ambivalence. The last and only time I'd tangled with Frankie, I'd been on the losing end until Raydean had showed her shotgun. How did I know he didn't want to pay me back? In fact, given the death of Denise's ex, how was I to know he hadn't killed Leon and maybe even Denise?

"I can't lose him, Frankie. Don't you think I've thought of that?"

"Just do like I tell you," he said. His voice didn't sound like there were going to be any options. It wasn't a polite request.

My curiosity got the best of me. I'd find nothing out if I stuck with my tail. Why not take the chance?

"Cross the bridge like you're heading home. Go your normal speed. Don't let him think anything's unusual. When we get to Beck, turn right." He was taking me to Old St. Andrews, a residential area filled with renovated older homes that lined the bay.

"That's your plan?" I asked.

"No, Sierra, I didn't want to give you too much at one time."

"Well, we're over the bridge and passing the college now." I glanced in my rearview mirror. "He's not too far back," I said.

"All right, listen. When you turn onto Beck, make a left pretty quick, cut your lights, and pick up speed. You know that area?"

"Well, kind of, but it's not where I usually hang, if that's what you mean."

Frankie sighed impatiently. "What you want to do is put some distance between you and him, then cut into a driveway or the back of a vacant lot and hide until he goes past and loses you."

"Yeah, right." Did he think I was James Bond?

"Sierra, he's not planning on this. You've got the surprise element working in your favor."

Frankie was right. When I veered suddenly onto Beck, raced for a side street, and cut the lights, I found myself behind the older homes in total darkness. I slid around darkened streets, looking for my opportunity. My heart was racing and my palms were sweating as I gripped the steering wheel. With a quick lurch, I turned into the gravel parking area of a big home, pulling my little Toyota up alongside a ramshackle former garage. As I peered out the back window, I saw the brown Ford glide by a moment later.

"Done," I said proudly.

Frankie's head popped up from behind the seat. He wasn't smiling.

"Don't get cocky. That boy's on the radio right now, and in two minutes every squad car in Panama City'll be down here looking for you. Come on." He pushed the back door open and hopped out into the dark humid night.

I saw no option but to follow him. We stayed close to the side of the garage, edging our way out toward the road. Frankie had grabbed my arm and was guiding, pushing, me forward. He'd been right about the police. Three squad cars moved quickly past the old home, responding to the detective's call.

Frankie waited until the third car had passed, then pushed me forward into the light of a lone streetlight and across the street onto the beach that rimmed St. Andrews Bay. It was a cloudy, moonless night, and the black water of the bay seemed to drink any available light down into its depths. Frankie climbed over some fallen tree limbs, all that remained of Hurricane Opal's rampage, and pulled me down and almost under the pile of debris.

"It'll be hard to spot us here," he said, "even if they come looking."

I crouched down among the branches, resting on the

moist sand. Above us on the road, I could hear the intermittent sound of a car's powerful engine, slowly cruising down the street. John Nailor was going to be pretty unhappy about this development.

"Where's Denise?" I asked.

"You tell me," Frankie answered, his voice a harsh staccato. "I haven't seen her since I moved her into her new room. She was supposed to sleep for a while, then meet me after work. She never showed up. It's been over a week, Sierra." Even in the darkness, I could see the anxiety on Frankie's face. "I've got to find her."

Frankie leaned over to peer into my eyes. "I've got to find her," he said again, but this time his tone was harsh. "If you know where she is, then you've got to tell me."

"Why would I hold out on you, Frankie? I told you I don't know where she is."

The nervous feeling was back in the pit of my stomach. Did he really not know where Denise was, or was this a careful manipulation?

"Did she say anything about me to you?" he asked suddenly. "Did she tell you anything about what's going on?" What was he talking about?

"No, she didn't say anything about you, except that she was happy and she felt safe with you." I stared through the dark-ness, trying to read him. "Why? Is there something she should've told me?"

Frankie backed up a little. "No," he said. "I wondered because you seem like you're keeping something back. Maybe she said something to make you not trust me."

My stomach churned away. None of this made sense. One thing I knew, Frankie wasn't being honest with me. I didn't answer him; instead I waited.

"Sierra, Denise needs me," he said softly. "She don't know how badly she needs me." His words were both menacing and pathetic at the same time.

"Frankie," I said into the dark space between us, "have you stopped to think that maybe she's dead? Maybe some rival dope dealer killed Leon and Denise."

"No." Frankie's voice jumped out into the darkness. "No, that's not possible. I would know if she was dead."

"Bullshit, Frankie," I said. "How would you know? What do you mean you would 'know'?"

"I would just know, that's all," he answered softly. "She isn't dead. She needs me. And she's in big trouble."

"So you're psychic, are you, Frankie? Now you can see Denise alive and in trouble, but you don't know where she is? Give me a break, Frankie. You're holding out on me. You know a lot of things you aren't telling." I reached over and snatched at the lapel of his leather vest. "You hurt her, motherfucker, and I'll kill you."

Frankie's eyes glittered in the darkness. For a moment we stayed locked together, then Frankie threw back his head and laughed. It was a harsh, angry sound that tore at the night air.

"You'll kill me, will you? You're mighty protective of someone you don't know half as well as you think. I'm not Denise's problem. Denise is in trouble all right, but she created it. And I'll tell you one other thing, it'll take more than guts and good looks to pull her out of it."

There was the sound of a car door slamming and footsteps running along the side of the road. I'd forgotten for a moment about the police. Frankie looked up, then reached across the short space between us. He grabbed me by both arms and pushed me roughly back onto the wet sand. I was only aware of his strength and size as he rolled his body on top of mine and roughly pushed his lips over mine.

I struggled and he pushed harder, seemingly oblivious to the approach of the police. A cold white light washed over us, illuminating Frankie. Frankie turned his face to the light.

"Hey, man," Frankie said, his voice slow and good-natured. "What gives?" Frankie's body shadowed my face, leaving me in the darkness. "Me and my woman was passing a little time, if you know what I mean." He chuckled and was rewarded as the officer moved the light away from us.

"Sorry," he called, "I was looking for someone. You or your lady friend see anyone down on the beach?"

Frankie laughed a deep throaty rasp. "Buddy, I ain't seen nobody and I can assure you my old lady wasn't looking at nothing but my ugly face. Ain't that right, baby?"

"No, baby," I answered, "I didn't see nobody but you."

That was good enough for the officer. He spoke into the mike on his lapel and then turned to leave.

"You folks have a good evening," he called. "Don't do anything I wouldn't do."

Frankie rolled off me and sat up. I pushed myself up and brushed the sand from my hair and back. The rough feel of Frankie's mustache on my mouth lingered; his leather-and-sweat smell clung to my skin.

"We'd better be gone before they come back and ask for identification or something. I'll get you back to your car."

"What about you? How will you get back?"

Frankie laughed his mirthless chuckle. "Southern Tattoo's right up the road. I'll call Rambo from there." He set off walking quickly across the road and I had to run to keep up.

"What about Denise?" I asked.

Frankie didn't look back. "Like I said, Sierra, Denise is in a lot of trouble. If you hear from her, tell her I'm looking for her. Tell her I'll help her."

"Help her what?" I said to his back.

"She'll know," he answered, then veered off abruptly to the right. "There's your car."

The Toyota was no longer hidden by darkness. Two cop cars stood parked behind it, their blue lights flashing and their spotlights trained on my bumper. When I turned back toward Frankie, he was gone, leaving me to face the music alone.

Twenty-one

$\mathcal{D}$etective Dennis Donlevy, my tail, and I had something in common: We were both in hot water with John Nailor. The young detective, when summoned by the officers surrounding my car, introduced himself with barely suppressed rage. He was no happier after speaking to his boss and finding that he was to follow me out to my trailer and wait for Detective Nailor to join us. Donlevy was just plain miserable after we arrived at the Lively Oaks Trailer Park. He slouched in the front seat of his car, staring straight ahead, waiting for the inevitable reprimand.

I thought about apologizing, but it wouldn't do any good. I'd tried explaining and that fell on deaf ears. He didn't buy that I'd been walking along the bay, thinking. It was almost a relief when Nailor's unmarked car rolled down the trailer park road and turned into my drive.

I sat on the stoop by my back entrance and watched the fireworks. They were quiet but unmistakable. John Nailor was unhappy. Donlevy listened while Nailor spoke, looked his boss in the eye, and, when the sermon ended, nodded. Nailor then appeared to say something funny. Donlevy looked in my direction and laughed. Nailor put his hand on Donlevy's shoulder and the tension was broken. I had no illusions that our chat would go so easy.

"Coffee, Detective?" I asked when he reached the foot of my steps.

We stood for a moment, me at the top of the steps looking down and him looking up, taking stock of each other. I broke free first, turning to unlock the trailer door and motion him in.

"Coffee'd be nice," he said.

No one spoke as I went about the business of making coffee and he wandered through my living room restlessly fingering my knickknacks. Fluffy, who had joyfully trotted out of the bedroom when I unlocked the kitchen door, stood warily at the edge of the hallway into the living room, making her own assessment.

"You take cream?" I called.

"No, black." He moved back into the kitchen and perched on a barstool, watching me pull the coffee and the milk out of the refrigerator.

Although it was once again almost five A.M., Nailor didn't seem at all tired. His eyes were clear and he was dressed in a freshly pressed white shirt and tie. As I walked toward the table, I caught the whiff of cologne or aftershave, and I noticed that his cheeks were smooth and unlined.

"You're mighty dressed up for this early in the morning," I said. "You out late or up early?"

He hesitated for a moment, then shrugged his shoulders.

"I've got to go out of town on business. My flight's at six-thirty."

I climbed up onto the barstool across from him and took a sip of coffee. It was time to stop playing cat and mouse and see if I could get him to listen to me.

"You know," I said, "I wasn't walking on the beach at St. Andrews by myself." Nailor looked up, his eyebrows raised like question marks and his eyes wary. "I know, you're thinking I'm gonna hand you more bullshit, and maybe you'll take it like that, but I'm hoping maybe you'll just listen."

Nailor took a sip of his coffee and waited for me to continue.

"When I pulled out of the parking lot, Frankie, Denise's boyfriend, was lying on the back floor of my car."

"How in the world—" Nailor began, but I cut him off.

"It doesn't matter," I said. "He could've gotten into my car any one of a thousand ways. What matters is he was there and I talked to him. Now," I said, resting my elbows on the table, "I figure that what Frankie had to say might be worth something to you."

Nailor frowned. "This isn't Philadelphia, Sierra. We don't pay informants."

"And I'm nòt asking for money, Nailor, I'm asking for some consideration, a concept which, I might add, seems foreign to you."

"Consideration?"

"Yeah, where I give you something you need and you do likewise." Nailor was listening, but he didn't seem happy. His eyebrows melded together in a frozen frown and his whole body was rigid with caution.

"See, you know by now that my blood wasn't at the murder scene, or at least I hope you do." Nailor's body language said nothing. "So I'm not a suspect, at least not as the murderer. You could still be thinking I'm an accomplice or whatever, but if I'm not the killer, and I'm cooperating with your investigation, do you really need to dog my tail with a cop every minute of the day and night?"

"You're not cooperating yet," Nailor said.

"I tell you what Frankie said and you back off my ass."

Nailor put his coffee cup down and laid his hands palms down on the table. "You tell me what Frankie said and I'll figure out what it's worth."

We were at a standoff and I was desperate. The trailer was silent while I tried to make an evaluation. I looked over at Fluffy, but she didn't seem to have an opinion. I had to do something before the weekend and this seemed like the best shot. So I started talking.

When I finished, John Nailor pulled out his notepad

and made a few notes. He looked up at me when he finished, as if by looking he could judge whether I was
telling the truth or not.

"How were you supposed to reach Frankie?" he asked.

"I don't know. We didn't get that far. I suppose he'll
reach me."

"What kind of trouble did you think he meant when he
said Denise was in trouble?"

"I don't know. Maybe it had something to do with
Leon."

Nailor looked at his watch, closed the notebook, and
stood up.

"Thanks," he said. "I don't know what it'll do for us,
but everything helps."

"So I'm off the hook?" I asked. I slid off the barstool
and followed him across the kitchen.

"We'll see," he said.

"We'll see?" I said. "What the hell is 'We'll see'? I've
got my boss breathing down my back to get the heat out
of his club and all you can say is 'We'll see'?"

Nailor looked at me, his eyes calm, his face set and
determined.

"I'll make a decision when I get back in town," he
answered.

"When will that be?" I said, fuming.

"I don't know," he said. "It depends on what I find
when I get there. Relax, Sierra, I'll get back to you as
soon as I can."

I slammed the door shut behind him, feeling frustrated
and trapped. "The policeman is your friend," I parroted in
a child's voice. What a load of crap. I went to the window
and peaked through the curtains at the street in front of
the trailer. Nailor was leaving and Donlevy was in his
same spot, watching.

The sky was beginning to lighten, giving the street a
dull gray cast. Soon the trailer park would come alive as
the nine-to-fivers left for work and their children waited

for the school bus. In my upside-down, late-night world, it was bedtime.

I wanted to believe I could sleep, but there are those times, before the head even touches the pillow, when you know it's not to be. This was one of those times. I lay in my room, listening as the sun slowly warmed the trailer, making it crack and creak as it expanded with the heat. I heard each car leave for work. I heard the children laughing and yelling as they waited for the school bus. Finally, I heard my answering machine log a phone call.

Usually I can block out the machine's click. I'd already turned off the volume and cut off the ringer on the phone, but my sleep-starved ears heard the tiny switch that signaled an incoming call. My curiosity overwhelmed me, forcing me to reach over and turn up the volume.

"Sierra," a male voice echoed, "it's me, Lyle. You didn't stick around last night and I really wanted to talk to you." There was a brief silence as Lyle decided what to do. "Maybe we can talk tonight. I'd really like that." The machine cut him off. For a moment, I felt guilty, but then I figured, What do I owe a guy who leaves me in a jam? I'd talk to him when I was ready, on my terms.

A few minutes later the machine clicked again. This time the caller hung up. A few minutes later another hang-up, then another.

"Oh, what the hell, Fluff," I moaned. "It's no use." I picked up the alarm clock and looked. Nine forty-two and I was still awake. "Might as well get something accomplished, Fluff," I said. "Let's clean out the rental car and go look for something reliable."

This suited Fluffy fine. After all, she'd slept most of the night like a normal person. She had energy to burn. She followed me outside, her little short tail wagging, her tongue dripping in the mid-morning heat.

The sun was blinding and the heat well on its way into

the eighties as I walked out into the driveway. I glanced down the street and noticed that a new officer had arrived to relieve Donlevy. I didn't recognize him. He had salt-and-pepper hair and seemed to be reading a book. I toyed with the idea of giving him the morning's itinerary but decided that would take all the fun out of the man's day. Nope, let him follow me down Fifteenth Street as I wandered from one used-car lot to the next. Hell, maybe he'd even give me a lift after I dropped off the rental.

"Okay, Fluff," I said, "here's the deal." Fluffy stood in the shade by the bottom step, watching me open the car door and bend over. "We get all my shit out of here, make sure I didn't drop one of my prize pasties or nothing under one of the seats, and then we're off to buy a real car."

Fluffy sniffed, which I took for a chuckle. I pulled my makeup bag out of the backseat and the coffee mugs that had accumulated in the past few days. When I reached down to pull the last mug out from under the passenger-side seat, I found the package. A square lump of brown-paper-bag wrapping, the same kind of package I'd send home at Christmastime, only flatter.

I didn't touch it for a moment. I leaned closer, as if by looking I could tell what it was. I thought about package bombs and the detective in the car down the street. It wasn't wrapped carefully, more like someone had folded a bag around a bundle and quickly taped it shut. I didn't suppose it was a bomb, more likely something left behind by another rental customer. But in case it wasn't, I straightened up, made like I was placing another mug on the car roof, and looked down the street. The detective in the unmarked sedan didn't appear to be paying careful attention.

Fluffy, sensing something was up, walked over and sniffed the bottoms of my feet as I knelt on the driver's seat and peered under the passenger seat again. Maybe with my ass in the air the detective wouldn't be so focused on what I was pulling out of my car. I tried to twitch attractively as I pulled the package from under the seat. I scrambled from the car, piled the mugs and makeup bag on top of the parcel, and walked casually back up the steps and into the trailer.

"Home free, Fluff," I muttered. "Now let's see what we have here."

I tugged at the tape that bound the package. Someone hadn't wanted it to come undone easily and I was finally reduced to using scissors. The bundle, while bulky, was light and fairly soft, and it took almost no time to cut a path through the bag.

"Oh Holy Mother of God, Fluffy, look!" I cried. Fluffy's ears perked up and she wandered closer to the table. With a quick shake I dumped the contents of the parcel onto the kitchen table. It was money, lots and lots of money, gathered into bundles an inch thick and secured with rubber bands.

"There must be thousands of dollars here, girl," I said. "Hell, we don't have to buy a used car now, we can buy a Porsche." I picked up the packets of money and riffled through the bills, all hundred-dollar bills, crisp and new. Any fatigue I'd been feeling slipped away, replaced by the euphoria and paranoia of newfound wealth.

Whose money was this? It seemed inconceivable that it had been left behind by some forgetful rental customer. Why would someone with this much money rent an economy Toyota, anyway? Frankie? I had to think about that one.

True, he'd been the last person in the car, the only person besides me in the car, but why would he leave money behind? This couldn't be clean money, I reasoned. Clean money resided in the bank, where it left only in small amounts and accompanied by a checkbook. This was dirty money. Of course it was Frankie's. He'd probably be looking to retrieve it anytime now. It burned me up the way he'd left me to face the cops alone and now dumped dirty money in my car, assuming nothing would happen to it. I should show him. I should go off and spend it. Right, I thought, and explain to Frankie and his club president that I thought it was a charitable contribution to my well-being.

And if it wasn't Frankie's? What then? Was there a lost and found for dirty money? An expiration date at which time the money would automatically become mine?

"Fluff, I say we count it quick, then hide it. If no one claims it in, say, a year, then we'll go house hunting. I'm thinking a little retirement condo on the waterfront. Maybe a small business." Fluffy grinned and I started counting.

"One hundred thousand large," I said finally. "Fluffy, that's a small business and a down payment on a condo. Hell, girl, now you can go to college if you want." Fluffy frowned. "Well, it was a thought. A dog as smart as you?" I was giddy and apprehensive, stupid with fatigue.

"I know the perfect place to hide this, Fluff." I got up and headed for my toolbox in the hall closet. "We stash the cash, and then we go car shopping, just like we planned. Just like normal." Only nothing was normal anymore. I'd lost sight of that boundary the day Arlo disappeared.

Twenty-two

*E*very year, like ants streaming to a cake crumb at a church picnic, the tourists arrive in Panama City. They stream south from Alabama on Highway 231. They flood west on Highway 98, or they pour south on Highway 77. They come with their vans and families, their surfboards and roommates, and most of them race through town blindly scurrying toward the beach. They funnel into one narrow little line that inches slowly across Hathaway Bridge and clots to a complete standstill somewhere near Thomas Drive.

From April through September they come, spilling their money and beer onto the sugar-white sands of Panama City Beach. And when they finally return to their homes and offices, they tell everyone they spent their vacations in Panama City. No, they didn't.

They missed Panama City completely, and for most of us locals, that's fine. They raced across the surface of Panama City and entered Panama City Beach, another town entirely. They never turned down a side street and saw the Spanish Art Deco mishmash that forms the heart of Panama City. They didn't stop at Panama Java for an espresso, or browse through the art galleries and antique shops. They didn't drive by the civic center or the city marina.

Thankfully, few see the elegant homes that line St. Andrews Bay or listen to music at the Bayview Cafe.

Instead they race past the car dealerships and pawn shops, shaking their heads and keeping their eyes peeled for the bridge and the beaches. This is a good thing, I think to myself.

One part of Panama City that seems most ironic is the area of Fifteenth Street and Balboa. That is where the car dealers have clustered, one after the other, next to and across from the forestry station. Amidst the loudspeakers and billboards, the freshly waxed vehicles and polyester pants of the salesmen, looms the wooden watchtower of the Forestry Service. Tall pine trees, dusky green service vehicles, and the pine-needled pathways to the ranger station all bumped up against the shiny metallic car lots.

Fluffy and I edged our way along the strip, looking for a deal. It wasn't going to be easy to replace the old Trans Am, not on my salary.

"Fluff, we need to stick around three or four thousand," I muttered. Fluffy moaned. "Don't worry, girl, I got a plan, a really good plan." A plan that involved the broken headphones to my handheld cassette player, a tape, and the unwitting assistance of Panama City's finest.

I looked in the rearview mirror before I pulled into Big Ed's Cars, Home of the Itty-Bitty Payment.

"Fluff, there's a sucker born every minute," I said. "Let's do it to them before they do it to us." I pulled into the lot and watched the unmarked car roll into the lot next door. "A piece of cake, Fluff."

Fluffy and I stepped out of the Toyota and surveyed the territory. I counted two salesmen to every vehicle, or at least it felt that way. It didn't take long to scope out the situation. There were three cars in my price range: a Cavalier, an older Mercedes with a dented-in passenger-side door, and in the back of the lot, my new car, a Z28 Camaro. It was silver, with a black interior, and it was calling my name.

A thin reed of a man with black hair nosed his way

ahead of the pack that threatened to converge on us, smoothly making his way across the lot. He wore tassel loafers and plaid slacks. His tie dangled loosely around his neck, a contrived attempt to let me know that we were at ease here, just two friends chatting. A cigarette he held casually in his hand was tossed aside right before he reached me and Fluffy.

"Well, hello there," he called, the last wisps of cigarette smoke escaping his lips as he spoke. "What can I do you out of?" He laughed at his joke and stared openly at my breasts. Fluffy started to growl low in her throat.

"Cute dog," he said, not at all convincingly. "I'm Neal Roberts, and you are?"

I smiled. It was all going according to plan. "Sierra," I murmured.

"What'cha looking to spend, Sierra?" he asked, his eyes still glued to my cleavage.

"Well, I really need to stick around three thousand." Fluffy strained at the rhinestone leash, ardent in her desire to nip at Neal's calf.

Neal's mental calculator took stock of his bottom line as he looked around the lot. First up, he tried the Mercedes. He lifted the hood, cranked the engine, and stood there raving about the leather interior and what fine shape the car was in.

"Honey," he purred, "now don't you worry about that little ding in the door. Auto body shop'll take it right out and you'll be good as new. Why, if·we had a shop here, we would've pounded it out ourselves, then this car'd be way outta your range."

I stooped and peered under the car; it was dripping transmission fluid.

Next he tried the Cavalier, but when we took it for a test drive, it pulled so firmly to the left and shuttered that I suspected it had been in an accident. Finally, I was ready to make my move.

"What about the Camaro?" I asked. Fluffy sighed softly; perhaps she'd seen it.

Neal glanced across the lot, almost too casually. "That, young lady, is an '83 Z28 with a V-8 engine. You wouldn't like it, honey; it drinks gas and it can really get away from you if you don't know how to handle it."

To my credit, I didn't kill him. I wanted to, but it wasn't in the Sierra Car Procurement Plan.

"Aw, come on," I begged. "Let's take it around the block."

As I suspected, it ran like a scalded dog. Somebody had taken care of this car. The interior was almost in good shape—a few tears, a snag in the headliner—but overall the radio and air worked. I checked the engine while Neal pretended to lean over and show me the dipstick. His nose was almost inside my shirt, but still I didn't flinch.

"Let's go inside and talk it over," I purred. Poor Neal's nuts were about to get squeezed by a pro. I almost felt sorry as he led the way into the air-conditioned dealership office.

Once inside, Neal pretended to consult a notebook. "Honey, you're in luck," he cried. "It's thirty-eight hundred dollars, American." Again the knowing chuckle. He pulled the calculator that rested by his arm around to the center of the desk and started crunching numbers.

"We could get your payments down to a hundred and fifty-eight fifty." He looked up at my chest, his eyes twinkling with expectation. It was time for me to remove the gloves.

I placed my index finger to my lips, cautioning Neal to be silent. I stood up and shut the door to his tiny office and Neal's entire body went rigid with expectation and desire. Still keeping one finger to my lips, I reached up with the other hand and began unbuttoning my top. Neal was salivating.

When I'd undone the top two buttons, I pulled the blouse apart enough for Neal to see the two wires I'd taped to my chest. The fact that they were wires from a broken set of headphones didn't appear obvious to Neal. I motioned to the earpiece, now a fake microphone, then covered it with my fist.

"Come here," I whispered, rising and walking over to the tinted glass window. "Look out there," I said, pointing to the unmarked sedan. "Your agency is a target of investigation. They told me if I didn't cooperate, I'd do time on account of I have some pending legal business."

Neal gasped and his face went pale. I walked back over to my chair and sat, waiting for him to collect himself.

"Neal," I said, "your dealership's crooked. They're just looking for confirmation."

"What? Why, we're not—"

"Save it, Neal," I barked. "I'm doing you a favor 'cause you've been sweet to me." I batted my eyes and Fluffy sighed again.

"What do I do?" he asked my breasts.

"Neal, I'm up here, buddy," I said. "Now, I can't hold this mike forever. They'll know something's up. Just do the deal squeaky clean. In fact, cleaner than clean."

Neal was a mass of trembling anxiety. "Yeah, all right," he said.

I let go of the mike. "No, really," I said, as if we'd been talking all along. "Is that the best you can do?"

Neal didn't waste a beat. "Let me go talk to the manager," he said. "I'll be right back." He scuttled from the room like a little crab, like somebody'd grabbed his testicles and squeezed really tight. I watched him walk up to the platform where the quasi–finance manager reigned. There was a huddle, a few thinly disguised glances from me to the sedan parked outside, and a hasty arrangement.

Neal trotted back into the room, his eyes met mine for the first time, and he sat down.

"Miss Lavotini, in view of your excellent credit, and because we hope to have you as a customer for many years in the future, I have received approval to sell you the Camaro for a mere two thousand nine hundred and ninety-nine dollars, to be financed at the low rate of six-point-nine percent over thirty-six months, no money down."

"Does that include a warranty?" I asked.

Neal blanched. "Twelve months or twelve thousand miles," he croaked.

I smiled and stood up. "A pleasure doing business with you, Neal," I said. The Camaro was mine.

I strolled out into the early-afternoon sunlight and made my way down the street to the car lot where my unwitting assistant waited.

"Yo," I said as he rolled down the window, "I gotta return this rental car. How about you follow me, then give me a lift back over here so I can pick up my new car."

He frowned and looked uncertain for a moment. I could see the wheels turning. Was this against departmental policy? He decided in my favor.

"No problem," he answered. I glanced back at the car dealership, aware that every eye in the place was on us. I gestured to the Z28.

"Nice car, huh?" I asked.

"Yeah," he said. A real talker this guy was. He'd probably been warned about me. I looked on the seat next to him. Facedown on the passenger side was *Men Are from Mars, Women Are from Venus*. He saw me look and reddened.

"Let's get going," he huffed.

"Indeed," I answered.

The day was complete. I had wheels again and one hundred thousand dollars lay stashed behind the motor of my nonfunctional Jacuzzi. What more could I ask for?

Fluffy stood on the front seat, her tiny body quivering, her lips pulled back in a snarl. I started the Toyota and pulled into the early-afternoon traffic. What was her problem? I wondered. Things were finally starting to go our way.

Twenty-three

The light on the answering machine was flashing when I finally pulled myself out of bed. Four hours of sleep hadn't been enough, but I was due onstage in an hour. I hit the play button and listened while I brushed my teeth.

"Sierra, it's Al," the message began. "Pick up if you're there." There was a pause while my brother waited for me to answer. "Sierra, this ain't no time to be fooling around. It's four-thirty. Call me at the station. I got desk duty until midnight. Sierra, this is really important."

I heard the urgency in his voice and tried to decide if Rosie had finally dumped him or if there was a real emergency. Hell, maybe Ma was sick, or Pop. Maybe one of my brothers had been hurt in a fire. My mind started racing as I considered the possibilities. If Rosie'd left, Al would've said so in his message. No, he considered this far too important to say in a phone message.

I had the phone in my hand, dialing his number, before I was really aware of my action.

"Precinct Four, Officer Lavotini speaking. May I help you?" His voice was controlled and professional, and it almost sounded like he was in the room with me. How bad could it be? I chided myself.

"Al, it's Sierra. I got your message. What's up?"

There was an instant change in his voice, from professional to near panicked.

"Sierra, Jesus Christ, I thought you'd never call. I've been trying to reach you all day. I didn't want to leave a message, but finally I had to."

"Al, calm down. What's wrong? Is something the matter with Ma or Pop?"

"Worse," he said. "I had a visit from a Detective John Nailor today. He was asking a whole bunch of questions about you."

"He what?" I screeched. I could feel heat coursing through my body, burning my face and ears.

"No shit, Sierra. What the hell trouble are you in down there? He wouldn't say much, only that you were part of an ongoing investigation. Sierra, I know what I know, and they don't fly cops around unless it's something big."

I sank down onto the lilac satin comforter that lay rumpled across the bed. What a mess. How dare that guy go disrupting my family, scaring my brother.

"Sierra," Al said, "this has something to do with Leon Corvase, doesn't it? That's why you were calling me about him, isn't it?"

"Yeah, Al," I said. "Leon Corvase was found dead in my friend's apartment."

"So what's that got to do with you?"

Al was a bulldog, intent on following the scent until he had the complete picture. If I told him too little, he was liable to come check out the situation for himself. If I told him too much, he'd come to straighten things out. Neither option looked appealing.

"Al, I'm the one found the body. I guess that made me a suspect or something." Al didn't need to know about the other body, or Arlo, or the car accident.

"You ain't being straight with me," Al said. "Just finding a body ain't grounds to look at you this hard."

"Don't I know it," I said, and sighed for effect. "The cops here are different than in Philly. They don't get too many murders. I guess they're being thorough."

This was not enough for Al.

"Then why they don't go after your friend, the one who was involved with the guy?"

"They can't find her just now, Al."

There was a moment of silence while Al added it up.

"So you're the link. They think you're involved. Sierra, you aren't holding out on them, are you? Sierra," Al said, going into lecture mode, "you should cooperate fully in a police investigation. That's the only way to get them out of your hair."

"Right, Al," I said. "Al, what did Detective Nailor ask you about me?"

"He already knew a lot, Sierra," Al said. "He asked if you got into much trouble when you were a kid. How you did in school—the social part, not the grades. He already knew about those." Al paused, hesitating. "He asked about Tony, Sierra. He wanted to know if that was why you left town."

I didn't need this. An icy fist wrapped its fingers around my gut and squeezed. Of all the things I didn't want to talk about, of all the things that would make the situation look worse for me, Tony was it.

"What'd you tell him, Al?" I asked, holding my breath for his answer.

"Aw, Sierra, what could I tell him? He'd probably picked up half of it at the Beaver. Anybody worked with you or knew you coulda told him."

"I know," I said dully.

"Sierra, the guy's not all bad," Al said. "He was a really nice guy, and I know from cops; I could tell if he was working me and he wasn't."

"Yeah, yeah, yeah," I said. "He's a nice guy and he's just doin' his job, but Al, you know I couldn't whack nobody. The guy needs to be looking for my friend Denise. He needs to be chasing guys that do that kind of thing. He knows I couldn't have stabbed Corvase. Women ain't that strong. Bottom line, Al," I said, "he don't have no right to be asking questions about Tony."

"Sierra," Al said, "cops ask whatever they feel is pertinent. Tony, being part of your past, and being a shaky part at best, is pertinent. And I'll tell you one other thing, John seemed to feel you were in a lot more trouble than you're saying."

"John? What's with you calling the guy by his first name?"

"Don't get wise with me, Sierra." Al was forgetting that he was my younger brother and was starting to sound like Pop. "I'm sayin' this: I'm callin' John in two days, and if you're still in this mess, then I got no recourse but to tell Pop. It's wrong, me not telling him now, but 'cause you're my sister, I'm giving you two days' head start."

"Aw, Al, don't pull this crap," I argued. "Pop don't need to know nothing about this."

"Sierra, I should call Pop now. I'm warning you: Clean it up or I turn it over to the old man, and you know how he feels about trouble. Remember how it went about Tony."

I remembered, and there weren't going to be any repeats of that fiasco. I moved to Panama City to avoid the very situation that now hung over my head.

"I gotta go, Sierra," Al said. "I got the Sarge looking at me. He don't like us conducting personal phone calls. I meant what I said, kid, you got two days."

He was gone before I could argue, leaving me with a dead phone and twenty minutes to shower and make it to work. No matter how I cut it, I was going to be late and Vincent Gambuzzo wasn't going to be happy, just what I needed. The way I saw it, it was all John Nailor's fault.

I drove the Camaro like a drop of water streaking across a griddle, hot and fast. I didn't give a wet rat's ass if Detective Donlevy kept up or not. I was late and I was angry. I held imaginary conversations with John Nailor all the way to the Tiffany. When Vincent Gambuzzo attempted to read me the riot act for being half an hour late, I blasted him back. If it was gonna be a bad night, let it be the worst.

I flew into the dressing room, looking for my outfit and attempting to regain my composure. One thing I could do, one area of my life that I could keep under my control, was my dancing. In order to knock their eyes out, I had to focus. I needed to sit out on the fire escape and meditate, center myself with my inner child, but tonight there wasn't time. I had to close my eyes, take five cleansing breaths, and hope that did the trick.

Rusty stuck his head in the door, trying not to stare at my naked ass and failing as usual.

"Five minutes, Sierra," he said and quickly withdrew.

I settled for elegance, pulling on the long black velvet sheath and pinning my hair up into a twist. Tonight I would be cool and unattainable. I would stand before them and wait until every man in the house had to beg. I would be their mistress, their trembling virgin, and their unfulfilled fantasies, all wrapped into one streamlined package. I would titillate and hurt them, just because I could.

I walked backstage wrapped in my professional persona, untouchable. Right before I walked on, I saw Vincent signal me, probably wanting the last word, but I ignored him and strode out onto the stage. Whatever he had to say could wait. I had a job to do and money to collect.

The fog machine softly thrust mist across the stage, spilling around me and caressing my body. The music started, a slow throb that pushed its rhythmic beat deep into the souls of the men who waited. I stepped forward and surveyed the audience, looking for the big spenders, the ones I would play to solely because of the depth of their pockets. In the second row, his now-familiar drink resting in front of him, sat John Nailor.

For a moment my brain refused to accept his presence, thinking instead that in my anger I'd imagined him.

When I realized that he was indeed in the house and watching me, I froze for an instant and just as quickly resumed my act with a vengeance.

The strobe lights flashed across the stage as I edged closer to the audience, my eyes fixed on John Nailor's face. The music pulsated as I pulled off one black satin elbow-length glove and tossed it in Detective Nailor's lap. His features flickered briefly but then went back to their smoldering appraisal. He had decided that if I could dish it out, he could give it right back. I loved the challenge.

Some women like to say that you should strip for yourself in order to more fully appreciate your body. In my experience, that's never been what turned me on to my own body and power. It's the look in a man's eye when you finally hook him, that moment when he gives over to wanting you and loses sight of himself. I was stripping for John Nailor, waiting for that one moment when he lost control.

He sat there at the table, his hand tightening around his glass, his skin dark against his crisp white shirt. I reached up behind my back and undid the zipper of my gown with one slow fluid movement, letting the dress slip over my breasts and past my hips, descending like a velvet water-fall to the floor.

I lifted one leg out of the puddle of material and stood spread-legged in front of the crowd, towering over them in my stiletto heels. Bruno, sensing the heat in the room, moved protectively forward. I sought out John Nailor, locking eyes with him, daring him to follow me deeper. I brought my hands up, sliding them along my waist, caressing my breasts, gliding them along my neck, until I felt the lone pin keeping my hair in its tight coil. I let my gaze wander across the room, then back to Nailor. With a quick motion, I pulled the pin and let my hair cascade down over my shoulders.

Nailor didn't flinch. He casually lifted the glass to his lips and drank, his eyes never breaking contact with mine. I began unhooking my bra. As it unfastened I reached around and held it in place, taking a step forward so I could be seen clearly, standing where the men could stick money in my garter. Again I let my eyes slowly slide around the room, trying to make contact with every man who watched, then letting my eyes fasten back on John Nailor.

"Do you want me?" I asked.

There was a chorus of shouts as men tumbled over themselves to stick money in my garter. Bruno moved closer still, with Big Ed bringing up the rear.

"Take it off!" they yelled.

"Do you really want me?" I cooed. I looked at Nailor. His face was tightly controlled, his eyebrow casually lifted as if I amused him, but was that a thin sheen of sweat I saw dampening his brow?

I let my hands slowly drop, and the bra fell to the floor, revealing my 38DDs and my black sequined pasties, the smallest made in the business. It was time to move in for the kill.

Men stood crowded around the base of the runway, their faces blurred by the fog machine and the glare of the twinkle lights that edged the stage. I knelt before them, cupping my breasts, then reaching my arms back to support myself as I slowly arched my back.

For a moment, I let myself go, envisioning myself walking slowly toward John Nailor, letting him reach for me. That was enough. It was as if a current surged through my body, disorienting me, and filling me with feelings I didn't want to acknowledge.

With one fluid movement I rose to my feet. I sought out John Nailor's eyes and saw that there had been a change. There was one brief instant when the veil of suspicion and professionalism dropped, and in that moment a promise was extracted and sealed away for another time.

My heart was pounding. I slid my hand behind my neck, scooped up my hair, and pulled it high on top of my head. The music rose to a crescendo, pulsing with energy and intensity. The lights wove across the stage, crisscrossing the audience and returning to focus on me. I glanced at Rusty and he gave me the nod. It was time.

I let my head fall slightly back, ran my tongue slowly across my lips, and moaned. The men surged forward as one, and Rusty flooded the stage with a gigantic cloud of fog. When it cleared, I had vanished. Bruno and Big Ed did crowd control as I slipped into my purple kimono and headed for the dressing room, weak with the effort I'd made to break John Nailor.

Vincent Gambuzzo waited outside in the hallway, his dark glasses quivering against the sides of his head as his jaw twitched violently.

"What in the hell did you do that for?" he asked. An unlit cigar dangled from his pudgy hand.

"I don't know what you're talking about," I said, and attempted to push past him. He grabbed my sleeve, twisting me around to face him.

"You and that cop," he said. "What was with you playing to him? Have you lost it completely? He could've busted us. All's he would have to do is cite lewd and indecent, and we'd be shut down. That's all I need," he fumed.

"Vincent, calm yourself," I said. "Do you see him back here issuing a citation?" Vincent didn't answer. "No, you don't, and you know why? It's 'cause I know men. It's my job and you gotta trust that." The twitching was slowing but not gone. "You think I wanna be out of a job? What you saw tonight was me letting that guy know I got limits and I don't scare."

Vincent shifted from one foot to the other, moving his three-hundred-pound body from side to side.

"I don't know what's going on, Sierra," he said, "but

I don't like it. You got two more days to get them guys off your back and away from my club, you hear me? Two days."

I pushed past him into the dressing room. Nobody had to remind me that the clock was ticking. I could hear it pounding in my head, louder and louder.

Twenty-four

To his credit, John Nailor was not a runner. He was still waiting when I walked out into the house. I made my way to his table, walked around to his side, and stood so close that it would have taken almost no effort on his part to reach out and sample the merchandise.

"Did you like what you saw, Detective?" I asked.

He ran his eyes over my body, slowly, so I should know that he was back in charge.

"I told you I'd get back to you," he said.

"So you did," I said. "I like a man who keeps his word."

For a short time, onstage, I'd forgotten how angry I was with him. Now it flooded back, overwhelming me with helpless fury. If he sensed the change, he didn't acknowledge it.

"I've decided to take you off surveillance," he said.

"Oh," I said, almost choking on the bitterness that threatened to spill over, "is that what my brother Al said you should do?"

Nailor didn't flinch. "Sierra, I was doing my job—maybe even less of my job, because I should've interviewed your parents. I decided I could get the information I needed from your brother."

"Oh, I am so lucky," I said. "Do you not think that it'll be all over that you were up asking the nuns about me? I mean, I can see you checking my work record, but school?"

"I told them it was a background check. Your brother's the only one who knew any different."

"And what about Tony?" I asked. "Was that necessary?"

Nailor regarded me cautiously. "Why don't you tell me, Sierra? The man was a felon. You could've been involved in his illegal activities. I say that's relevant to my investigation. Your past history and relationships follow you wherever you go."

I looked up and saw Vincent hovering near the bar. This was no discussion to continue in the Tiffany.

"You know I was cleared of any involvement," I said. "You wouldn't be calling off the watchdogs if you thought I was dirty." I looked over at Vincent and back at John Nailor. "The boss don't like you dogging me at my place of employment. I could lose my job."

Nailor stood up and smiled. "Now, that would be a loss," he said. "I'll be in touch."

"Do that," I answered, but he was already walking away, nodding casually to Vincent Gambuzzo as he pushed through the door and out into the night.

Lyle ignored me. All I could figure was his feelings were hurt because I hadn't made time for him to explain his aversion to law-enforcement officials. When I wandered up to the bar, he turned away, making like Rambo, who was sitting in front of him, was saying the funniest thing he'd ever heard.

"Hey," I called, "what's a girl gotta do to get some service around here?"

Every head at the bar swiveled. The customers smiled and some started asking what kind of service I was looking for, but not Lyle. He was too cool to make a scene, so he walked slowly to my end of the bar, but he wasn't going to make like everything was okay, either.

"What can I get for you, ma'am?" he asked, his voice stiff with insincere civility.

"Aren't you being a little formal, considering as how I'm standing here in a G-string and a silk kimono?"

Lyle pretended not to hear me and waited for my drink order.

"A Coke with a twist of lime," I said finally. If he wanted to be a prickly cactus, so be it.

He fixed the drink and brought it over, extending his arm to hand it to me while standing as far away as possible. This was ridiculous.

"Lyle," I began, "look, I wasn't up for talking last night. I got the message you left on my machine and that's why I came over here. I wanted to set a time for us to talk."

Lyle looked like he could be considering it. He swiped at the bar with a once-white cloth, his brows furrowed with cowboy angst. After a few moments he looked over at me.

"Well, when, then?" he asked. I was forgiven.

"How about tonight, after work? Do you have to close?"

Lyle looked down the length of the bar at his bar back. "No," he said in his cowboy drawl. "Harv'll do it. He owes me from last week."

"Good," I said. "We'll go somewhere and grab a bite to eat." Lyle relaxed enough for a slight smile. "Meet me out in the lot when you're done, I got a little something to show you." I meant the Z28, but Lyle and the rest of the bar thought otherwise. It don't cost nothing to dream, I guess, but they would only be dreaming. For now, Lyle was on my personal back burner.

I'd have to say I drifted through the rest of the night. I'd reached my personal best and used up most of my energy on Nailor. I pulled out my Little Bo Peep routine for the second set and used Goldilocks for the closer. The tips were great as usual, but I could've worked the crowd for more. The problem was my heart wasn't in it.

I was whipped by the time I headed for the parking lot. Maybe I'd lean back on the headrest, crank up the Camaro's Bose speakers, listen to some Bruce Springstein, and reenergize. Maybe hash browns from the Waffle House, scattered, smothered, and covered, would do the trick. I was beginning to feel sorry I'd told Lyle we could talk. All I wanted to do was go home and sleep.

Maybe I dozed off. I'd parked the Camaro in the far corner of the Tiffany employee parking area so nobody would ding my doors or anything. It was dark, the music was good, and I was so dead tired. Something jerked me awake and I sat up trying to figure out what time it was. Where was that Lyle?

My watch said it was nearly three-thirty. The parking lot was almost empty. The dancers had long since left, and only the cleaning crew and the bar closers would be inside. This was ridiculous. I was going inside to tell Lyle he could just can it for another night, I wasn't waiting. The least he could've done was come tell me he'd been delayed. On the other hand, he didn't know about the Camaro. Maybe he thought I'd left him. He'd really be pissed if that was the case.

I hopped out of the car to go check, and that's when my evening ended. I heard a sound behind me, half turned to look, and felt something hot explode inside my head. There was nothing after that but darkness.

I was aware of pain, radiating from my head, raking through my body, and gravel, little stones that bit into the side of my face, chewing my arms and legs as I struggled to move. It hurt everywhere.

I was trembling uncontrollably and moving was agony, but somehow I heaved myself up, clinging to the side of the Camaro for support. It was no longer dark, but not quite light. The parking lot and the back side of the Tiffany were bathed in shades of predawn gray. What in the hell had happened to me?

I pulled weakly at the door handle, finally using both hands to open the door. I sank down into the driver's seat, my head resting on the leather-padded steering wheel. I brought my fingers up and tenderly felt the right side of my head. There was a knot the size of half a golf ball that brought tears to my eyes when I accidentally touched its angry center. No blood, I thought, bringing my hand down in front of my eyes; that's good.

You grow up on the streets of northeast Philly and you are not exactly immune to brutality. Life has its share of hard knocks and punches. In the old days, I'd run with a pretty rough crowd. Somehow, here in Panama City, where the crime rate is low, I hadn't expected to be a victim. Now in the space of ten days, I'd been battered more than I had in ten years in Philly.

I raised my head slowly and what I saw brought a fresh round of tears. Someone, some person or persons, had tossed the car. My pretty Bose speakers dangled from red and black wires. The contents of the glove compartment were strewn across the seats. The floor mats were ripped up and thrown across the front passenger seat. Even the backseat had been ripped up out of place. My purse and dance bag were empty, their contents sprinkled throughout the interior of my brand-new baby.

That was the last straw. Denise, Arlo, Leon, whatever and whoever, it no longer mattered because now it was personal; now they were messing with me and my car. I reached for the door handle again, pried myself out of the car and onto my feet. It was slow going, but I made it to the back entrance of the Tiffany and up the black wrought-iron steps to the door.

It took forever to fit the key in the lock, open the door, and punch in the alarm code, but when I had, I made straight for the phone outside the dressing room. I started to dial 911, then stopped. Why go through the trouble of calling a patrol unit? They'd only call Detective Nailor anyway. I had his card in my locker. It'd save us both a lot of trouble if I just called him directly.

I didn't have to worry about being able to focus on the numbers of my combination lock. Someone had been there before me, leaving the door wide open and my belongings scattered across the floor. John Nailor's card lay in a pile of broken makeup bottles, a crimson streak of blush all but obliterating his name.

I woke him out of a deep sleep, and when he spoke it was as if from a great distance, yet he recognized my voice.

"Sierra?" he murmured sleepily, as if thinking perhaps this was a dream. Then more alert: "It's after five in the morning. What's wrong?"

I gave him points for knowing that it would take a major act of God to make me call him at any time, let alone at five A.M.

"I knew if I called nine-one-one they'd call you anyway. I'm saving them the trouble." There was a problem. Something was taking my voice away and huge black spots were floating in front of my eyes. I leaned against the cool concrete block wall of the hallway, cradling the phone against my neck. I was going to be sick.

"Tell me where you are," his voice demanded.

"The Tiffany," I whispered. It was worse than I thought. I was going to be sick all right, but I was also very afraid that I might cry. Cry or pass out. Something was wrong because my knees were jelly.

"I'll be there in five minutes, Sierra," he said. "Can you hold on five minutes? You want me to send a patrol car?"

It didn't matter. From a long tunnel I tried to answer,

tried to keep the phone in my grasp and failed. The black spots converged and I felt myself sliding down the wall. The worst part was I could still hear. As darkness swirled around my head, I heard the rush of footsteps, running, and the sound of two voices whispering.

Twenty-five

After Tony was killed I had a miscarriage. It was all the more tragic because I had not known I was pregnant. I don't know what I thought, because I knew I was late, but with Tony around, you forgot about normal. He treated me so good that I didn't even care after a while that he was married. We had our life together, and then he had his other two-dimensional world in New Jersey.

When he got shot I found out about the other Tony, the one with not just a wife, but two little girls, the Tony connected to a crime syndicate out of Newark, the Tony who lay dead outside a nightclub after a rival family decided to make a statement and end his life. I guess the shock brought on the miscarriage. Anyway, I ended up alone, terrified, in the emergency room of Thomas Jefferson Hospital in Philly, because who was I going to tell?

The doctor and the nurses were kind, but there wasn't a thing they could do except give me something for pain. I lay there for hours crying for Tony and the baby, mad at the world for taking him and mad at Tony for lying to me. I was alone and afraid and I hated myself for being such a fool. That was three years ago.

Of course my family found out about Tony; they'd seen me with him at the club where I worked. When his picture was plastered all over the *Inquirer*, the rest of the secret was out, but they never knew about the baby. I couldn't do that to them. I lived with it and I live with the guilt and the what-might-have-beens every day of my life.

Maybe God was trying to make life catch up with me. Maybe that's why everything was coming to a head in Panama City, Florida. Maybe I should let it happen. I thought all these things and more while I was lying on the floor of the Tiffany, drifting in and out of consciousness. The whispering voices of my attackers were gone, but I didn't know where. Maybe they were gone. Maybe whoever hit me was coming back. Maybe they were going to kill me before the cops could come. It didn't matter because I was powerless to lift a finger to stop them.

In the distance I could hear the wail of sirens. Nailor must've sent a car, I thought. The sounds grew louder and stopped. Footsteps clattered up the fire-escape stairs and in through the back door of the club. I struggled to open my eyes, blinking at the sudden surge of light.

"Sierra." It was John Nailor's voice, soft by my ear, his arms scooping me up by the shoulders and supporting my head.

"Tell the EMTs to get in here," he barked to someone. I blinked, opening my eyes and trying to focus.

"I'm all right," I protested, but it was a waste of breath. "Someone hit me, out by my car."

"Yeah, it's a mess. It looks like they were searching for something," he said. "Don't talk anymore. We're going to get you to the hospital."

"No," I said, mustering all the strength I could find. "No more ambulance rides. I'm fine, really."

The EMTs arrived and started their prodding and poking. I lay there feeling too weak and nauseous to fight.

"Someone broke into my locker, too," I said.

"Todd," Nailor said, turning and addressing a young uniformed officer, "tell the lab guys to check the dressing room." The patrolman nodded and vanished. One of the

EMTs, a dark-haired, tanned man, turned to Nailor.

"I think it's probably a concussion, but she oughta have an X ray, get checked by a doc."

"I'm not going in an ambulance," I said to them. "I'll drive myself later." Who was I trying to kid?

John Nailor spoke up. "I'll see she gets there," he said. He patted my shoulder, more a warning to keep my mouth shut than sympathy. Carla Terrance, who picked that moment to come inside, thought differently.

"How sweet," she said, her voice dripping acid. "John, if you can pry yourself away, I need you outside."

Nailor didn't like the intrusion, but he followed Carla silently. They were gone for almost five minutes, leaving me to try and figure out what was going on. Whoever'd ransacked my locker either stayed behind, hiding after closing time, or knew the security code, or knew how to disable the alarm system. Did they hit me and then riffle through my locker? I'd heard two voices; maybe one had done the car and one the locker. My head ached with the exertion and I was almost grateful when John Nailor returned.

"Okay," he said, "let's get you to a doctor."

At this point I thought I was feeling strong enough to take it under my own power. I stood up and promptly started to sag. Nailor jumped forward and caught my arm as I went down, and he was laughing.

"You don't learn, do you?" he asked. "Let's do it my way. You lean on my arm and I'll walk you to my car. I'm gonna drive you to the hospital, check you into the ER, and then I'm going to come back here."

As he spoke, he started leading me slowly toward the door. His shirt felt smooth and his muscles taut beneath the fabric. I wanted not to like leaning on him, but I was having trouble doing that.

"How will I get back to my car?" We were outside now and I could see that the Camaro was covered with crime scene technicians.

"I'll come get you," he said. "Listen, do you think you could take a look at the interior of your vehicle and see if you notice anything missing? It'd speed things up for us."

"No problem," I said weakly. We walked slowly across the parking lot, coming to a stop beside the hood of the car. Carla Terrance stood, her back to us, slowly examining my few belongings.

"This is the inventory of the interior," she said, her voice tight with controlled anger. "Anything of yours missing?"

I stared at the assortment of cosmetics, papers, pens, and lifestyle detritus. Nothing appeared to be missing. My wallet still had ten dollars and my lone credit card in it. No, nothing was missing, but as I looked I saw that something had been added. In the middle of the assorted junk lay a gold dangle earring with an amethyst teardrop, Denise's amethyst earring.

I didn't let my eyes linger. Instead I reached for my wallet.

"I'll need this," I said. "It's got my insurance card and my checkbook." Carla frowned but made no move to stop me. "Can I take the rest of my things?" I asked.

"Go ahead." Carla sighed. "You're sure nothing's missing?" I picked up a few pens, a notepad, and finally the earring.

"No, not a thing," I assured her. How had Denise's earring gotten into my new car? Had it been in my dance bag or my purse? Surely I would have noticed it. The earring was huge. I was starting to feel dizzy and leaned against the edge of the fender to hold myself steady.

"Let's get you to the hospital," John said. "I'll be back in a half an hour," he told Terrance. She appeared not to hear him, turning instead to Detective Donlevy, who'd made his appearance along with the rest of Panama City's police force.

"Here we are." Nailor opened the car door and lowered me into the passenger seat. My head was spinning again and I wasn't sure I'd make it to Bay County Medical before I threw up.

He started the engine and pulled out onto Thomas Drive. The police radio was spitting out a staccato stream of numbers and street addresses, the law-enforcement chatter designed to keep the rest of the world at arm's length. The car radio played a jangled country melody, and I knew for certain I would not make Bay County.

We rounded the corner onto Joan Avenue, leaving the junky part of Thomas Drive behind and spinning past a little residential section.

"Would you mind pulling over a second?" I asked.

Maybe he saw the color had drained from my face. Whatever it was caused him to ask no questions. He lurched to a stop in front of a tractor tire painted topaz blue that held blood-red geraniums, someone's idea of a flower bed.

I jumped out and tried to make it to the end of the car before I hurled. I hate throwing up in front of an audience. I was leaning on the car for support when I felt his arms wrapping around my shoulder and holding my waist.

"It's all right," he said, as if comforting a child. "This happens when you have a concussion." I was in no condition to comment.

When I'd finished he reached into his pants pocket, pulled out a crisp white handkerchief, and handed it to me. He led me back to the car, gently deposited me in my seat, and returned to the driver's side. I didn't even want to look at him. This was one of the low moments of my life.

Nailor slowly pulled the car back onto the road and headed at a slower pace toward Bay County Medical Center. He reached over and flicked off the car radio, then turned the police radio's volume down to just a whisper. I tried closing my eyes, but it made me dizzy, so I focused on the early-morning ride from Panama City Beach over Hathaway Bridge to Panama City. When the bridge crossing made my head start spinning, I watched Nailor drive. I liked watching the way the muscles on his tanned forearms moved against the white of his rolled-up shirtsleeves.

He pulled into Bay County's emergency-room parking area like someone who'd routinely visited, and I guessed in his line of work that was par for the course. When he led me inside, he seemed to know several of the nurses and admitting clerks. This was standard procedure for him, I thought.

When I was safely settled in an examining room, he stuck his head in the door.

"I'm going. I'll be back to pick you up and take you home. An officer will transport your vehicle to your trailer." Detective Nailor was back on duty, there was no doubt about it. I lay back on the gurney and closed my eyes.

I had a concussion. At least my assailant hadn't fractured my skull. I should try and stay still for a few days. I listened to the nurse drone on as she signed my discharge papers and handed me back over to Nailor. The whole process had taken two hours, and it was well into the morning when we emerged from Bay County and headed back to the Lively Oaks Trailer Park.

Fluffy'd be pissed for sure, I thought. Her food dish would be empty and she was not one to miss a meal. By the time Nailor turned into the entrance of the park, I was remembering the feel of my sheets against my skin and thinking how good eight hours of sleep would be for my headache.

"I really appreciate this," I said as we rolled onto my parking pad. "I'm sorry about hurling on the way to the hospital."

John Nailor smiled. "Sierra, really, don't think anything more about it."

He came around to my side of the car and helped me out.

"I can make it from here," I said. "Thanks."

"I'll get you inside," he insisted, taking the key from my hand. "Maybe you should call a friend to come stay with you." Yeah, right, I thought: One friend's missing, presumed dead or wanted for murder, one friend's not speaking to me, and my other friend's just as likely to hallucinate and think I'm an alien invader.

"I'll do that," I said. He needed to get back to work and I needed to sleep, then figure out why I had one hundred thousand dollars and an amethyst earring belonging to my missing buddy.

He swung open the door, then turned back around to me so quickly I almost tripped and fell backward.

"Go back to the car," he barked, not really seeing me.

"What?"

"You can't go in there right now, so I want you to wait in my car for a minute."

"Don't be ridiculous," I said. "It's my trailer and I'm going inside." I tried to push past him, but he held my arm. He wanted to move and get to the radio in his car, but he wasn't going to risk leaving and having me decide to go inside.

"What is it? Let me see."

I pushed his arm hard enough that it moved and I could crane and look inside. Whoever'd done my car and my locker had moved across town and torn my trailer apart.

"Fluffy?" I yelled. John Nailor still hung on to my arm. "Fluffy, where are you?" I pushed at Nailor, desperate in my need to reach my baby.

"Sierra," Nailor said, "it may not be safe for you to go in there." As he spoke he dropped my arm, reaching inside his suit coat for his gun. "I'll look for her. You sit here." He went inside the trailer without waiting for my answer.

What? Did he really believe I'd sit there and let him play Tarzan to my Jane? Oh, I think not. I stepped over the sill and saw what some creep or creeps unknown had done to ruin my home. The kitchen drawers were pulled out, the contents strewn haphazardly around the room. Cabinets were torn apart. Even the refrigerator and freezer were emptied.

I looked into the living room and realized it had received the same treatment. The cushion ripped off my futon, the plants upended out of their pots. From the other end of the trailer, I could hear Nailor moving slowly, opening doors, searching for Fluffy and any sign that the intruder could still be in the house.

"Fluffy, baby," I called.

Nailor yelled out from my bedroom. "Goddamn it, Sierra,. I told you to stay out. You're contaminating the scene."

"No, I'm not, I'm looking for my dog. I don't care about your scene. I care about Fluffy."

He came walking down the hallway toward me, sticking the gun back into his holster. "Well, it probably doesn't matter. Whoever did your car and your locker didn't leave prints. I'm sure the same guys did this. But we need to check anyway." He walked past me, into the kitchen, and picked up two overturned barstools off the floor, placing them back at my table. He motioned me into a seat and I didn't resist; I didn't have the energy to fight everything.

"Sierra, who did this and what are they looking for?"

I wanted to tell him, but I had to think. I wanted to say Frankie, but what if I was wrong? Even if I was right, I had a feeling I knew what the money was for: It had to be for Arlo's ransom. Maybe Frankie was trying to help Denise. But why hadn't he come to ask for the money back? He didn't need to tear up my trailer and my new car. What good could Frankie do Denise if Nailor had him in jail? And what if someone had Fluffy? I needed the leverage of the money.

"I don't know who did this," I answered after a few

moments. "I tried to think and I don't know." I looked him right in the eye and lied.

It was just as bad lying to him, after all he'd done for me today, as when I used to try and pull the wool over Sister Mary Margaret in second grade. Sister always knew when I was lying, and from the disappointment in John Nailor's eyes, I figured he could read me, too. Whatever closeness we had started to build would disintegrate now. He knew I didn't trust him and he was probably tired of trying to get me to.

"They could have killed you, Sierra," he said softly. "This was a warning. If they didn't find what they were looking for, then you can count on them coming back. I can put a cop in your driveway, but I can't guarantee your safety. You should tell me what's going on and let me help you."

I said nothing. I couldn't even trust myself to look at him. I was going to have to find Frankie and straighten the mess out by myself.

"I guess your mind's made up, then," he said. "I'll call and get the lab guys out here." He was resigned, on autopilot. "I'll get someone over here to watch your place as soon as possible."

I didn't know what else to do. My head was spinning with fatigue and pain and I couldn't think. I wanted to reach across the table and touch his hand and say something that would make him understand how I felt, but I couldn't. He stood up and walked out the kitchen door, looking like the same tired man I'd seen the first time we met.

There was nothing that I could do immediately except wait for the forensics team and look for Fluffy. I searched through the trailer, calling and whistling, but she wasn't there. I wandered out into the trailer park, dark glasses shielding my eyes from the sunlight that threatened to make my head explode. I found her sitting on Pat's back stoop, shivering in the tropical heat.

"Who was it, Fluff?" I asked. "Who's doing this to us?" Fluffy shivered, moaning with fear. I held her close, carrying her like a baby all the way back to the trailer. At first Fluffy didn't want to go inside, struggling against my grip as we mounted the stairs.

"It's all right, girl," I murmured. "They're gone." I held her tight, carrying her through the devastated trailer, surveying the damage. When we got to the bathroom I leaned down to check the Jacuzzi motor housing. It was untouched.

"Well, I got the money and I got you," I whispered. "The rest I can deal with."

Fluffy whimpered like she'd lost faith and I couldn't blame her. I wasn't in any shape to be holding a revival meeting in the Church of Lost Causes.

Twenty-six

I had a plan. I'd been awake now for an hour, listening to Fluffy snore and trying to fight off the king-sized headache that threatened to gnaw its way from the right to the left side of my head. As soon as I could swill enough coffee to get motivated, I was going to find Frankie. That was the sum total of my plan; whatever came after that would be pure guesswork and luck.

The entire trailer was a wreck and would have to stay that way for now. I cleared enough counter space to resurrect my coffeemaker, found the remains of a bag of ground coffee and one unbroken mug. I found the paper lying outside on the stoop, the only part of my afternoon ritual left intact.

"Come on, Fluff," I said, opening a can of dog food, "you can sit up here with me." I emptied the can into her dish and placed it at the table, then picked Fluffy up and perched her on a bar-stool. "Special occasion, Fluff," I said. "You eat with Mama."

Fluffy felt this was only fitting. She preened and reached her two front paws up until she maintained a balance between the stool and the table. I poured myself a cup of coffee and opened the paper. We were silent for a few moments. Every now and then Fluffy would peer over at the paper, as if inquir-ing about the daily news, and then turn her attention back to her dish.

"Holy shit, Fluff," I said. "Listen to this." In the local

section of the paper, down at the bottom of the third page, was a small article. "Local Man Seriously Injured in Motorcycle Accident," it read. I pulled the paper closer, reading half to Fluffy, half to myself. "It says a local man, Frankie Paramus, thirty-four, was seriously injured when his Harley FBX-80's front tire blew out." Fluffy stopped eating and looked at me, listening.

"I don't know what you're thinking," I said, "but I don't know too many guys named Frankie who ride Harley FBX-80s in Panama City." Fluffy nodded in agreement. "Says he lost control and slid into the intersection of Fifteenth and Lsenby. That's right down from Southern Tattoo," I added. "He's in Bay County in serious condition."

Fluffy didn't appear to be listening. Her head turned toward the door and she started to growl.

"Fluff, forget about that dog down the street," I said. "This is much more important. How're we going to talk to Frankie if he's in intensive care or something?" I looked back at the paper. "It says he's been in there since yesterday afternoon." So he couldn't have trashed my trailer, or hit me outside of the Tiffany.

Fluffy erupted into frenzied barking and jumped down off the barstool, our cozy breakfast forgotten. Someone was knocking at the door and Fluffy wasn't at all happy about the intrusion. I leaped up and followed her to the front door, standing cautiously by the side and trying to peer through the bay window out into the driveway. My heart had started erratically racing and my stomach involuntarily began to knot up. I kept remembering Nailor's last caution: "If they didn't find what they're looking for, they'll be back."

It was only Lyle. He stood on my steps, his hat slung low over his face, his expression unreadable. Damn. Just what I needed, some moon-eyed cowboy wanting to give me his life history. And then, where had the son of a bitch been last night when he'd promised to meet me in the parking lot?

I reached for the chain and unhooked it, turned the deadbolt and swung the door wide open. Lyle was past due for a piece of my mind. Fluffy apparently agreed. She launched herself at his leg and sunk her sharp little canines into Lyle's calf, unfortunately biting boot and not flesh.

Lyle jumped, attempting to pull his leg away from my marauding guard dog. Fluffy couldn't have hurt him, but it had to frighten him a bit. Fluffy was growling like she could bite through the boot at any second.

"I'll tell you something," I said, leaning against the doorsill and enjoying the show, "just so's you know, if you hurt my little Fluffy, I will personally kick your ass."

Lyle looked up, a strained expression on his face. "And if she hurts me?"

"I'll give her a little something extra at suppertime," I answered. I turned to walk back inside, looking over my shoulder at the two locked together on the front steps. "You coming?"

Lyle half stepped, half dragged himself and Fluffy into the living room and stopped still, focusing on the disaster area.

"What happened?" he asked. Fluffy growled, intent on amputating Lyle's leg.

"Nothing," I said, pulling the futon mattress back onto its frame. "I'm just a hell of a lousy housekeeper."

"Aw now, you're mad at me on account of last night," he said, finally keying in. "Honey, I came out looking for you, but I didn't see your car. I figured you was fed up with me taking so long." His eyes were huge and liquid. Fluffy must've been making inroads on that boot.

"Don't call me honey," I snapped. "You didn't hear my stereo?"

"Sure, I heard something, but I didn't figure it to be you." He looked down at Fluffy and back up at me. "Honest, hon—er, Sierra, I wouldn't go off without talking to you. I needed to see you, bad."

I wanted to take pity on him, but Fluffy had no intention of giving up her quest for his shin bone.

"Well," I said, pointing to an armchair, "sit down and start talking. I got a lot to do today and a short amount of time to do it in. I'll give you five minutes, and if it ain't interesting, I'll shorten it to two."

Lyle looked around the trailer again, obviously wanting to ask some more questions but thinking better of it.

"Can you call off the dog?" he asked. "I cain't concentrate on what I gotta say with her gnawing on me." For the first time there was a hint of irritation in his voice. His request was bordering on a command.

I shrugged and snapped my fingers. "Fluff," I said softly, "save something for later, dear." Fluffy looked over at me, reluctant to let go of her prize. "It's all right, girl," I added. "I can handle it from here."

Fluffy released his leg but wasn't happy. She moved one step back, the low growl continuing in her throat, a warning to Lyle that next time she might move her attack to a more vulnerable location.

I looked at my wristwatch and over at Lyle, a signal that his five minutes were ticking away.

"Okay," he said, and his voice changed, deepening somewhat and losing its cowboy hesitancy. "I know you wondered why or how I could run off and leave you like that after you found that man's body." I nodded. "Well, I need to show you something. Might help explain why I didn't want to be around when the police showed up." He dug deep into the back pocket of his jeans, pulled out a slim plastic case, and passed it across to me.

I opened it, already suspecting. It was an identification card. Lyle Martin was a bona fide Drug Enforcement Agency special agent. I looked up at him and back down at the card case. Fluffy was still growling. No matter what his identification said about him, she wasn't letting up on him.

"And?" I said, tossing the case back to him.

"And so I didn't want to jeopardize an ongoing investigation, or blow my cover, so I had to leave you behind. I'm sorry." He didn't look particularly sorry. He looked matter-of-fact.

"So, aren't you blowing your cover now?" I demanded. "And what about last night? Where were you?"

Lyle's back straightened and his eyes hardened. "Sierra, there are certain things I am at liberty to discuss and others that must remain confidential."

"You guys are all alike," I said, "full of self-importance. Your reasons are more important than keeping a commitment to a woman. Now I've heard it all."

Lyle ignored me. "Sierra, our investigation is stuck and we feel you could be of some benefit. You are also, perhaps unwittingly, placing yourself at substantial risk. I don't know if you know Denise Curtis's whereabouts or not, but if you do, we need to get in contact with her."

I started to speak, but Lyle interrupted. "Sierra, you haven't told the police, and frankly, I doubt you'd tell me, so let me give you some more information and then you can make your decision." He wasn't waiting for a response from me.

"Your friend Denise isn't as innocent as you might think, or as uninvolved," he said. "She knew the first guy they found in her hotel room. He was a former associate of Leon Corvase's, a drug courier, like Denise, who'd become an informant. Denise knew he'd flipped to avoid prosecution. We think Leon had the guy executed, then transported to Denise's room to send a message."

"Why would he want to send Denise a message?" I asked. "She wanted to stay clear of Leon. She was scared to death of the guy. When she heard he was out of prison she freaked."

"Did she really?" he asked. "Or did she just put on a good act for you?"

"It wasn't bogus," I answered firmly.

"Then how was it that Denise was seen in Fort Lauderdale, on board the *Mirage,* two weeks before she disappeared?"

"You're mistaken. The information is wrong."

Lyle reached in his pocket and produced a snapshot. There was Denise, her long red hair flowing in the wind, on the back deck of the *Mirage,* laughing, a drink in one hand and her arm around Leon Corvase.

"It's an old picture," I said.

"No, it isn't," Lyle answered calmly. "Denise was there. Two weeks later, Leon's so unhappy with her that he sends her a message. Two days later, Denise is gone."

"What about her dog, Arlo?" I asked.

"Maybe he was the first message."

Fluffy growled a bit louder but subsided when I snapped my fingers again. My stomach was a mass of knots. I couldn't sort it all out. I couldn't see what was going on, and yet something had to be wrong with the picture. Denise with Leon? It didn't make sense. She had seemed to be so genuinely scared of him.

"Sierra, if you know where she is," Lyle continued, "we need to talk to her. We've formed a task force with the Panama City police force. John Nailor and our liaison, Carla Terrance, decided it was time to give you more information to work with. It isn't a matter of you covering for a friend anymore. We're thinking Denise may have killed Leon Corvase, or have been killed herself."

It was like the Discovery Channel special I'd seen on spiders, I thought. Two spiders mated, but who ate who? Was Denise really a spider? I thought of little Arlo. What was a nice dog like him doing with a spider like Denise? Fluffy wouldn't have stuck with me had I been a mean person. Dogs sense these things. And yet Arlo wasn't with Denise anymore, was he?

"Lyle," I said, "I don't know where she is."

"Well, apparently," he said, surveying my ruined trailer, "we're not the only ones who think you do."

Lyle stood up and shoved his identification back into his pocket. He tossed the picture of Denise and Leon Corvase onto the futon.

"You can keep that," he said. "We got plenty of copies."

I stared at Denise's laughing face. The photographer had caught the true Denise, the drink-you-under-the-table, don't-give-a-shit Denise. I looked closer, trying to figure out how someone could've pasted Denise's head on someone else's body, but I knew this was no trick. Denise was looking straight out of the picture, laughing right in my face.

Twenty-seven

*I*t was a different thing, walking through the front entrance of Bay County Medical Center as a visitor instead of a paying customer. Not that I shouldn't have been a paying customer. My head ached, I still felt nauseous, and I knew I wasn't supposed to be up running around. But Lyle's visit had given me a sense that time was running out, and I was feeling desperate.

Frankie Paramus had a private room and bodyguards. As I attempted to open the door and walk in to visit, a burly, hairy arm reached across the doorway and held the door closed.

"There's no visitors allowed in there, Miss."

I hadn't even seen anyone near Frankie's door. I'd been in such a hurry to get to Frankie, I'd overlooked the other human beings surrounding his room. Now I was forced to stop and look around. Standing in the hallway, flying full colors, were three of Frankie's nearest and dearest. I recognized two of them from their visit to my trailer the time Frankie met Raydean.

"He'll want to see me," I said, not at all sure that that would be the case.

The biggest guy, a stocky man with a full thick brown beard, his hair covered by an American flag bandanna, stood in front of me, his beer-barrel gut practically assaulting my 38DDs. He didn't look like he was going to take any argument.

"He ain't feeling up to company," he insisted.

"Tell him Sierra Lavotini wants a word," I said. I didn't back off. I stood there in my five-inch stilettos, glaring at him.

"Aw, go ask him," another man interceded. "Maybe it'll perk him up." There were some muffled snickers as the big man seemed to mull it over.

"Yeah," another one said, "maybe she's come to do a table dance."

The bull moose turned and disappeared into Frankie's room, leaving me under the watchful eye of the others. A tall skinny biker, his front tooth rimmed with gold, stepped up, seizing the opportunity.

"You know," he said, attempting to be smooth, "if Frankie ain't up to you, I could use a little attention." He lifted one hand and casually pinched my left nipple. The others snickered.

"Back the fuck off, asshole," I said. The man's face reddened. He wasn't about to lose face in front of his compadres.

"Bitch, I—" He was interrupted as the door swung open and the first man returned.

"Frankie says you can come in." He held the door open and I walked past. The others crowded into the door frame, ready to cash in on Frankie's unexpected good fortune, but the big guy stopped them. "Frankie says he wants to be alone," he said, laughing, a dirty little snickering sound. "He don't want no intrusions while he's with the lady." The door swung shut behind him and the room was empty except for the figure in the hospital bed and me.

I took a few hesitant steps into the room and stopped. Frankie looked bad. His face was ashen beneath a two-day growth of stubble. The right side of his face was an angry mass of red scrapes and purple and black bruises. He appeared to be sleeping, but opened his left eye when he heard me step closer.

"Come here," he muttered. I took two steps closer,

pulling a chair up to the foot of his bed. "No," he whispered harshly, "closer. I don't want nobody hearing what I got to say to you."

I moved the chair up by Frankie's head and sat down.

"What happened to you?" I asked softly. "How'd you dump your bike?"

"Is that what they say?" he muttered, a harsh cough-like laugh escaping his lips. "I guess it worked, then." His closed his eye briefly, then reopened it. "It wasn't no accident. Somebody shot my tire out."

"Who?" I asked.

"I don't know for sure," he whispered. "It happened in front of Southern Tattoo. One of the guys in the club owns it. Your dog's friend, Rambo. There's bikers in and out of there all the time. Could've been anybody, from our club or anywhere else. It don't matter. I got to tell you something and we don't have much time. Them assholes'll be back in here wanting to see if I got you naked."

"Did you leave something in my car?" I asked. After all, I came to see him. I had the agenda.

"What?" he asked, surprised at the turn of conversation. "No, I didn't leave nothing in your car. Take off your shirt."

"What? Fuck you, Frankie. This ain't no peep show."

"No," he muttered impatiently. "Take it off so if they look in they'll see we're having a little private time and go away. And it would help if you laughed now and then, like something good was going on."

I didn't like it, but I did as he said. I stripped down to my black lace bra and laughed wickedly. Frankie wasn't about to pretend he wasn't eyeballing my chest. He stared for a moment, long enough for me to know he wasn't in any life-threatening condition, and then continued his talk.

"Denise is in trouble," he said.

"I know that, Frankie," I said. "We already covered this."

"Hush," he said. The door swung open and the bandanna stuck his head in. I laughed and looked around guiltily.

"Can't you see we're busy?" I asked. Frankie reached over and fondled my breast like we were old buddies and the bandanna withdrew quickly. I laughed again, loudly, and turned to Frankie. "Touch me like that again," I hissed, "and you really will need a doctor."

Frankie ignored me. "Denise is trying to rip us off," he said. "She's dealing again, only this time it isn't small stuff. Right before she disappeared she set up a deal for our club. Now she's missing, and along with her went the front money."

"How much?" I asked, the trip hammer banging in my chest.

"One hundred thousand dollars," he said.

The door started to swing open and this time I jumped out of my chair, leaning across Frankie's torso, my breasts within inches of his face. The door closed and I took my seat.

"Sierra," Frankie said, "the club ain't gonna let Corvase's organization get away with ripping them off. If Denise is in on this, she better find a way to make it right and then disappear. I can't help her from here," he said. "You'd better find her." He looked away for a moment, then back at me. "It might be almost better if she was dead," he said softly. "They tend to make an example of them that's done the club wrong."

Outside I could hear an angry woman's voice engaged in an argument with the self-appointed bodyguards. I scrambled around, pulling my shirt on, before the nurse could win out and enter the room.

Frankie watched me, no longer interested in anatomy.

"Sierra," he asked, "what got left in your car?"

"Oh," I said, startled, "that. I found an earring in the car and I guess I just hoped . . . Well, I don't know what I hoped."

That was enough of an answer for Frankie. As I turned to leave a nurse burst into the room red-faced with anger.

"Mr. Paramus doesn't need visitors," she sputtered. "He doesn't need to be excited in any way." She eyed me up and down like I was an undesirable lab specimen.

"Don't get your panties in a wad," I said, walking past her. "I was just leaving."

Frankie laughed softly, then groaned as the nurse did something to him. I stepped out into the hallway and headed for the elevators. Frankie's boys didn't try to mess with me as I passed, choosing instead to utter low catcalls and whistles as I sauntered off. I felt like a deodorant commercial: "Never let them see you sweat."

I leaned against the wall of the elevator, my head pounding along with my heart. It was Thursday afternoon, one day before Vincent's deadline for me to clean up my act and lose the cops. The cops were back on my tail, this time trying to function as protection. The DEA had their eye on me. Somebody or bodies weren't satisfied that I didn't know where Denise was and had decided to tear up my life looking for her. All in all, it was a hell of a mess, and I had no clue what to do to set it all right.

Twenty-eight

$\mathcal{J}$ohn Nailor walked into the Tiffany as I was getting ready to do my last set, but this time I had advance warning. Marla, her silver-sequined G-string and pasties glinting in the backstage lights, marched over and made the announcement.

"Your boyfriend's here," she said, all sugar and spice. Marla would be the last one to catch on that Nailor was heat.

I peered out into the house and saw him chatting with Vincent. Neither one looked happy.

"Rusty," I called, "give me two minutes. I got company." Rusty cranked up the bumper music and nodded, his eyes glued to the house curtains.

Vincent's entire body was twitching by the time I walked up. Whatever Nailor was saying went against Vincent's good nature. And Nailor wasn't looking too happy himself. His suit and shirt were immaculate, and his tie was a dark wine that added luster to his tanned skin. But he was angry with Vincent, and it showed in the rigid way he held his shoulders.

"So," I said, hooking my arm through Nailor's and trying to edge him away from Vincent, "you didn't get enough the other night, and now you're back." Vincent watched us walk off, his eyes narrowing warily. I led John Nailor over to a front-row table and gently pushed him into a chair. I pulled up another chair right next to his, flipped it around, and straddled it.

"I thought I told you not to come in here," I said. "It isn't good for my job security. And you pissing off Vincent is going to be very bad for me indeed."

John leaned against the back of his chair and smiled. He was in a dangerously unpredictable mood.

"Maybe I'm so taken with the talent, I can't keep myself away," he answered, then leaned forward, his face so close to mine that I could taste his breath. "Or maybe it's time to turn up the heat."

"Turn up the heat, Officer," I purred, "or turn the heat on?" Nailor didn't give, didn't move an inch. "Well, stick around, big man," I said. "I'm about to do my last set. Maybe I can help you raise your thermostat."

"Oh, I'm not going anywhere," he said. "I'm taking you home." His steely eyes went right through me and I felt my stomach flip over.

"Is that right?"

"Absolutely," he said. "I'm gonna stick so close to you, you'll think I was skin."

"Really?" was all I could get out. The scent of his cologne, the warmth of his breath on my cheeks, the nearness of his hands as they wrapped around my chair-back, framing my own—they were all signs. I was losing control of the conversation and I wasn't sure my legs would carry me backstage.

"Yeah," he said, sensing victory and suddenly pulling back, "I got more questions for you than you can ever answer, and I'm going to stay on you until I ask every one."

"And to think I thought you were back for more of me," I said, feigning disappointment.

He smiled and leaned back comfortably in his chair. "I wouldn't want to give you more than you can handle in one night," he said. "You just focus on giving me answers."

I'll give you answers, I smoldered silently. I'll give

you every answer I've got. I made my way backstage and took five cleansing breaths. When the curtain went up and I walked to the edge of the stage, John Nailor had vanished.

He turned up again as I was leaving. I found him sitting on the hood of my Camaro. His tie was loosened and he sat with one foot on the ground and the other on my bumper.

"Hey, watch it with the car," I yelled. "You could dent my hood."

Nailor didn't move, just watched me walking toward him, his eyes casually wandering down my body and up to look at my face. He was making me uncomfortable.

"This thing as fast as your mouth?" he asked.

"Could be close," I said, stopping within a foot of where he stood. "You wanna go for a ride?"

"Yeah," he said, his eyes continuing their inspection, but always returning to stare directly into mine. Nailor cocked his head to the side and smiled slightly.

"You're a little bit intimidated by me," he observed. "That's good, I think."

"Bullshit," I answered, my heart racing in my throat. "Get in the car and we'll see who scares who."

I walked over and hopped into the driver's seat.

"Remember you've got an escort," he said.

I glanced in the rearview mirror and saw the unmarked police car start up and switch its headlights on.

"Well," I said, "looks like I got a little dilemma. You want to see what I can do, and he doesn't want to lose me. That's a real problem." I cranked up the V-8. "But I figure," I said, revving the engine and suddenly letting up on the brake, "you can fix the ticket if he can catch us." I floored the accelerator and tore off out of the lot and onto Thomas Drive. Sierra Lavotini was behind the wheel and fear was not even a factor.

"Where are we headed?" I asked as we rounded the

corner onto Joan Avenue. The T-tops were off and the windows were down. The cool late-night air streamed into the car, blowing our hair back and making conversation almost impossible.

"Your place," he yelled. I looked over at him, but he was staring out the window at the road in front of us. My place it was.

I concentrated on driving, enjoying the power of the Z28 and the thrill of being uncatchable and invulnerable for one brief stretch of night. I reached the Lively Oaks Trailer Park in ten short minutes, coming to a stop inches from my bottom stoop.

"Not bad," Nailor said. "Where'd you learn to drive like that?"

"I dated a NASCAR driver for a little while," I said, opening the car door and stepping out. "Come on in."

"Sierra, wait," he said. His hand was reaching inside his suit coat, unhooking his holster. "Just for my peace of mind, let me go in first and make sure it's all clear."

"As a favor to you?" I said. "Knock yourself out." I stepped aside, handed him the keys, and let him go first. We both turned at the sound of crunching tires behind us. Faithful Detective Donlevy had arrived, catching up at last. The lights on his car went out and he sat, two car lengths away, with the motor running.

Nailor raised his hand and waved, then turned and walked inside the darkened trailer. Lights went on, one at a time, as he made his way through the length of the mobile home. Two minutes later, he appeared at the back door.

"Coast is clear," he said.

I'd spent a little time cleaning up in the afternoon, but that only meant that the kitchen was reassembled and the living room habitable. The back of the trailer needed work.

"Take a load off," I said, gesturing toward the living room. "You want a beer or something?"

"No," he answered, "I want you to come in here and

sit down." He pointed to the other end of the futon. "I want to talk to you."

"All right," I said, taking a seat. "Start talking."

"Not like that," he said. "Move in a little closer."

Butterflies started fluttering against my rib cage as I slid closer to him.

"Give me your hand," he said.

"What?"

"Just do it," he said. "I won't bite you." He stretched out his hand to me, palm up, and waited for me to place my hand in his.

"Good," he said as I gently rested my fingers on his palm. His fingers tightened slowly around mine. "Now I want to play a game." His fingers tightened again, gently enfolding my hand. In spite of myself I felt a little nervous. His hand was firm and strong.

"I used to play this when I was a kid," he began. "It's kind of like truth or dare." I attempted to snatch my hand away, but his grip tightened again and this time I couldn't move.

"Let go," I said, squirming.

"No. Listen to me." I made an effort to relax and act like he was boring me. "I'm asking the questions," he said, "so I hold your hand. If you lie when you answer, I'll feel it in your fingers."

"No you won't," I said. How could that possibly be true?

"Yes," he said, "I will. They'll twitch. Here, I'll ask you some easy questions and then I'll tell you if you lied."

"Oh, go ahead," I scoffed.

"How old are you?" he asked.

"Twenty-eight," I answered, watching my fingers.

"Good," he said. "How long have you lived in Panama City?"

"Two years, three months," I answered.

"You like me, don't you?" he asked suddenly.

"Get out," I laughed, trying to pull my hand away.

"Ah, you do," he said, laughing, "your fingers twitched. You don't think I'm all bad. Now, wait," he said, his face serious again. I focused on making my fingers go limp. "Did you really learn to drive from a NASCAR driver?" he asked.

"Yes," I answered, looking into his eyes.

"Not so," he said calmly. I could have sworn my fingers never moved. How could he know?

"Where is Denise?" he asked finally.

"I don't know," I said, fear rising in my throat. "I really don't know."

John Nailor's grip on my hand changed. He turned my palm over, face up, and gently stroked my fingers. He looked up, his eyes sinking into mine.

"I know you don't," he said softly.

For a moment we sat still, my hand in his. The sound of a muffled groan interrupted the stillness in the room.

"What in the hell?" John said.

We both looked around, trying to determine the source of the sound. I stood up.

"It sounded like it was coming from underneath us," I said. The noise began again, this time different, more of a squeak and growl. Abruptly, Fluffy came skittering out from under the futon. She turned and looked at the sofa as if expecting it to come after her.

"What is it, girl?" I looked over at Nailor. "I think whoever tore up the trailer last night must've scared Fluffy. It's not like her to do this. She's usually right out if she hears me come in. She must be doing this because you came in first."

"Probably," he said. He bent down, offering Fluffy a hand to smell. When she wandered over to be petted, he scratched her head and talked softly to her. Fluffy's little tail wagged happily. She'd found a friend.

"I'd better get going," he said, straightening up.

"I thought you had questions," I said.

"You answered the one I was concerned about."

"You need a ride back?" I asked, wanting to prolong my time with him.

Nailor laughed. "I'll take my chances and have Donlevy call someone to take me back to my car. You're probably tired."

"No, I just got my second wind," I said.

"Sierra, you're lying again," he said softly. He didn't need to hold my hand to see the truth in that statement. I could feel my eyes burning with fatigue, and I knew the makeup had long since worn off my face.

"Don't get into any more trouble for a while, okay?" he said.

He didn't need to convince me. My headache was beginning to return, reminding me that I was supposed to be taking it easy.

I stood watching the door after he left, finally plopping down onto the futon and pulling Fluffy up onto my lap.

"He likes you," the futon said. "And you like him, too, I can tell. You get that fuzzy tone to your voice."

I jumped up and whirled around.

"Denise, where are you?" I yelled, pulling the futon away from the wall. Denise lay wedged behind the sofa, her tiny frame pulled up into a ball.

"Oh God," she groaned. "Help me up, will you? I thought you two were going to sit on me all night." She turned to look at Fluffy. "And you," she said, pointing her finger. "You shouldn't eat food that doesn't settle well. Stinker."

Denise, aside from her voice and stature, was not the Denise of almost two weeks ago. Her beautiful long red hair was gone. In its place was a choppy mop of black. She wore a tight faded pair of blue jeans and a white T-shirt, and no makeup or jewelry. At a quick glance, she almost looked like a small boy.

"How'd you get in here?" I asked.

"You still keep your spare key under the propane

tank," she answered, grinning. "Jesus, you've been hard to get to. You got cops all over you." She looked around the trailer. "And who did this?" Denise was in overdrive. "You got my package, didn't you? And the earring? I figured you'd know I was all right if I left you a sign, you know?"

Here was Denise, in my living room, totally fine, without so much as an "I'm sorry" or "Hope I didn't freak you out too bad."

"Sit down," I commanded. "We'll get to your questions when I get done with mine." Denise stopped and looked at me. "You think you can run out on me, leave me to face the cops, get my tail in a sling, and scare me to death without so much as a 'Kiss my ass'? I don't think so."

Denise arranged her face to appear contrite, but I wasn't having it.

"That guy you think likes me is a cop, remember? He's looking for *you,* as you may have overheard. They think you killed your ex-husband. I thought you were dead. I want to know, right now, what the hell is going on?"

Denise sank slowly down onto the futon, her shoulders slumping. On closer inspection, she looked the worse for wear. Her jeans were fashionably ripped out at the knees, but they were dirty, as were her running shoes. She was thinner, much thinner than before, and her eyes were rimmed with dark circles.

"All right," she said, sighing, "no bullshit, but you aren't going to like it."

"I don't have to like it," I said. "I need to know what I'm dealing with."

Denise nodded, running her fingers through her close-cropped hair.

"Leon was on me the day he got out of prison. He'd never intended to leave me alone. That was obvious when Joey V., Leon's other drug courier, showed up and insisted that I accompany him back to the *Mirage*.

Joey wasn't any too happy about coming to get me or having Leon back on the outside. He said Leon was crazier than ever, that he was going to go right back into the business even with the feds all over him. Sierra, I was scared." Her big green eyes stared up at me. "You couldn't imagine how Leon can terrify you, hurt you until you'd do anything he asked, just to get away." I thought back to my brief encounter with Leon in Fort Lauderdale and nodded.

"I had some time to think on the drive down, and I decided that I had to get away, far away, once and for all. I figured that if I could get enough money, I could get lost somewhere, maybe another country. I don't know. I just knew I had to get far away. So I talked Joey V. into working with me. Then I went down to the *Mirage,* and I let Leon think I was glad to be back."

I remembered the picture of Denise, smiling with her arm around Leon's waist. She put on a good act.

"I did whatever I had to do to make him think I was glad to see him. I told him I'd always known he'd get off and that we'd be together. I told him I divorced him to throw the cops off my trail. I told him I did time for him rather than flip for the DEA, and he believed me." Denise's eyes filled with tears. "I slept with him, Sierra. I made myself forget about Frankie, just so I could save my own ass." Denise scuffed at my carpet with her shoe, not looking at me.

"I told Leon I had a contact with the Outlaws and that they were looking to score something really big. He liked that, but he was having trouble getting his organization to front him more dope 'cause the last bust was so big. I told him that if we brought new business into the organization, then it would restore their confidence in him." Denise had to be telling the truth. No one could talk that fast and lie at the same time.

"I told him I'd go get the front money from the bikers

and put it with whatever he could come up with, and then maybe Mack 'the Fish' Tunnato would do business. It was Leon's idea to send me to Mack with the money instead of using Joey V. He said Tunnato always liked me anyway. You know what he meant, Sierra," she said, moving restlessly on the couch. "He meant I should sleep with Mack.

"There was no turning back then. I let him think that I was going to go along with it. Leon said he'd send Joey up with the money for Mack. He figured Joey would keep an eye on me; he sent Joey because he didn't really trust me. Then I went to Frankie and told him I was back in the business. He wasn't happy about it, but he finally agreed to introduce me to the club president so I could set up the deal."

"You were lying to me," I said. "You were planning to disappear all along."

"Sierra, I couldn't tell you how it really was. I couldn't tell nobody. Not you, not Frankie. Leon was poison, Sierra. He'd kill or torture anybody or anything I loved, just to see it eat away at me. It would only be a matter of time before he decided to pay me back for deserting him. He was using me to get back in business. I had to leave or stay and let Leon kill me.

"I thought I had it all together, the timing and everything, until Arlo disappeared and somebody stiffed Joey V. and left him in my room." Denise shook her head slowly. "There I was, holding a hundred thousand dollars and too stupid to run off and leave my damn dog. Time was running out. Leon thought Mack the Fish had his money. Frankie's club thought I had their front money. If I didn't show back up in a matter of hours, they were going to get squirrely." Denise hit the couch with her fist. "I guess somebody didn't trust me. Joey V. was a warning and Arlo was the insurance."

I was seeing another Denise and I wasn't so sure I

trusted her. "So why did you come back? How do you know that Arlo's even alive? And why'd you put a hundred thousand in my car?"

Denise got up and started pacing the length of the living room. "I got to think that Arlo's alive. I can't leave until I know for sure. I put the money in your car 'cause I hoped you'd know I was around. I figured it was safer to stash the money there in case something happened. If it didn't work out like I planned, well, I knew you could use the cash. I was going to try and see you, but you been covered over with cops. Sierra, I'm sorry. I was so scared that I guess I didn't think about anything else."

"So, what," I said, "you're here for your money?"

Denise sighed and ran her hands impatiently through her hair. "No, I need help, Sierra. I can't pull this off by myself. You're the only one with balls enough to help me. If you don't want to do it for me, then think of Arlo. I know he's alive, Sierra. I just know it."

"Denise," I said, "who killed Joey V. and Leon?"

"I don't know," she said, her fingers nervously twitching at her frayed jeans. "At first I thought Leon had somehow found out what me and Joey were planning, but then when Leon got killed I couldn't figure it."

"Denise, did you kill them?"

"No." Denise's eyes blazed with anger. "Do you want me to say I'm sorry they're dead? 'Cause I can't say that. Maybe Mack Tunnato did it. Maybe Leon's own people. I don't know."

"What about Frankie?" I asked.

Denise's eyes filled with tears. "Not Frankie," she whispered. "He's not like that."

I couldn't believe her. "Denise, wake up," I said. "If Leon's dead and Mack Tunnato didn't kill him, then Frankie's your next best bet. He knew where you lived. He knew you were crazy for Arlo. He knew you got the dope from Leon. And Denise, you ripped him off."

Denise was openly crying now. "Not really," she said. "I didn't really rip him off. I ripped off his club."

"Same thing," I said. "And Frankie's gonna be the one they're gonna turn on when you don't show up." I thought of Frankie, his front tire shot out from under him. Perhaps they were already cutting him out of the pack, keeping him alive, hoping he would lead them to Denise.

This line of thought clearly hadn't occurred to Denise. Her eyes widened.

"What are we going to do, Sierra?" she said, sinking back down onto the futon. "What in the world am I going to do?"

Twenty-nine

I found myself at seven-thirty the next morning rolling up in front of Bay County Medical Center, half asleep and cranky. I didn't care what Denise thought—no mobster worth his salt would hold a dog hostage. Frankie had to be behind it; nothing else made sense.

I stepped off the elevator, wishing I'd had one more cup of coffee, and found Frankie's bodyguards sleeping in the visitors' lounge. If someone had really wanted to get to Frankie, it would've been a piece of cake, because I sailed right past. It occurred to me that maybe the guards weren't sent by the Outlaws to keep others out. Maybe they were there to make sure Frankie didn't leave.

Frankie was awake, trying to force down the lukewarm breakfast the hospital was trying to palm off as food. He looked up when I walked in, and stretched to see behind me.

"They're sleeping," I said, answering his unasked question. "You want me to take my blouse off, or can we have a decent conversation without all the hoopla?"

Frankie still looked bad. His bruises were turning gray-green and his contusions were a rusty brown color. He tried to smile and failed, then reached into the bedside table drawer for his cigarettes and lighter.

"You can't smoke in here," I said.

"You think they're really going to try and stop me?" he asked. I watched him go through the ritual of tapping the cigarette on the filter end, then sticking it in his mouth, and flicking the silver-and-turquoise lighter until the flame caught and held.

"No, I guess not," I answered. "So when are you getting out?"

Frankie took another long hit on his cigarette and squinted at me through the haze of smoke.

"Probably tomorrow morning," he said. "They were watching for internal bleeding." He shifted in the bed. "So, did you hear from Denise?" he asked.

"No, nothing like that." I pulled a chair up by his bedside. "I was here getting some blood tests run and thought I'd stop in on you."

"Is that right?" Frankie didn't look like he believed me.

"Well, I guess I had a couple of questions," I said. "I mean, maybe I can help you find Denise."

Frankie raised himself up in bed and blew smoke rings toward the ceiling.

"Maybe you can," he said slowly. "So, ask me."

"All right, where was Denise supposed to meet you?"

"She wasn't supposed to meet me, she was supposed to meet Rambo, back at the clubhouse, and do the deal."

Rambo, I thought, my favorite. The image of his boot connecting with Fluffy flashed through my head.

"Where's the clubhouse?" I asked.

Frankie frowned. "Well, it's not a clubhouse like the Masons or nothing, it's a house where some of us live. Behind Tan Fannies."

"The strip club?" Definitely two steps down from the Tiffany.

"Yeah, convenient, huh?" Frankie leered.

"You couldn't pay me to live there, but it's your party, I guess."

Frankie's features clouded over and he glanced toward the closed door to the hallway.

"I don't know where I'm going after this. The president's pretty pissed that Denise took off with the money. He's not sure I didn't have something to do with it. Rambo and some of the others think I did. They're going to hold a tribunal when they get back from the rally in Daytona this weekend."

"What's a tribunal?" I asked.

"Like a biker court," he answered. "They'll have a trial and decide if I was involved with Denise in ripping them off or not."

"And what if they think you were?" I asked.

"They'll kill me," he said simply.

"Why don't you take off?" I asked.

Frankie laughed caustically and stubbed his cigarette out in his scrambled eggs.

"Why do you think those guys are out there?" he said. "Sierra, it isn't the money. With the Outlaws, it's the principle. They'd as soon kill somebody for taking five bucks as they would for taking a hundred thousand. They've got to make an example out of someone. If it isn't Denise, it might be me. Hell," he said, "I might've been gone a long time ago if I hadn't wanted to stick around and try to protect her."

"Did Denise know that?" I wondered aloud.

Frankie laughed. "She left before I could tell her. Story of my life, I guess. Something good finally happens and boom, it ends before it starts."

"Where's Arlo, Frankie?"

"You don't need to worry about Arlo, Sierra. We needed to get Denise's attention."

"So you took him?"

Frankie glanced toward the door again. "No, that wasn't my idea, but when the decision gets made, you got to go along with it. I'm keeping an eye on him."

I didn't point out that it was hard to keep track of a dog from a hospital bed. And Frankie wasn't in any shape to influence what happened to Arlo. They seemed to be in the same sinking rowboat.

"You sure are asking a lot of questions about me and the Outlaws," Frankie said. "Sierra, if you know where Denise is, or if you've heard from her, tell me and then let me handle it. Don't go getting any ideas about saving Arlo. That would make the situation a lot worse for everyone."

"Frankie," I said, "I'm not stupid."

I slipped out of Frankie's room and past the still-sleeping bodyguards. There were worse places to be than in a hospital, I thought. There was no way I'd want to be in Frankie's boots. The elevator slid open and I stepped inside. As the doors slowly started to close, I watched an aide pushing an empty breakfast cart down the hallway. He wore the faded blue uniform all the other aides wore, but something stood out about him. It was the slow way he moved, as if going nowhere but watching everything. He drew even with the elevator as the doors were closing and I could see his face. If I hadn't been quite so tired, I would have sworn it was Lyle.

Something didn't sit right with me about Frankie. There was something he'd said, something he'd done that had set alarm bells off in my head. I couldn't quite put my finger on what it was, but something was very wrong with the picture he was painting.

Thirty

At one A.M., Saturday morning, Dennis Donlevy began to think he was in trouble. Raydean, her favorite Easter bonnet perched atop her frizzled gray hair, a yellow raincoat the only covering between her and mankind, had left her home and was singing "Onward Christian Soldiers" at the top of her lungs. To further complicate the situation, she had entered the carport, released the emergency brake on her vehicle, and was now pushing it down the slight incline of her driveway and into the street.

At 1:05 A.M., young Detective Donlevy began to panic. Raydean's Plymouth Fury had completely blocked the road, making it impossible for young Donlevy to follow his assigned protective duties. As I smoked tires and sped off down the Lively Oaks Trailer Park Drive, Dennis Donlevy was standing in the middle of the street, screaming at an unresponsive Raydean. By the time he returned to his car and radioed for assistance, I had vanished.

At one-fifteen A.M., Denise and I were parked around the corner from Tan Fannies, watching the Outlaws' clubhouse and trying to determine if anyone was still inside the faded wooden building.

"We look ridiculous," Denise said, looking in the passenger-side visor mirror. "What if someone sees us?"

She was right. It was my idea to dress in black and blacken our faces. I figured we needed all the help we could get. Of course, if someone spotted us crossing the street and creeping up the dirt front yard to the Outlaws' house, we'd stand out like sore thumbs.

"No one's going to see us," I said. "We'll make damn sure they don't."

Denise started to giggle. "Did you see the look on that cop's face when we drove off and Raydean wouldn't move her car? Man, that was great."

"Hush, Denise," I hissed. "Keep your mind on what we're doing. Let's go." I reached for the door handle and started to open the car.

"Wait, Sierra," Denise said, her face pale around the edges of her makeup.

"What?"

"Nothing, I guess," she murmured.

We stepped out of the car and into the humid night air. The side door of Tan Fannies stood open and the sound of music and men catcalling the dancers drifted out into the neighborhood. I moved swiftly across the street with Denise right behind me, into the sheltering darkness of the trees that surrounded the Outlaws' front yard.

There were no motorcycles in the front yard, only a large white Lincoln parked under the lone light shining onto the gravel driveway. A small garage marked the end of the driveway like a mausoleum. There was no sign of life on the inside of the faded wooden house. It stood eerily silent, its front porch casting an ominous shadow over the bushes that lined the front of the house.

Denise and I moved quickly past the front of the house and began edging closer to the windows along the side. One small window was open about six inches.

"If I boost you up, can you open it more and crawl in?" I asked Denise.

"Me?" Denise squeaked.

"Well, I'd go myself," I whispered sarcastically, "but I got eight inches and twenty pounds on you, so it'd be hard for you to lift me."

"Twenty-five," she whispered caustically. "Let's go."

I braced my back against the side of the house, laced my fingers together, and hoisted Denise as far as I could. With a harsh thud that seemed to rattle the ancient house, Denise heaved her tiny body across the windowsill. There was the sound of a soft splash, then Denise's voice swearing. A few moments later, the thick mop of black hair appeared at the window ledge.

"Wouldn't you know it," she called softly. "Right in front of the friggin' toilet. I'm soaked."

"Forget about that," I said. "Get to the back door and let me in. And be quiet. Somebody could be in there." Denise's eyes widened and she disappeared. I crept cautiously around to the back door and waited. In a matter of moments the door creaked open and Denise beckoned me in.

"God, you stink," I whispered.

"I don't think they worry about flushing, Sierra," she said softly.

"All right, did you hear anything? See anything?"

"You can't see a freaking thing in here," she answered. "How're we going to find anything?"

"Stand still and listen," I commanded. We were both silent, listening for anything we could pick up. Somewhere above us I could hear the faint sound of a dog whining.

"Oh God, it's Arlo," Denise breathed. Before I could stop her she was gone, racing through the darkened house, bumping against furniture in her haste to reach her baby.

I followed her, pulling the penlight I'd brought out of my back pocket and using it to pick my way through the house. The place was a shambles. Dirty sofas, ripped armchairs, and battered end tables lined what was intended to be a living room and dining room area. The banister shook and nearly came loose as I attempted to climb the steps. I could hear Denise crying and talking— I hoped to Arlo.

I followed the sound of her voice down the central hallway, past bedrooms that appeared to have mattresses on the floor and little else. I found Denise in the corner of a front bedroom, on her knees, with Arlo firmly clutched in her lap.

"Sierra," she cried, her voice choking with tears, "I think he's dying."

I stepped over to her side, squatting down beside the two of them. The room reeked of dog urine and feces. The small wire cage that had been Arlo's prison was covered with dog shit. I shone the flashlight on Arlo and realized that he was indeed in bad shape. His ribs stuck out through his encrusted fur and his eyes were sunken into his head. He stuck out his little pink tongue and tried to lick Denise's hand.

"What have I done?" she cried. "This is all my fault."

"Denise," I said, "you can't do this. We've got to get Arlo out of here, right now." I stood up, reached to help her up, and froze. Someone was walking down the hallway toward us.

It was too late to react. There was nothing we could do and nowhere to hide if we'd wanted to try. The room was filled with the glaring light of a single lightbulb that hung from the ceiling. Even as I blinked, trying to adjust to the brightness, I knew our intruder. His boots were the first thing I saw and the last thing I remembered about him.

"I knew you'd be back," Rambo said to Denise. "I see you brought the SPCA along with you." Behind him I could hear the snickers of his companions, and I knew then that we were trapped. When I'd thought it was only Rambo, I'd figured maybe we could take him, but with three or four on two, there'd be no chance.

Rambo stepped easily into the room and looked around. Two other men followed, chains dangling from their back pockets and guns in their hands. Rambo paid no attention to his entourage. He was looking at Denise while he pulled a pack of cigarettes and a lighter from his shirt pocket.

"There's a bounty on you, you know," he said. "Walt don't like it, you being a bitch and ripping us off."

"I didn't—" Denise began.

"Shut up!" Rambo screeched. In two quick steps he'd covered the distance between us and stood inches from Denise's face. His breath was sour with alcohol. His eyes were narrow pinpoints and his breath came in quick shallow gasps. Rambo liked his cocaine, I thought.

"How'd you know we were here?" I asked, hoping to draw his attention away from Denise and Arlo.

He looked at me and blew smoke right in my face. A thick, black-handled knife had materialized in his hand. He stepped closer, bringing the knife up close to my face.

"How do you think them titties would look if I was to carve my initials in them?" he rasped.

I didn't move, didn't say a word. One of his companions sniffed uneasily and this distracted Rambo momentarily. When his attention returned, his mood had changed.

"You think we'd leave the clubhouse unprotected?" he asked. "You were seen. Sam, here, just walked on over to Tan Fannies and let me know you'd arrived. We've been waiting."

"Look," Denise said, "I've got the money. I was going to tell you that Leon couldn't do the deal and give it back."

"What kind of dumb ass do you take me for?" Rambo asked. "You two ain't going nowhere until Walt comes back from Daytona. No, you two ladies are our guests for the weekend, so enjoy yourselves. I can assure you, me and the boys are going to enjoy ourselves." Rambo reached out and flicked the material of my shirt with his knife.

"Rambo, you up there?" a male voice yelled out from downstairs. "You got company."

"Shit. It's them damn Mexicans, I bet," he said to the others. "Come on." Rambo walked briskly from the room followed by the two men. "Lock up," he barked.

One of the men pulled the door shut, and from the outside I could hear the sound of a key being inserted into the dead-bolt lock. Denise began to tremble uncontrollably. I felt a chill move through my body. Below us, the house began to fill with loud voices and music. The bikers were partying, and when they reached their peak and finished with whoever had come to see them, we would be the next item of interest.

Two minutes passed in which neither of us said a word. Denise perched on the edge of the filthy mattress, rocking Arlo back and forth like a baby. Finally she looked up at me and I saw the fear was gone from her eyes.

"Well," she said softly, "I'm thinking the window."

I stepped softly over to the window and looked out.

"I'm game if you are," I said. "We're over the porch roof. It's steep and it looks kind of rotten, but if we could make it to the edge, it would only be about an eight-foot drop."

"What about Arlo?" she asked.

"I got an idea about that, too," I said. I pulled the black turtleneck I wore off, stripping down to my black sports bra, and tied the neck hole closed. "Put him in here," I said, holding the bottom end of the shirt open, "then turn around." Arlo was too weak to move or put up a struggle as I strapped him to Denise's back, papoose-style.

"Ready?" I asked. Denise nodded and I moved to the window and slowly raised it. The high-pitched squeal it made filled the room, echoing off the empty walls. I stuck my head out and looked down. The porch roof was a four-foot drop. It would be easy as long as we didn't land on a rotten piece of shingle or slip on the thin layer of moss that coated the disintegrating shingles.

"Go first," I said. "I'll try and help." The short drop to the porch roof was nothing Denise couldn't handle if the roof held.

Denise swung one leg over the windowsill and stopped. Arlo was tied to her back and not moving.

"Sierra?"

"What?" Another sound was filtering through, past the sounds of bikers partying. It was the sound of someone in the hallway. Denise looked up at me, her eyes wet with unshed tears.

"Thank you," she whispered. "Nobody ever went out on the line for me before."

The footsteps were definitely coming closer, stopping outside the door. We had to move quickly. I gave Denise a little shove.

"Someone's coming, hurry," I urged.

Denise lowered herself over the edge and dropped softly onto the roof below. Crouching down, she began to inch her way toward the end of the house and the sheltering branches of a pine tree.

I was halfway out the window when the door to the bedroom swung open. I didn't wait to see who it was. I swung my other leg over the sill and jumped, barely catching myself as I hit the roof. My left foot slammed into a rotting shingle and sank two inches down into the roof's surface. The porch wasn't going to take much more abuse and might not even hold the two of us as we tried to climb down.

There was a muffled shout and then Rambo stuck his head through the window.

"Don't even try it!" he yelled.

I didn't look back, just kept heading for the edge of the porch where Denise waited under the sheltering arms of the pine tree. I knew he was coming. I reached the lowest edge of the porch and laid down.

"Denise," I said, "hang on to my wrists and the edge of the gutter and drop down. It's only eight feet."

Behind me I heard Rambo swear and swing his leg over the windowsill.

"Hurry," I said. Denise wasted no time. She grabbed my wrist with one hand, anchored herself alongside the gutter, and swung over the side of the house. Light spilled out into the yard from the lower floor, and the loud sounds of bikers drinking and yelling echoed through the tiny yard. No one would hear her drop.

Rambo swung himself over the edge and dropped onto the roof behind me. One foot landed in the rotten hole and sunk up to his ankle.

"Goddamn it!" he roared. "I'll kill you." He lurched across the roof and I didn't wait to see if he'd make it. I grabbed at the gutter and prepared to swing off into the darkness.

"Not you." I felt my head jerk backward, throwing my body off balance. Rambo's hot sour breath coated my face. "One down, one to go," he snarled. Wrapping my hair firmly around his thick hand, he led me, stumbling backward, across the rotting porch roof and toward the gaping window where the others waited.

I couldn't fight back. I could barely keep my balance as he dragged me. Down below, I could still hear voices and the sound of men running and shouting to one another. I didn't hear a sound from Denise. Had she made it? Could she possibly have gotten away before the others knew what had happened? I wasn't much for praying, not in any organized sort of way, but I found myself muttering the rosary from childhood. She had to get help for me. She'd do that, wouldn't she?

Rambo pulled me through the open window, not caring that he scraped my back against the sill, not easing up on my hair.

"So I got you," Rambo said, sneering. "We'll get your friend, too. She couldn't have gotten too far. Then we'll have us a real party." One of Rambo's men laughed and I felt my stomach turn. "What d'you say we have a little entertainment?" Rambo asked his friends. "Wouldn't them Mexicans love a little T and A before they go?"

He turned back to me and took his time looking me over. "I hear you can dance," he said softly, tightening his grip on my hair. "Well, I got a hungry audience downstairs. I think we oughta let them see you, one last time, before you go." He laughed, a high-pitched evil laugh that shot out over the others' laughter.

One last time before you go. The words echoed through my head. What happened when the music stopped? I didn't want to think about it. Instead I turned my head as far as I could, given that my hair was wrapped around Rambo's grease-stained hand, and looked him dead in the eyes.

"You assholes are in luck," I said, " 'cause I'm the best that's ever been. Now let go of my hair."

There was a moment of silence. Rambo just stared at me, like I was too brain-damaged to know what happened when the act ended and I was alone in a room with a bunch of bikers and their coked-up friends. Then he nodded slightly, let go of my hair, and pushed me toward the door. Where in the hell was Denise and how long could I stall these morons?

The excited rumble of voices and noise stopped when Rambo shoved me into the living room. There had to be twenty men and maybe five women, although calling them by gender was giving them the generous benefit of the doubt.

"Over there," Rambo said, pointing toward a long table. "Do it on there."

"Yeah, then we'll do you," someone yelled out and the others laughed. I had no doubt that he was speaking for all the men in the room. What a fucking way to go.

"Wait," I said. "Let me see the music. I gotta have music."

Rambo hesitated, then pointed to the stereo and CDs that lined one side of the wall. I wandered over and squatted down, pretending to peruse the selections. I waited until I heard Rambo walk up behind me, then I stood up and turned, a CD in hand.

I couldn't tell you what I picked, just that I knew it had a good beat and a playtime of over four minutes. It was going to have to be the longest and best performance of my life, because when it ended, if Denise hadn't gotten to the cops, I'd be beyond saving.

I jumped up on the table and looked out at the rest of the room. It was hot and crowded with sweaty, smelly bodies, all as close to the table as they could be and still see me. A few people hung around a coffee table, snorting clean white lines of coke that littered a mirror. Slowly the music began and I began to sway with it, trying to let my body go through the motions while my mind worked overtime.

It didn't seem to matter that I wore black shoe polish on my face, or that I was scraped and bruised. My audience was watching me move, watching my hands move over my body, waiting for the opportunity to tear me apart. Right down in front stood Rambo, a sickening leer on his face.

I had to get out of here. If Denise didn't reach the cops in time, if they didn't believe her, then I'd die. I let my eyes roam around the room. It was littered with motorcycle parts, cans of various shapes and sizes, tools and old furniture. At one end of the table stood a floor lamp, the kind with a halogen bulb. I moved rhythmically, my plan suddenly in place.

I reached out and grabbed the lamp, pulled it up onto the table, and began using it like a pole. The men started yelling, a few of them grabbing their crotches and making obscene movements. I threw the lamp over on its side, letting it drop down into a pile of rags, and grabbed my bra straps, yanking my bra down around my waist. Every eye in the house was on me. Even the women stopped and watched. I inched my hand down inside the waistband of my jeans and slowly licked my lips. The music had increased in intensity, building toward a climax.

When the rags caught fire and the first can exploded, no one saw it coming, except for me. I jumped down off the far edge of the table, letting my weight flip the table on its side. In the confusion and pandemonium, I hitched up my bra, ran toward the open window, and vaulted out into the cool night air.

I felt myself falling and braced myself to land and start running. Instead I felt a pair of strong large hands grab my waist and guide me to the ground. I turned, wild-eyed in the darkness, ready to lash out, and saw Frankie's face with Denise just behind him.

"Come on," Frankie hissed, "this way." He turned and vanished into the trees.

"Run!" I yelled as bikers swarmed into the dirt yard like fire ants. We tore off, through the pines that surrounded the yard and out onto the street, running faster than I thought possible. Ahead of us, Frankie hopped onto his Harley and jumped to start the engine. I could hear sounds behind us, the rush of footsteps, the roar of bikes suddenly pushed into action. Denise and I never looked back. She jumped into the car while I started the ignition. We were off and on the open road before they could catch us, but it would only be a matter of moments before they did.

I tore out onto Fifteenth Street, the Camaro's tires smoking as we left long black marks through the inter-section. I was running wide open, through intersections, topping seventy-five miles an hour, and praying that a cop would see me.

"They're behind us!" Denise screamed into the wind. "They're going to get Frankie. Sierra, oh God!" Denise was frantic, turning around backward in her seat watching the road behind us. I looked in the rearview mirror for a second and saw Frankie purposefully weaving across the road, trying to keep the others from passing him.

"I only need one more minute!" I yelled. "When I tell you to, jump out and run inside." We raced past the forestry station, past the Blue Marlin, and finally cut a sharp left into the police station parking lot. I pulled right up to the front door of the squat tan building and jumped out, racing through the front door, then flattening myself against the rest-room door, away from the glass entrance. Denise followed me, pushing the rest-room door open and running inside.

In the lobby I could hear the insistent voice of the officer on duty yelling, "Can I help you?"

"Yes," I called from the rest-room doorway, "get some help out here fast." In the parking lot I could hear the sound of bikes roaring up, then loud backfiring or shots ringing out. Then the bikes seemed to turn around and speed off. We'd made it, but there was no sign of Frankie.

The watch commander and several officers burst through the office doors, filling the lobby with their uniformed presence.

"You guys get that man in here," the watch commander barked.

Frankie Paramus half walked, half crawled through the front doors, collapsing on the floor in the center of the police department lobby. As he fell, his lighter tumbled out of his pocket and clattered onto the tile floor by my feet. I stared at it; then back at Frankie. The final piece fell into place.

"I'm Sierra Lavotini," I said, stepping cautiously out from the rest room, "and I would appreciate it if you would call Detective Nailor and ask him to come down here."

Thirty-one

I could hear John Nailor arrive. From his office where we sat waiting, I could hear his voice as he rushed through the building, asking for details, and then suddenly stopping yards from his office.

"What in the hell is that odor?" he asked. "Aw, you didn't . . . Man, you put them in my office?" There was the muffled sound of laughter and then suddenly there he was, standing in the doorway.

"What in the world?" he said, staring into the small room. There we sat, reeking of dog shit, covered in black shoe polish, wearing black clothes, and me minus a shirt, wearing a black sports bra. Denise's hair was windblown and sticking straight up. My own hair must've been in a similar state.

"Ladies," he said, composing himself, walking into the room and taking a seat behind his desk, "to what do I owe the honor? I understand that you arrived with an escort and that you parked your new Camaro on our front sidewalk, Sierra."

Denise, remorseful in her past neglect, strove to make up for it now.

"Don't get on Sierra, Detective," she said. "This was all my fault and I'm responsible."

Nailor turned his attention to her. "Ms. Curtis, lovely to see you again. You've changed your appearance."

Denise froze momentarily, then with a big sigh, began to talk. She seemed to tell him every detail, all without pausing for a breath: Leon, the phony scam to get her safely away from the man she was certain would eventually kill her, Arlo's rescue. Denise was cleansing her soul.

I listened but I was getting impatient. I wanted to get things wrapped up and over with as soon as possible.

"I think I know who killed Leon Corvase and the other guy," I said suddenly.

"Finally, she says something I want to hear." Carla Terrance's voice floated over my shoulder as she stood in the doorway.

Nailor looked at her briefly, frowning. "What was that, Sierra?" he asked.

I looked over at Denise. "I'm sorry, honey," I said softly, then turned back to face Nailor. "The man who was with us, Frankie Paramus. I think he killed Leon Corvase."

Denise stared at me, her eyes filling with tears.

"What proof do you have of that?" Carla Terrance asked.

"He has Leon Corvase's cigarette lighter," I said. "It's turquoise and silver, with a big filigree C on the back. I saw Leon with it in Fort Lauderdale."

Nailor looked over my head to Carla. He nodded slightly, then turned back to us. Carla vanished from the doorway. Denise was slowly becoming hysterical. She looked at me and I could see she was about to go off.

"Denise," Nailor said, apparently sensing what was happening, "look at Arlo." Denise's eyes sharpened and she looked down in her lap. "We need to take care of Arlo, Denise, and we need to get the EMTs to take a look at you, too." Denise looked at Nailor, then Arlo, then me. Tears streamed down her cheeks.

"Not Frankie," she sobbed brokenly.

Nailor walked around his desk and gently knelt before Denise. "Come with me, Denise. I'm going to have one of my officers help you. We'll get Arlo some water and get him cleaned up. Come on." Denise slowly rose and Nailor led her to the door. As they walked away, I could hear Nailor's voice calling to someone and Denise's quiet sobbing.

I sat, looking around the tiny office, and wishing I were home with Fluffy and the whole mess had never happened. The hallway outside Nailor's office had become a rush of police officers brought in to handle the evening crisis. I gradually became aware of two voices, growing closer as they neared the room where I waited.

"Look," Carla was saying, "we need him. He's critical to our investigation. If he agrees to testify in return for a slot in the witness protection program, then I can close my case."

"Not if he's a murderer," Nailor answered firmly.

"We'll see about that," Carla answered. "Your people are jeopardizing our investigation. They've got him so paranoid, he won't talk to anyone. Lyle's already been in to talk to him. Frankie says he wants a lawyer or he wants out."

"I don't care if he talks or not," Nailor said. "If the DNA matches, then it's a go and I don't need squat from him."

"And if it doesn't, you'll have held up my investigation for nothing. The Outlaws'll run and six months of effort will go in the toilet. I don't have that kind of time."

They reached the doorway and the conversation broke off. Nailor walked back into the room, his face a rigid mask. Carla glared after him for a minute, then turned and walked off.

"You could let me talk to him," I said when Nailor sat down.

He didn't try to pretend he didn't know what I was talking about. He stared at me for a moment, then picked up his pen and started writing something on a pad of paper.

"That's out of the question," he said finally.

"Don't be ridiculous," I said. "I might actually save you some time. That would get you out of a bind with your buddy Carla."

He scowled and looked back down at the paper in front of him. He was making up his mind.

"Guess it won't hurt anything," he said at last. "But I go in with you."

"Oh, he'll really be comfortable then," I said.

"Take it or leave it," he said, standing.

Frankie sat in an interview room staring straight ahead. His battered face was set in a tight scowl, his hands clenched tightly together in front of him, gently pounding on the scarred interview table.

Frankie," Nailor said, "Ms. Lavotini wanted to talk to you." Frankie didn't acknowledge our presence. He kept his eyes glued to the table, tightening his fist until the knuckles of his hand turned white.

I took a step toward the table and pulled out the chair across from Frankie and sat down. Nailor hovered behind my left shoulder.

"Yo, asshole," I said harshly, "I don't give a shit if you go down for killing them two guys, really I don't, but you got no right to hurt Denise like this."

Frankie looked at me, his eyes filled with unspent rage.

"You stonewall everyone and get sent to prison, probably for life, and Denise will always think you were just a creep like every other man she's ever known. She'll wonder if she was next on your list."

Frankie was still staring at me, but he was listening hard.

"I don't know you well," I said, "but I got a hard time believing you killed those two men over dope money."

"I didn't kill nobody," Frankie roared.

"Then why didn't you say so?" I asked.

"Why bother? These people don't believe me. First some guy named Lyle comes to my hospital room, identifies himself as DEA, and tells me he knows I'm in trouble over a dope deal. He says if I'd agree to testify against the club, he could set me up anywhere in the country with a whole new identity. I tell him to kiss off. I can take care of myself.

"Then all I do is try and help you and Denise out of a jam. I bust my bike and myself all to hell, and what happens?" Frankie looked at me and Nailor. "I wind up in here. I got cops and some bitch from the DEA all over me, saying I got Denise's ex-husband's cigarette lighter and I'm looking at murder one." Frankie snorted derisively. "It's all a part of the setup. Won't matter what I say. If I don't testify against my brothers, then I'm down."

"Frankie," Nailor said, "that's not how it is at all."

"Really?" Frankie spat. "And now, even if I was to walk, I'd be dead within an hour because I helped some woman who jacked my club and thinks I murdered her ex. My own friends are looking to take me out. Oh yeah, my trust level with you people is real high."

"Frankie," I said, "Denise doesn't want to believe you killed Leon. She's down the hall, hysterical, because she thinks you're innocent. See, she actually thought she needed your forgiveness on account of she messed you up with the club. She had the idea you two would run off together." I laughed bitterly. "Well, I guess there's a sucker born every minute." I sat still for a moment and let the words sink in, then I stood up and made like I was leaving.

"Wait, Sierra," Frankie said quietly. "Rambo gave me

to the hospital and gave it to me
ttes. Now let me talk to Denise
ns you want to ask."

drove me home in my
detective in an unmarked
still at the police station,
EA. Frankie'd agreed to
long as he had witness

mbers had been picked
l was being matched
lin crime scene. The
he Tiffany the night
tch it to Rambo or
l of this did to the
aling activity in
stified, then the
anama City at

d Fluffy. No
ers, no more
be boring,

the wheel
uld miss
itement
nd find
other
ively
r up
o. I

-

chest and squeeze hard. My d
streaming from the trailer into

"No," I answered, "I did
locked it and I know the ligh

Nailor's gun was drawn
car. Whoever was inside
heard us roar up. Maybe t
Nailor signaled to the un
other detective picked u
other detective left his
Nailor at the foot of th

I didn't stay in the
and I had to know
trailer, drifting out
distinct odor of fre

"Hit me, boys.

"Raydean," I
laughed softly a
pushed his gun
car to head o
hear in the di

I ran up
morning co
my pop.

Pop st
mitt and
brother
denly
caugh

"\
shir
he

o

trouble down here. He says you think you can handle it, but he smells different. He wises up and figures he needs to tell me. You're damn right he needed to tell me," he said, the scowl now directed at Al. "We come down here as fast as we could, not like two men on a vacation to the shore, no, like an old man coming to rescue his grown-up daughter."

"Pop, I—"

"Enough," Pop roared. Raydean straightened in her seat and looked like maybe Pop was one of them Flemish she was so concerned about. Al was making a face like didn't he tell me so.

"And who is this?" Pop asked, looking at Nailor.

"Detective John Nailor, sir. If it's any help to you, sir, your daughter's situation has been resolved successfully and she is no longer in any difficulty."

"You mean," said Pop, "she pulled her ass out of the fire, all by herself, like she always does, tempting Lady Luck again."

"Exactly," said Nailor, grinning.

Pop wandered a couple of feet over to one of my barstools and sat down, mopping his brow with a handkerchief.

" 'At's a hell of a note, isn't it, Detective? A man can't even protect his own daughter. Always the tomboy, always taking her licks and no helping her. Sweet Mother of God, it's all I can do to keep up." Pop started to laugh and then Nailor and Al started. The tension had broken.

"What the hell," Pop said, rising from his stool. "I made a pot of coffee and this lovely lady has entertained us all night long. Youse two draw up a couple of chairs, let's play a hand or two."

We followed Pop over to the table where Raydean dealt the cards. She was still wearing her shiny yellow rainslicker, but this time she had a housedress on underneath. When Pop sat down next to her, she reached over tenderly and patted his arm.

"Hit me, big man," she whispered softly. "Luck be a lady, right?"

Pop squeezed her hand and picked up the cards. "She was tonight," he murmured.

I picked up my cards and looked across the table at John Nailor. He was slowly picking up his cards, one at a time, and sticking them in his hand, but he wasn't watching the cards. He was watching me.

John Nailor and Vincent Gambuzzo are trying to drive
me crazy. If they were working together on this project,
I'm sure I'd be in a straitjacket somewhere, gulping
down Prozac cocktails. As it is, I'm still one up on both
of them, but they're gaining on me.

John Nailor is a detective with the Panama City Police
Department, and up until he kissed this little brown-
headed woman, I thought he was pretty interested in me.
It wasn't like we were dating. We had shared an
encounter of a personal and dangerous nature and I
thought that in the near future we would evolve into
something a bit more horizontal. But when he looked over
at me before he kissed her, I knew I'd gotten it all wrong.

I guess he's not really my type anyway. He's too
clean-cut. His hair is straight and brown, and he wears
suits, with crisp oxford-cloth shirts and ties. He's not
even quite as tall as me when I wear my five-inch stilettos, but still, there's something about him that makes me
forget that I prefer a biker with a panhead Harley. Maybe
it's his eyes. When I stare at him, he never backs down.
That is, until he kissed that woman right in front of me.
He looked away then.

Vincent Gambuzzo, on the other hand, drives me
crazy for an entirely different reason. He's my boss. He

figures it's his job to make my life a living hell. The Tiffany, where I work, is his little kingdom. He figures if he micromanages his exotic dancers, especially me, his headliner, then his club will one day be as well-known as the Gold Club in Atlanta. I say what Vincent knows about managing talent could be stuck on the head of a pin and you'd still have room left over.

Take, for example, tonight. I'm out on the runway doing my tribute to Dorothy and The Wizard of Oz when Vincent comes barreling right down front with some young guy in a black satin jacket. Vincent can never do anything small. He weighs about three hundred pounds, all of which he squeezes into a black suit and black silk collarless shirt. He talks loud and he wears black wraparound sunglasses 24/7, even with it dark as ink in the club.

"Hey, Rita," he shouts, "bring Mr. Rhodes here a gin and tonic. And bring me my usual."

Did he not have any respect for a working artist? Judy Garland is crooning "Somewhere Over the Rainbow," I'm reaching behind my back to undo my red sequin bra, and guys are down front panting. He completely blew the moment.

Vincent didn't even notice. He was too busy arranging for Mr. Big Shot's comfort. For somebody who's always intimating that he's mob connected and therefore fearless, he sure was kissing up to this Mr. Rhodes. It was sickening, but then, I know Vincent is no more connected to the mob than my third-grade teacher, Sister Mary Rose. So he needs all the big-shot connections he can get. Of course, that still doesn't justify why he saw fit to drag me into the whole thing. If Vincent Gambuzzo hadn't dragged me into his little plan for Mickey Rhodes and the Dead Lakes Motor Speedway, then I wouldn't have seen John Nailor kissing that bimbo and I certainly wouldn't have gotten myself in such big-time trouble.

Vincent waited until I was down to my pasties and my

red sequin shoes to point me out to his visitor. He leaned across the table and bellowed: "Now you'll want her for sure. That's what you get when you use the Tiffany talent."

I'm thinking whatever scheme Vincent Gambuzzo is trying to promote, Sierra Lavotini will avoid like the black plague. I don't do lap dances and I don't have nothing but a hands-off relationship with the clientele. Vincent had to be out of his mind, and the dirty look I shot him told him so.

Vincent laughed. "She's a feisty one, that Sierra, but she draws a crowd."

I'm thinking to have a little talk with Gambuzzo after his friend leaves, maybe remind him that Sierra Lavotini is perhaps connected to the "Big Moose" Lavotini syndicate out of Cape May, New Jersey. That usually kept Vincent in his place. He didn't need to find out that I was in no way related to Mr. Moose.

When I clicked my heels three times for the finale and started saying "There's no place like home" to my crowd of admirers, Vincent started talking again. I'm sure he ruined my tips by a good fifty percent.

"Sure," he was saying. "Pick any two girls you want. I'll have them up to the Speedway for opening night. It's no problem."

I snapped my garter, trying to get Vincent's attention, but he ignored me. If he thought I was going up to some race-track and stand around while greasy-fingered motorheads rubbed their hands all over my ass, well, he was mistaken.

Of course, if the money was right, I might consider it.

* * *

Ruby Diamond was born to strip. I knew it from the moment she walked into the Tiffany. You can tell a natural at a glance. It's the way she moves. Ruby's walk was a caress. She was comfortable with herself and vulnerable, all at once. When she got up on stage to audition, the men in the club stopped to watch, and not because her figure was outstanding, which it was. They stopped because something in them reached out to her.

Ruby walked out on stage and the music started, but she didn't move for a full thirty seconds. She just stood there, looking out like she was searching past the bright lights for something or someone. She stood there, biting her lower lip gently, wearing nothing but an FSU T-shirt and a bikini. She had long brown hair, coiled into a sleek French twist, and large liquid brown eyes. For one moment, every man in the place imagined that Ruby was a virgin and she was going to offer herself to only him.

They moved, like a herd, down to the front of the stage, their faces changing into soft, comforting older-but-wiser lovers. She seemed to look at each man, a smile playing softly across her face, and then she began to move. She held those men in the palm of her hand, and before she'd even lost her T-shirt, her garter was full of bills.

The men didn't whistle and call out like they do the ones who strip to get naked. They whispered encouragement. They smiled like newlywed husbands on their honeymoon night. They were entranced. Ruby, in her soft, open way, was seeming to give herself up to them, but I was watching her eyes and I knew the truth. Ruby was a pro, just like me. She was new and her act lacked refinement, but she was pro material nonetheless.

Later, after Vincent hired her, I gave her the backstage tour. That's when I got the scoop, just like I do with all the new girls.

"So what do you think?" I asked. I swept my arm around the locker room, including the long makeup bar with its wall-to-wall mirror and the rusty metal lockers.

Ruby was glowing. "It's great. Just great." In the light of the dressing room I could see she was no more than nineteen, about the age I was when I started.

"First job?" I asked.

She turned to me, her eyes gleaming with the knowledge she'd just conquered the room.

"Yeah," she breathed. "Yeah. But I won a wet T-shirt contest on the beach last month." As if that counted for something.

I knew the look. She'd just discovered that there was something she could do really well. She could make men want her, and for that, she could make a lot of money. I felt the same way my first time. Most of the time I still feel that way. There's nothing like standing at the edge of the runway, towering over a crowd of men, and realizing they're yours. You own them.

"I just moved here from Wewahitchka," she said abruptly. "I got my own place and everything, but my roommate, she took off on me. I didn't know how I was gonna make the rent. Then I saw the audition sign, and it was just like my psychic said: 'Don't turn down any opportunities; this is your lucky cycle.' "

Ruby was running on adrenaline now, driven to give me every detail of her short life.

"I don't know if I can really do this," she said honestly. "I mean, Mr. Gambuzzo said we were supposed to have themes and choreography and, well, I can dance and I took lessons from Miss Loraine at the Wewa Dance Studio, but this is different." Her voice slowed and she seemed overtaken by the enormity of her situation. She looked at me as if she were seeing me for the first time.

"What in the world am I gonna do?" she asked. Her legs seemed to give out under her and she sank into one of the chairs by the makeup bar. "Aw, man," she sighed.

"Ruby, get a grip," I said. "You're new. You're green. And you got talent. Without talent, technique ain't nothing but T-and-A working a pole. Vincent is a windbag, and nobody expects you to be a pro right off. You'll learn the moves from the rest of us. Pretty soon it'll come natural, from inside somewhere."

"Like when you know something but nobody ever

taught you and so you start thinking you must've done it in a past life?''

No, I thought, nothing like that. "Past life?" I shrugged."Whatever. All's I know is, when I stepped on stage my first time, I felt just like you did. At first you're scared, but when you see their faces, and you see that money sliding into your garter, you get this rush that's better than anything you ever did before. That's when you know you're a dancer. If you don't fight it, it'll come and take you over. Then you're on a big stage making big bucks, and don't nobody own you. Not ever.''

Ruby's eyes were silver dollars. "Yeah," she said, sighing,"that's it exactly. That's what I want.''

From that moment on, Ruby attached herself to me like a young puppy. When I came to the club to practice, she was there. When she worked out her first routine, I helped her. A lot of the girls ignored her, or worse, snubbed her. But that's life when you work this business. There's a lot of jealousy. I figure it this way: If you can dance, if you've got it, can't nobody take it away, and can't nobody ruin your stuff. The no-talents will move on or be moved out, so there's no sense in sweating it if they take an attitude. It's the real dancers who look out for each other. We're a family of loners and outcasts. We have to stick together to survive.

Ruby was good, but she was young and inexperienced. What I knew took years to learn; not that I'm old, but twenty-eight is light-years ahead of nineteen. I could do the vulnerable virgin for days, but I could do Aphrodite's night of a thousand pleasures, too. You don't learn that stuff at nineteen.

When Mickey Rhodes picked Ruby Diamond to appear at the Dead Lakes Motor Speedway along with me, I couldn't have been happier. My protégée was going to make her first publicity appearance. She didn't know enough to realize how fast those things can get old.

"Why did he pick me?" she kept asking. "Why not

Marla, or Yvonne? They're bigger acts than me." We were lying on the floor of my living room, exhausted from working on a new routine, when I decided to finally answer her.

"Ruby, Vincent and Mickey Rhodes are looking to do a business deal. The Tiffany sponsors the opening race and one of the drivers. In return for Vincent laying out a small amount of cash, the Tiffany gets a lot of publicity. You and me are just the pawns in this little game. It's not an honor or a privilege to get picked out by Mr. Rhodes. It is more or less a pain in the ass compounded by the fact that we ain't making enough extra jack for submitting ourselves to God knows what kind of physical and mental harassment by redneck racetrack fans."

There was a moment of silence while Ruby considered this. Then she laughed. "Oh, go on," she said. "Sierra, don't you know nothing about racing? Mr. Gambuzzo is sponsoring Roy Dell Parks. I went to high school with his little brother. Roy Dell Parks is gonna be the next Richard Petty."

She was serious. I turned and looked out the bay window, biting the inside of my lip so I wouldn't laugh and hurt her feelings. Ruby Diamond actually thought some three-quarter-mile dirt track driver was a threat to the Indy 500. I didn't know anything about racing, but I sure as heck knew one thing: The big racers didn't come out of little bitty racetracks in North Florida.

Ruby rolled over and sat up, looking at me with her big brown eyes. I suddenly had the feeling we were on dangerous territory.

"Sierra, I grew up in Wewa. Those people out at the race-track, I went to school with them. A lot of them talked bad about me behind my back, and you know why?" Ruby wasn't waiting for an answer. "Because I was adopted out of foster care when I was three. That was the only reason. Well, that and because I used to make believe I was reincarnated."

"Reincarnated?"

"Yeah," she said, her tone a bit defensive. "Reincarnated. You know, like I had a past life as somebody else. Madame Jeanette thinks I was Mata Hari."

I was biting the inside of my lip hard now, and I would've laughed if my hairless chihuahua, Fluffy, hadn't picked that moment to come into the room and distract us. Fluffy skidded into the room, sliding to a halt on the wooden floor by Ruby's side. It was a credit to Ruby that Fluffy accepted and liked her. Fluffy doesn't like just anyone. In fact, I have considered myself such a bad judge of character, particularly men, that I usually subject them to the Fluffy Test. If Fluffy doesn't like you, I don't date you.

I'd only seen Fluffy make an error once; that was when she took to John Nailor right off. Even I could've told her that was a mistake. Of course, Fluffy didn't see John Nailor plant one on that bimbo at the Dead Lakes Motor Speedway.

* * *

Most folks consider Panama City to be a small town, despite its reputation as the Redneck Riviera. We get people flying in here all the time from L.A., but around here, that just means Lower Alabama. We are a village made famous by a strip of white sand beach and MTV. Most people drive right past the real town in their rush to stake a claim on the sugary sands, and that suits the locals just fine. Better the tourists should not know about the huge Victorians that line St. Andrews Bay. Better they should stay away from Uncle Ernie's or Joe's. Leave the good living to those of us who can appreciate it.

I don't think the people of Wewahitchka feel like that about their town. When your biggest local attraction is a three-quarter-mile dirt track, you've got problems from a

Chamber of Commerce perspective. Having dancers from the big metropolis of Panama City was not their cup of tea either. I could tell we were unwanted right away. When I pulled up to the pit gate in my '88 black Camaro, there was a small crowd already waiting. Their signs read: Nudity is Everyone's Problem, and God So Loved the World That He Clothed Adam and Eve.

They were blue-hairs, mainly, who carried the plac-ards, but there was a sprinkling of dark-haired, fresh-scrubbed Christian righters. The younger ones looked mean, in particular a man with a bull horn and black-rimmed glasses. I'd heard about protests, but usually they happened outside of clubs. Surely they didn't think Ruby and I were going to get naked here? Ruby sank down in the passenger seat as we approached the gate.

"Oh Gawd," she moaned softly, "that's Brother Everitt, from my Mama's church."

I looked over at her. She sat slouched down in the seat, a scarf around her head and huge dark glasses covering the top half of her face.

"Didn't you figure this might happen?" I asked. I stared out the window at the tiny crowd of protesters. The women were wearing pastel polyester, their eyes focused rigidly in front of them, ignoring the cars backed up behind us in line, seemingly oblivious to the incredibly loud sound of engines being pushed to their limits.

"Well, I'd hoped not. I mean, Brother Everitt is bad to do stuff like this, but I just thought with the race-track being technically outside the Wewa city limits, and closer to Panama City than anywhere, he wouldn't come." She sighed again, and her hand went nervously up to touch her hair. She was wearing a Dolly Parton blond wig.

"So that's why you wore a wig?"

A small grin played across her face. "Yep. Pretty slick, huh?"

No, not really, I thought. "Yeah, kid, slick," I answered. "Now put them idiots out of your head and get ready to work your ass off. These gigs aren't for your lightweight."

Ruby straightened up in her seat and took a deep, cleansing breath, just like I taught her.

"Feel your inner child," I said as we pulled into the pit entrance. "Be at peace with yourself." It might have worked had we not come face-to-face with Roy Dell Parks, the self-proclaimed King of Dirt.

I had gunned the accelerator of my Camaro and was just starting to cross the track to get to the pit area, when out of nowhere a dusty yellow Vega, vintage 1972, appeared, barreling across the straightaway, seemingly out of control.

"Sierra, look out!" Ruby screamed. "Oh Gawd, Roy Dell's spun out!"

There was no time to slam the Camaro into reverse. Instead I braced myself, anticipating the shuddering thud that would jar every bone in my body. At the last second before impact, I saw a wild-eyed man with a bushy red beard and hair frantically fighting to turn the wheel of his battered yellow Vega. It was no use. Roy Dell Parks careened off the front right side of my car, throwing us backward into the line of waiting vehicles.

For a moment I was too stunned to move. The impact had shaken me, but other than that, the only damage seemed to have affected my precious '88 Iroc Camaro. Once I realized that a piece-of-shit Vega had demolished the front right side of my car, I was out of the door, heading for Roy Dell Parks and vengeance.

Roy Dell had managed to extricate himself from his car, which to my amazement seemed to have suffered no damage, and was directing his pit crew and the others who'd raced onto the track to offer assistance.

He saw me coming and headed toward me, his hand outstretched as if to shake mine.

"Roy Dell Parks, ma'am," he said. "That Vega'll run like a scalded dog, won't she?"

That's when I decked him. I pulled my arm back as far as I could and sent it steaming forward, hoping to punch right through his solicitous face and into the middle of the track.

It was pure pleasure to connect with his big fat lips. Roy Dell Parks was a bleeder. His mouth gushed blood, his eyes rolled up backward in his head, and ever so slowly he pitched forward as his knees buckled under him.

This brought about an instant reaction from his supporters. Half of them rushed to Roy Dell where he lay on the dirt track, and half just watched, trading looks of amazement for grins of admiration. I guess they didn't see many women punch men in their neighborhood. Where I come from in North Philly, growing up with four brothers, learning to deliver a punch was as much a way of life as going to Catholic school. I just happened to have paid more attention during the defense part of my education.

Ruby was standing by my side, her Dolly Parton wig slightly askew and her eyes wide.

"Good God Almighty," she said, "they're gonna kill us."

"Kill us?" I said. "Because some self-proclaimed king of racing hit my car?"

As if on cue, a scrawny man with thick muscled forearms and a wealth of tattoos stood up and headed in my direction. In the distance I could see two sheriff's deputies walking quickly toward us.

"What in the hell kind of thing to do was that?" the scrawny man asked. Others were falling in behind him, and the mood seemed to be heading toward a good old-fashioned lynching. Ruby jumped behind me, and I was thinking about how fast I could make it back to the car and grab my tire iron, when Roy Dell Parks rejoined the living.

"Now, Frank," he said weakly, "let me handle this. Can't you see the little lady was acting out of shock?" He chuckled as he stood up and swayed ever so slightly. "And a hell of a shock it must've been, too, if that punch was any judge."

Frank looked at me and snarled, just like Fluffy does when she disapproves of someone. Roy Dell walked slowly in between the two of us and once again stuck out his hand.

"Roy Dell Parks, ma'am, King of Dirt."

I looked at his outstretched hand for a second, then ignored it.

"Sierra Lavotini," I said, "the Queen of I Really Don't Give a Shit."

Roy Dell laughed, then winced and touched his lip.

"Don't be mad, ma'am," he said. "It really wasn't nothing I could control. One of my boys must've left a bolt off the steering column." He held up a hand as if to forestall any further comments from me. "I know, you're worried about your vehicle, but ma'am, honest, ain't nothing to it. Hell, the boys here'll take that car over to the pit and have it right as rain before the night's out."

Despite myself, I could feel my anger easing.

"Thanks, Roy Dell," Ruby said, taking over. "I know Sierra'd feel a lot better if you took care of her car. You know, Sierra's car means the world to her."

Roy Dell seemed to see Ruby for the first time. His eyes widened and he wiped his beefy hand on the front of his coveralls before extending it toward her.

"And who might you be, darlin'?"

Ruby blushed and placed her hand in his. "Ruby Lee Diamond," she murmured softly. "It sure is a pleasure to meet you."

I was gonna be sick. There was enough love juice and chemistry oozing out between the two of them to gag any self-respecting person. Roy Dell still hadn't let go of Ruby's hand, and she hadn't taken her eyes off of him. If Mickey Rhodes and his entourage hadn't joined us, accompanied by the sheriff's deputies, we might have stood there all night waiting for the blessed consummation of Roy Dell and Ruby's newfound romance.

"Ladies," said Mickey, "I am so sorry for this mishap." His pudgy little face was wrinkled with concern. "Of course, the track will absorb any cost incurred by Mr. Parks's negligence."

This snapped Roy Dell Parks back into the here and now. He whirled around to face the track owner, his face turning scarlet.

"Let's us just get one thing clear," he said, his voice dropping by two octaves and assuming a menace I hadn't thought possible. "This was an unavoidable accident. Weren't nothing to it but a loose bolt, and Miss Sierra and Miss Ruby know that. I'll be fixing this Camaro up better than new, and ain't none of your money needed."

Mickey puffed up like a rooster, and I was thinking that Roy Dell could fix my car for me, but there was no call to be turning down the track's money. After all, I could be the victim of delayed whiplash. One could never be too careful.

"Ouch," I moaned, grabbing the back of my neck.

"Sierra, what is it?" Ruby asked, rushing to my side. The little crowd had fallen silent, their total attention turned to me.

"Ow, I don't know," I said, massaging the back of my neck tenderly. "I just felt this sharp pain."

Mickey Rhodes's face paled as he smelled his liability burning. "Hey, Meatloaf, call them ambulance attendants over here. Looks like we might have a casualty."

A thick, tall man broke loose from the crowd and moved off at a trot toward the pit, and I stared off after him. From where we stood, at the top of the slanted dirt track, I could look down on the pit area and up over at the grandstands. Even though no cars were on the track, the sound coming from the pit where crews revved car engines was strong enough to feel as if it hit me square in the chest, pounding away like a bass drum.

"I'll be all right, I think," I said. Ruby hovered by my side, her wig now completely twisted.

"Miss Lavotini, I don't want to take any chances on you being injured," Mickey said. "We'll get you checked out and your car towed over to Roy Dell's crew."

There was no way I was letting some motorhead drive my baby. I'd worked too hard to obtain that car, and I wasn't taking any more chances.

"Nope," I said, "no way. I'll drive the car myself."

The EMTs arrived, accompanied by the man Mickey Rhodes had called Meatloaf.

"Miss Lavotini may have a neck injury," Mickey explained. I grimaced and allowed them to tilt my head this way and that.

"Ow, fellas, take it easy," I said. "You could do more harm than good here."

We were sailing along just fine with them prodding and me wincing, when I caught a flash of familiar movement on the edge of the pit where a crowd of onlookers had gathered. For just a moment, I thought I saw a man who looked a lot like John Nailor. I snapped my neck to the left suddenly and almost forgot to moan while I scanned the crowd. The man stood just on the back fringe of the crowd staring, if I was not mistaken, at me. If it wasn't John Nailor, then it was his spitting double. Only thing was, I couldn't imagine a man like him at a dirt track. It just didn't match up.

My stomach did that little flip it always does when I'm around him, the true test that my unconscious recognized him, even if my eyes were a little slow.

"You know," I said, pushing the prying hands away from my neck, "I think I'll be fine. Moving my head back and forth seems to have fixed the problem. Let's get moving."

Mickey Rhodes looked relieved. In fact, if I was any judge of human character, I was guessing there was going to be a very hefty tip from him at the end of the evening. Fluffy'd be chomping on gourmet dog food this week.

"Come on, Ruby, let's get to work." I said. Ruby smiled happily and hopped back into my car. If John Nailor was at the track, then it could only be for one reason: He'd come to see me.

"Follow us," Roy Dell called, jumping into his battered Vega. Driving slowly, he led us to the pit entrance and down a narrow dirt lane. There were cars everywhere, hoods open, with men hanging half into the mouth of the car, tinkering. Big panel vans sat behind some of the cars, with wrought-iron railings around their roofs and aluminum lawn chairs perched up on top. Small children played in the dirt, pushing little cars and trucks around. But there was no sign of John Nailor.

The track photographer rushed us as soon as I parked my battered baby. He was a short oval of a man, with a belt line that hit him just below the armpits, white socks, black sneakers, and a bald head. He looked like a brown shiny egg, and the closer he came, the more I realized that he smelled much worse than a rotten egg.

"Ladies," he said, but it sounded more like "lathies," due to a profound lisp. "I am Harold VonCopage. We're behind schedule. Follow me."

Harold quickly led us over to a small wooden platform, where he apparently intended to photograph us with every driver and crew member at the Dead Lakes Motor Speedway. I don't know how he intended to do this because I couldn't even see. Thick clouds of red-clay track dust whirled around us and car exhaust fumes made my eyes water. However, as soon as Ruby and I climbed the steps, men began appearing, lining up at the bottom of the platform as Harold had instructed.

"Are you ready?" Harold asked, an eyebrow arching as if daring us not to be. I looked over at Ruby, who was slathering on blood-red lipstick and hitching up the bra of her little Dutch girl costume. She nodded to Harold. I made an attempt to brush off the dust from my French maid's outfit. It was pointless.

"Just a sec," I called, more to irritate Harold than anything else, and pulled a compact from my purse. My long blond hair was piled high on my head, making me look even taller than my six-foot height in five-inch stilettos. It would be a rusty-red color by the end of the night. I licked my lips slowly and heard the men in the front of the line moan. I wanted to bend over and shift my cleavage even farther north, but this was a family event. My 38DDs probably wouldn't be appreciated by everyone.

I stowed the mirror, looked over at Ruby, and nodded. Then I stretched out my arms to the first man in line.

"Come to Mama, big boy," I crooned, and the night began.

We'd been standing and posing for about an hour when the smile faded from Ruby's lips.

"Sierra," she hissed between photo ops, "why didn't you tell me they pinched? My derriere is going to be black and blue, and my costume's gonna look worse. Honey, they didn't even wipe their hands off first!"

I smiled. "Welcome to the life, kid. You're building yourself a consumer base. They'll walk off with your picture, and within a week, half of them'll be in to see you. Think of your bruised ass as an investment in your financial future."

Ruby looked dubious, but she put on a big smile when the next driver climbed the steps. Throughout the evening I'd look over at her and she never lost that smile, although once or twice I saw her grab a man's hand and pinch the fleshy part between his thumb and forefinger, just like she'd seen me do. But she kept her smile, and the men smiled right back.

Roy Dell Parks was the worst. He kept finding reasons to wander over and talk to her, and Ruby didn't seem to mind him at all. She smiled and spoke softly to him. I couldn't figure what she saw in the big guy.

It was getting late in the evening when I spotted John Nailor for certain. There'd been God knows how many races, all announced over a loudspeaker that was too distorted to understand, and everyone was gearing up for the main event of the evening. Roy Dell Parks and about twenty others were getting set to go fifty laps around the track for the big money purse of the evening. In another half hour the race would take place, and then Ruby and I could leave. I was counting the moments when I looked up and saw John staring at me.

I opened my mouth to call out to him when I realized there was something very wrong with the picture. John, the same guy who'd come into the club on numerous occasions and not all of them professional, the same guy who'd driven me home after some bozo coshed me on the head, was standing not twenty yards away from me with his arm around some tiny brunette.

I should make it clear, here, that John Nailor and I were smoldering somewhere between chemical reaction and friendship with intent to distribute the affection into the physical realm at some point in time.

As such, I recognize the fact that I had no possessive claim on the son of a bitch, but the sparks that had passed between us on a number of occasions led me to believe we meant a lot to each other.

He was watching me now the same way he always did when we first met, from a distance, with an impassive expression on his face, as if I didn't faze him, but I knew different. I'd seen that same look on his face the first time we met, when he was investigating a murder and thought my girlfriend and I had something to do with it. Every time he came to talk to me, he'd look like that, but he kept coming back, even when he didn't have to.

So my mouth dropped open, and my eyes got wide, and I froze, staring at him. He looked at me with those dark eyes of his. Then his companion saw him looking and started to pull at his arm, as if she intended to bring him up to the stage to have his picture taken. He looked down at her, then back at me for just a flash, and that's when he turned away, leaned down, and kissed her.

He kissed her just the way I'd always imagined he'd kiss me one day: hard and like he meant it, like he played for keeps. Then he grabbed her arm and spun her around and they walked off. He was walking rough, and she looked a little surprised but was clearly enjoying this new side to his behavior. I could've told her I'd seen it all before, but I was busy having my picture taken by a smelly egg and my ass pinched by yet another psycho dirt racer.

You'd think by now I wouldn't let stuff like that get to me. It's not as if that was the first time some guy did wrong by me. Far from it. It's just that the kind and quality of man I usually associate with can be expected to be mean. John Nailor was about the last man I thought would deliberately hurt me, and I decided on the spot that I had to know why.

"Break," called Harold. "Big race is in fifteen minutes. We'll take one last round with the winner, and then you girls can go on home."

Ruby was looking wistfully after Roy Dell Parks, who seemed to be beckoning her toward his car. Mickey Rhodes was heading in our direction. He was leading Vincent Gambuzzo and some guys in suits. More publicity, and I was in no mood for it. I wanted to look John Nailor in the face, up close and personal, and see if he was as brave eye to eye as he'd been a few seconds ago.

"I'm outta here," I said, heading for the steps.

"Sierra, where are you going?" Ruby called, but I didn't answer. I kept walking off in the direction I'd seen John head with that perky little bimbo. If he could have picked the almost total opposite of me, he couldn't have done better. She was short, terminally short. I bet in heels she didn't come up over five feet four inches. And she was flat-chested. That is a problem I'll never have to worry about. Her hair was dark and mine was macaroni blond—natural, not bottle—courtesy of my northern Italian ancestors. And she looked like one little puff would blow her away, a real lightweight in your most Junior League sort of way.

I was searching for them and cursing myself. What was wrong with me that I'd let myself get so worked up over a guy? It was just not like me. No, I take it back, it was just like me, but the me of my North Philly days. Since I'd moved to Panama City two years ago, I hadn't made a fool of myself over anybody. In fact, I hadn't even dated anyone—hadn't wanted to, really.

I walked past the drivers and the pit crews, barely noticing the catcalls and the whistles. The smell of coffee and greasy hamburgers from the snack shack reminded me that I hadn't eaten since lunchtime. My stomach finally won over where my brain had not succeeded. It was a much saner idea to eat a burger, drink a cup of coffee, and reflect upon my loss of control with John.

I stepped up to the dirty white shack and let the girl working the counter shove a wax-paper-wrapped hamburger into my hand.

"They all got chili and coleslaw on 'em, hon," she said. "That'll be three dollars with the coffee." If my French maid costume seemed out of place at the track, she never noticed. Her eyes were glued to the track, where the last semifinal race had just ended.

"Aw, hell," she said, turning to a young teenaged girl who was wrapping hot dogs. "Meatloaf done lost to Frank. There'll be hell to pay at our house tonight. He'll come home drunk, I guess." The girl nodded, never looking up from the dogs. "Son of a bitch," the cashier muttered.

I turned away with my food and wandered out behind

the shack. The inner circle of the pit was reserved for parking. It was dark and the ground was a combination of gravel, red clay, and sparse grass.

"All I need is to trip in these heels," I muttered. I almost bumped into a cluster of three picnic tables and decided the safest thing for me to do would be to sit down and eat while my eyes adjusted.

The loudspeaker began to blare over the constant sound of engines being pushed to their maximum rpms. From what I could catch, the starting lineup for the last race was being announced. I didn't pay much attention. I just wanted the entire evening to come to an end so I could go home to Fluffy and the comfort of my double-wide.

As my eyes adjusted, I could see a trash bin about thirty feet away, and now and then I could discern shapes moving past, heading to or from the parking lot. Someone tossed a bottle and it hit the side of the Dumpster, clanging noisily above the dull roar of the pit.

I started to feel sorry for myself. I was sitting alone at a picnic table eating and thinking: What am I doing here? Why wasn't I home, curled up with a book? True, Vincent had bribed me with money to be here, but was it worth it to come all the way to Wewahitchka, just so I could have my fantasy shattered? I didn't think so.

I got up and started walking toward the Dumpster so I could pitch the rest of my hamburger and get back to the platform. I figured I might as well watch the race and talk to Ruby; that was better than stalking John and his new love interest.

"Son of a bitch," I muttered, thinking of the cashier at the snack shack. "They're all alike."

Someone giggled. It sounded like it came from the other side of the Dumpster.

"Why, I don't know what to say," a woman's voice said. It was Ruby. I started to say something, but hung back instead. If she wanted to ruin her evening by fooling around with Roy Dell, who was I to interrupt her? She'd learn soon enough that they're all alike. Or maybe she knew something I didn't. I doubted that.

I had turned to leave when I heard her again.

"I couldn't, really," she said, and I heard a different tone come into her voice, an edge. If that brain-damaged redneck thought he could mess with Ruby, he would be in for a surprise.

I whirled around and started back, only to hear her giggle again. I froze, uncertain about interrupting. A man's voice rumbled and I couldn't make out what he said. The loudspeaker had blurted out something, drowning out their conversation. I started to walk away again.

"Look here," the man said.

Another giggle from Ruby and then the horrible, unmistakable sound of bone snapping. I sprang forward, lurching to cover the distance to the other side of the Dumpster. As I rounded the corner there was a brief painful flash as I collided with something or someone. The last thing I remember as I slid into darkness was the word "No!" echoing soundlessly inside my head.